# A Noble Affair



JENNIE GOUTET

Printed in the United States of America

First Printing, 2016

*To Matthieu –*
*my own French noble man and real life hero*

# CHAPTER 1

"You wanted to see me?" Chastity poked her head into the principal's office.

"Yes, come on in." Elizabeth Mercer took freshly printed sheets out of the tray and checked them against a list in front of her. She swiveled on her chair and placed one paper on the stack behind her, and the other to her right. "You're settling in all right?"

Chastity nodded, hiding her fatigue. She didn't need to discuss her small worries with her boss.

"I saw your e-mail about meeting with Monsieur de Brase. Here—have a seat. And why don't you close the door?"

Chastity walked over and peered into the adjacent library where the voices swelled. "Hey everyone, keep your voices down." She gave a pointed look at the students clustered around a tiny screen, and their voices fell to a whisper. While her principal continued to sort papers, Chastity sat, staring absently out the window at the young children chasing each other with untrammeled glee.

"So, you're meeting him to talk about Louis's English grades, is that it?"

"His grades, yes," Chastity said. "But also the quality of his writing.

It's really below standard. How did he keep passing on to the next grade?"

Elizabeth pressed her lips together before replying. "He continued to scrape by. We helped him whenever we could, and it didn't seem like holding him back would make much of a difference. He's just never been a great student. Either way, it would've been hard to go against the wishes of his father."

Chastity frowned. "His father?"

"He refused to let him repeat a grade and said he trusted us to do whatever it took to help his son pass."

"But—why does the father have a say in whether his kid passes? I didn't think a parent's opinion ever swayed our decision-making."

"Ah. You don't know who Monsieur de Brase is." Elizabeth gave her a level stare, and if Chastity hadn't begun to know her principal better, she would say she was pausing for effect. "He owns the Château of Maisons-Laffitte."

"Oh. The viscount." There was a pause. "Still, we have other influential parents. I don't see why—"

"Because he donates a large amount of money to the school, and we depend on it. He's also on the board, and some of our largest donors are on it because of him. It's not worth the risk of losing that kind of support if we can avoid it."

"Okay, I'm sorry, but that just...irritates me. He's using his wealth and influence to push people around, but he's not considering what's best for his son." Chastity was breathless and wound up, which might have been the extra cup of coffee she'd had before her last class.

"You'll see for yourself," Elizabeth responded. "He's a nice enough man, but he's kind of hard to argue with." Chastity snorted delicately. "Just don't say anything to set him off. We do need his monetary gifts."

Chastity rolled her eyes, but smiled as she picked up her bag. "I'll try to be on my best behavior."

Once back in her office, Chastity realized she'd forgotten to tell her principal everything, but she didn't have time to fill her in now.

Only fifteen minutes remained before Mr. de Brase arrived, and she wanted to be prepared. She selected a colored file from the stack on top of the cabinets near the window.

Flipping through the papers, she came to the one she wanted. It was Louis's critical essay on Euripedes' play, "Medea," and she read it through once more. "You are kidding me," she muttered. "How could the school let him bulldoze..."

She reviewed her corrections—"There should be no first person in a critical essay. The beginning is too informal." —and added, "Louis, you need to improve your writing. These words are too simple." *At least this is ready to show his father. He can hardly argue with me on how bad—*

Elizabeth rang earlier than expected. "Chastity, Louis's father is here to see you."

"Okay, thanks. I'll be right down."

Chastity slung her purse over her shoulder and pushed her reading glasses on top of her head, which was starting to hurt. She wasn't sure if it was the upcoming meeting or if she had pulled her hair back too tight.

At the bottom of the spiral staircase, she rounded the corner and came abruptly against a tall, well-built man. What she noticed, when he faced her, was the shape of his nose—a Patrician nose that looked as if centuries of aristocracy had poured into the genes that formed it. *A nose made for snubbing people*. She barely took in his blue eyes and firm mouth.

A quick look at his Italian shoes and navy blazer with a little silk scarf caused her to glance at her own long skirt with a peasant top tucked in. *I should really start dressing like a French person.* His hair was his friendliest quality. It had a few strands of gray but was otherwise thick and tousled with boyish locks that made him look much less formidable.

She hid her nervousness and stuck out her hand. "Bonjour, Monsieur Brase."

"Monsieur de Brase," he answered, accenting the prefix, which denoted ancient nobility.

"Monsieur *de* Brase," she conceded, although she had known perfectly well how to pronounce his name. She had just been flustered by the fact that he appeared younger than she had expected. She turned to walk back up to her office. "If you'll follow me?"

They walked silently up the stairs, and she wondered if her shirt was tucked in properly in the back. A more amiable parent might have complimented her on her excellent French, but Louis's father said nothing. When they reached the top of the stairs, Chastity gestured forward. "Right in here, please."

Shutting the door behind them, she took a seat across from him and folded her hands on the table, trying to keep them still. *Why am I so nervous?* "I'm sure you know why I've requested a meeting?"

"I've no idea, other than your note, which said you wished to discuss my son's English language skills."

*He doesn't care a whit about his son,* she thought. "That's not exactly... it's not so much a problem with his language skills. It's that he doesn't seem to understand the material we're studying, and he rarely participates in the class discussion. When he does talk, his spoken English is pretty advanced, actually," she added.

"Yes, that's what I thought." Mr. de Brase spoke with complacence.

Irritated, Chastity began again. "Have you been following his coursework? His grades on the papers he's handing in?"

"My son is fifteen years old and doesn't need me to stand over him to get his homework done. He's been doing his own homework for a few years now and his grades were not worrisome last year."

*Then why do you keep getting called in for parent-teacher meetings?* She cleared her throat. "Something has changed, I guess. I don't know how he was last year, but in my class Louis is below-grade, and if he keeps on in this way, he's in danger of failing. I'm not sure he's reading the assignments. And the papers he hands in are not as advanced as other students his age."

"Mademoiselle Whitmore, English is not his mother tongue."

"Yes, but that's what I'm trying to tell you. He speaks English well enough, but he...he can't think critically, or analyze what he's reading, or...organize his thoughts well enough to write an essay that will get a passing grade." She grabbed the papers from her desk, slapping the colored file on the table with more force than she intended. Mr. de Brase jerked at the noise, which made her flush with embarrassment.

She heard her voice grow sharper. "Here, for instance." Flipping through the papers until she found the right essay, she pointed to a paragraph in his son's scrawl. He talks about Aegus being a god. But he's not a god. He's the king of Athens. Louis wasn't even able to keep track of the characters, which means he didn't read the play and needs to work harder. Or he did read it and can't understand it, and is therefore in the wrong class."

"I'm not familiar with—"

"And here." Chastity knew she was starting to become aggressive but couldn't prevent everything from spilling out. "He writes like someone in the sixth grade. There are fragments, and misused words, and punctuation in the wrong place." She stopped abruptly.

Mr. de Brase sighed. "Isn't this the teacher's responsibility to oversee all this? What do you expect me to do?"

Ignoring the implied insult, she leaned forward. "Help him with his homework. Take an interest in what he's reading and what he's working on. Be willing to hold him back, even, if that's what it takes."

Mr. de Brase folded his arms. *Oh, he did not like that suggestion.*

"It's your first year here?" he asked.

"Yes."

"Perhaps you don't know who I am."

Her eyes narrowed. "What..."

Mr. de Brase changed the subject so fast her head spun. "I'll talk to my son about his grades, but I won't start looking over his shoulder. I didn't raise him that way, and he doesn't need a babysitter. Besides, his work has always been good enough before."

Chastity bit back retorts like "father's coercion" and "gullible teachers." Clearly he was used to people eating out of his hands. She would not be one of them. She forced her shoulders to relax. "There's something else."

"Go on."

"For the past month or so, I've had this suspicion that your son is using illegal substances."

Mr. de Brase looked at her sharply, the first sign of possessing an emotion other than bored indifference. "My son doesn't use drugs. Where would he get them? He doesn't even smoke."

She looked at him in surprise. "He smells like smoke every time he comes into class. And this area is wealthy—a prime target for people who sell drugs. I've overheard students talking about weekend parties, and someone is getting drugs. That, in itself, is a concern. But when it starts spilling over into his school days it becomes a real problem."

"What makes you so sure Louis is using drugs? You mentioned smoke, but that's not the same thing as drugs."

"I can't be sure. It's true—I have no proof." Chastity took a deep breath, knowing that this admission didn't add to her credibility, but she was certain enough in her suspicions to insist. "Sometimes I catch a whiff of something that doesn't smell like nicotine. It's mostly his behavior in class. He seems so mellow at times, he's almost comatose."

"My son is reserved." Mr. de Brase shrugged. "As you said, you can't be sure that the smoke is what you think it is. Or even that it came from him."

"Yes, but—"

Mr. de Brase stood, ending the conversation. "I appreciate your concern for my son. I'll take into consideration everything you said, but I believe you're mistaken in the matter."

Chastity stood too, her eyes level with his chin so she was forced to look up. "Why? Why aren't you even considering the possibility that your son needs help? What have you got to lose?"

She saw his face flush with anger and wondered if she had been too pushy and whether Elizabeth was going to hear about it. Mr. de Brase walked to the door and turned back long enough to say, "Good day, Mademoiselle."

His broad shoulders filled the narrow corridor, and she watched him turn the corner and disappear from sight.

Perhaps that wasn't exactly my best behavior, she mused. *But really. How am I supposed to be nice to the man?*

# CHAPTER 2

The morning sun streamed through the tall windows of the Château of Maisons-Laffitte, and the small square windowpanes made a checkered pattern of sunlight on the wooden floor. It was a warm day for late October, and the crisp sound of birds chirping nearby intermingled with the muted squeals of children playing further away.

The Viscount Charles Jean Anne Monorie de Brase sat behind the Louis XIV desk, which was antique in structure but modern in disarray with cords and chargers strewn among the documents. Papers were stacked in what could roughly be called piles, and a steaming cup of espresso sat in the center of it all, yet untouched. Leaning back against his padded armchair, one leg crossed easily over the other, Charles idly flipped through yesterday's news articles on the tablet perched on his lap, raising his brows over one of the photo captions.

He dipped an end of the sugar cube in his coffee and watched as the cube turned brown. Then, stirring it with the tiny silver spoon, he drank the liquid in one swallow. As soon as the porcelain cup clattered on the saucer, a door in the wall opened that was so discreet you wouldn't notice it unless you knew where to look.

"I don't imagine you want to be involved in this, monsieur, but the *élagueurs* are here from Versailles to trim the trees and bushes. I told André to show them what to do."

"You're right. I don't need to be involved. They know what they're doing."

"Oui, monsieur." The butler walked over and picked up the empty cup and saucer. "That just leaves your visit with the stable manager this morning before your family arrives for lunch."

Charles focused on some distant point out the window. "I wonder if we can keep the meeting at the stables to under an hour. Or better yet," he muttered under his breath, "skip the family reunion entirely." He sighed, and the butler waited silently.

Noticing his employer had gone back to reading the news, Paltier ventured, "May I ask what time lunch should be served?"

"My mother won't arrive until one o'clock, so we'll eat shortly after that." Charles smiled by way of dismissal, and Paltier nodded his gray head, leaving the room through the discreet passageway.

By the time the sounds of his mother's arrival filtered up the stairs, the visit to the stables had been completed in record time, and his two sisters and the elder's husband had been there for a half-hour. A stout, graying woman climbed the stairs with difficulty and stood erect at the entrance to the sitting room where the family was taking refreshments.

"Hello, Maman." Charles rose to his feet and crossed the room to kiss her lightly on each cheek. "I hope you didn't hit too much traffic."

"The *péripherique* was slow, as to be expected." She glanced around the room shrewdly. "Ah. I see you moved that Cézanne as I suggested."

Her eyes narrowed, and she studied the painting for a moment before adding, "It needs to be closer to this armchair. It's not properly centered between the windows."

Charles sighed inwardly. He was respected in his field, and the owner of the nicest château on the outskirts of Paris, but his mother had the gift of making him feel like a boy as soon as she entered the room. She turned stiffly in her cream-colored Chanel suit to where a teenager with headphones was lounging on the sofa by the window.

"Louis, aren't you going to greet your grandmother?" Her tone was acerbic as she addressed the boy's father. "Perhaps a few hints on etiquette from time to time would serve him well. That's how I raised you, if you'll remember."

"How could I possibly forget it?" he murmured. *Or escape it?* Charles lifted a stemmed glass lying on a nearby table. "A glass of Porto, Maman?" She shook her head no, scrutinizing the young man who rose to his feet and slipped off his headphones before lumbering over to his grandmother and kissing her. "Bonjour, Grand-mère."

The matriarch turned back towards her son, her pale blue eyes boring into his. She didn't bother to lower her voice. "I've told you this before, but he needs a woman in his life. A mother. It's been fifteen years."

She walked across the room to kiss her daughters and son-in-law, who had risen on her arrival, and turned back with an afterthought. "But not that young actress of yours."

Charles felt his temper rise, but he kept his face impassive from years of training. "Shall we have lunch?" He gestured for his mother to lead the way into the dining room that was large enough to accommodate the massive table.

Over the first course, Charles's sister, Adelaide, who was older by four years and his closest sibling in affection, leaned over with a twinkle in her eye. "How *is* that actress of yours?" She grinned and poked her fork into the toast with melted *chèvre* and took a bite.

"You have salad in your teeth."

Adelaide knew not to be put off by his grumpy rejoinder. Turning her face from her mother, who sat across from them, she grinned wider showing all her teeth, now full of salad and cheese in the crevices. "Do you think she will like me, Charles?" She eyed him balefully, her mouth full.

"Please be serious." The stony face was belied by a smile in his eyes.

Adelaide suppressed a grin and murmured, "Don't rise to the bait, Charlie."

The dowager interrupted her son-in-law, who rarely paused for breath. "What are you talking about over there?"

"I was asking Charles if he could look in on Isabelle at Cambridge when he goes to England next weekend." Adelaide's daughter was in her first semester at university there.

"Why are you going to England?" his mother interrogated.

Charles shot his sister a look before breaking off a piece of bread. "Manon will begin filming in London. I plan on accompanying her just for the weekend."

"Louis, what will you do while your father's away?"

Louis shrank into his seat as all eyes turned towards him. "I didn't...I don't know." He scraped his fork against the plate, and everyone cringed.

Charles's eldest sister, Eléonore, who was six years his senior, spoke peremptorily. "Louis, you will come and stay with me."

Louis's face froze in alarm until his father rescued him. "Louis is perfectly fine here by himself. He's fifteen years old and doesn't need a babysitter. Paltier will be here if he needs anything. Besides—" addressing his son directly, "you have plenty of homework, don't you?"

Louis mumbled and inspected the table, spared from a further need to talk by the footmen bringing in plates of roast pigeon and potatoes seasoned with thyme.

"Charles, you know I don't like poultry with little bones," his eldest sister exclaimed.

Paltier had begun to fill the viscount's glass halfway with red wine, and he looked up at that. Charles drew in a breath. "I'm sorry, Eléonore. I had forgotten."

Adelaide hid a smile behind her linen napkin as her brother-in-law spoke bracingly. "It's not like quail, *mon chou*. You won't break a tooth this time."

"Paltier, I'll have some fish. Or an egg if you've nothing else." Eléonore inched backwards in her seat to allow the footman to clear the plate.

"My dear," continued her loving husband, "you are perfectly right to take no chances, especially with Mathilde's wedding coming up. Last time you chipped your tooth, you couldn't talk properly for a month."

"No loss," whispered Adelaide.

Charles was immune to Adelaide's attempts to make him laugh in front of their mother—the age-old game for their private amusement. He knew she wanted to chip through his icy exterior, and she knew his coldness was only a façade. Still, they slipped into the roles easily. Ignoring Adelaide, he addressed his mother. "The mayor asked me to serve on his advisory board for the city."

Eléonore looked up. "It's about time you got more involved in politics." Eléonore's husband, Raphael was the campaign director for the right wing political party in France.

"I'm not getting involved in politics," Charles said firmly. "I'm more concerned with the affairs in this town—preserving the forest, for a start."

"I thought that was a given," Adelaide said, serious for once. "I thought there were strict laws and that nothing could be built there."

"There are." Charles took a sip of his wine and separated the meat from the drumstick. Its brown sauce marred the pristine white of the china plate. "There are those who feel some of the forest could be sold off to build a new housing community."

Everyone became animated, except Louis, who examined his plate. "I have never heard of anything like this," the dowager spluttered. "Is no property—no piece of history to remain sacred?"

"Many people felt the same way when my father bought the Château de Maisons-Laffitte," Charles said in a spirit of mischief.

"I hope you do not regret he did so." His mother's tone was dangerous.

"No Maman," was the smooth reply. "I recognize the value of heritage."

His mother picked up her fork again but remained silent throughout the meal. Paltier brought in the cheese platter and everyone refused, except Charles and his brother-in-law, who apparently decided to ignore the straining shirt buttons. Everyone accepted an espresso.

The family lingered after their coffee for over an hour while Louis slipped away. Afterwards, the dowager walked down the large marble steps in the foyer and allowed her son-in-law to open the heavy iron and glass door that led to the courtyard. She turned to her son to receive his kisses and, glancing beyond him to the men trimming the trees, placed her gloved hand on Charles's arm and sighed. "The grounds have never looked as good as they did when Pierre was caring for them."

"Yes," he answered with a grim smile. "But Pierre took off one day without saying a word."

"I was never more shocked in my life." His mother gripped his arm. "After twenty-two years of faithful service to go off without a word. He left the hedges half-trimmed." She shook her head, and in spite of her sudden vehemence, seemed frail.

Charles waited for his mother to recover, and when she did, her voice held urgency. "See that you preserve the legacy of this place. It may not have been long in our family, but you owe it to the families that came before you—and you owe it to your son."

"I will, Maman." He led his mother to the back seat of her chauffeured car. He helped her into it and turned to kiss his sisters, and take leave of his brother-in-law, as they crossed the courtyard. As usual, there was little discussion between the men.

"Charles." Raphael shook his hand, his pompous voice booming out in the courtyard.

"Have a nice drive, Raphael."

The cars drove off, crunching on the pebbles until they reached the broad street. Charles stood on the stone steps, watching the iron gates close automatically behind them. He was plunged in thought, remembering the last time he saw Pierre before he disappeared.

The gardener had been on the ladder, trimming the hedges manually, which was, in itself, an ordinary occurrence. The younger version of himself rounded the corner with his childhood friend, Miriam, having just discovered she returned his deeper feelings. Pierre frowned when he spotted the young couple, and when they looked up, their newly clasped hands flew apart. The gardener removed his beret and studied its lining.

Charles and Miriam had been unable to subdue their excitement. Joy spilled out in their bright eyes and the large smiles of young love. Normally, Pierre would have risked a wink at Charles, celebrating his triumph, but on that day the gardener was somber and unlike himself —as if there had been foreboding that such happiness could not last.

Charles was frozen, recalling Miriam's brown eyes—the only thing he could remember clearly without looking at a photo. The grief he suffered was long gone, but there had never been any joy to take its place. Sometimes he wondered if that should worry him.

He turned to go inside and came up flush against the same set of eyes, causing his heart to skip a beat in surprise—a ghost rising from the past.

"Oh. Louis. You're here." He paused, his mind a blank. *I don't even know what to say to my own son.* "Sorry to spring it on you that I'm away next weekend like that." Charles shifted to the other foot.

"That's fine." A long lock of dark, wavy hair hid Louis's brown eyes, which didn't sparkle or laugh like his mother's, but rather turned downwards.

His son didn't offer anything else. Charles recalled his conversation with the English teacher and felt a flash of irritation towards her. He had the urge to lean forward and sniff his son to see if he smelled like smoke or something else. He resisted the urge. "I met with your English teacher."

Louis looked up, alarmed. He opened his mouth to speak but closed it and schooled his expression. His father was forced to go on. "Is...uh, everything all right in school?"

"Yes, Papa, everything's totally fine." Louis oriented his face towards the door.

Charles sighed, his eyes on his son. *He's just going through a phase, like all boys his age. He'll come about if I leave him alone.* He glanced at the iron gates that had closed behind his mother's departing car. *At least that's what I would have wanted. A bit of space and more trust.* "Make sure you do your homework for school tomorrow."

"Oui, Papa." Louis made his escape.

Charles stood on the steps surveying the beauty of his property and trying to shake off the ghosts it held. To the left, the *élagueurs* were now working on the rows of trees closest to the edge of the park. One man was standing in the bucket, perched on the arm of a small truck. He sliced the side of the tree with his electric trimmer in a perfect line. There were shouts as the men below cleared the area of falling branches.

Charles turned and entered the marble foyer, his footsteps echoing as he walked up the empty staircase.

Jean was sure it was him. The gentleman who leaned over the stone wall overlooking the Seine perfectly fit the description he'd been given. He had the straight black hair with a touch of gray, the Mediterranean skin color, the black leather jacket. He stood there, waiting. It couldn't be anyone else.

He watched as the guy pulled out a pack of cigarettes from his inside pocket. He could read the words FUMER TUE in large letters, even from across the street. Smoking Kills. The man tapped a cigarette out of the packet before tucking it back inside his jacket. Jean waited one more minute before heading over.

He was nervous. This was not a person you messed with—the man radiated power. Even if his reputation hadn't preceded him, every movement he made was decisive. Jean jogged across the street, dodging the last car that was anticipating the light before he reached the curb. Slightly out of breath—as much from nerves as from the light jog—he approached the wall at a respectful distance, leaving enough space not to threaten the man if he had misjudged.

"Jean." As if he had sensed his presence, the man turned and reached out his hand, his greeting a confirmation rather than a question. "Let's walk." He jerked his head East towards the *Notre Dame* and began heading in that direction.

"Are you clear on what Etienne told you—your end of the deal?"

"Yes." Jean's voice cracked. He cleared his throat and continued in a deeper tone. "It's perfectly clear. There shouldn't be any problem."

"I don't want to rush this. I want every step in place before we proceed. You're not to deviate from the plan. Is that clear?"

"Absolutely." Jean gave a firm nod. "That's precisely how I operate. When I—"

The man cut him off. "Good. I'm glad we agree on that. Take your time. Build those relationships you talked about slowly. It's been sitting there for twenty-five years, and it can wait a few more months. The important thing is that this time we pull it off without anyone getting caught." The man studied Jean and lifted his stubbled chin. "Any problems you can foresee?"

"None at all," he replied quietly. The man cut across the street without another word, and Jean watched as he disappeared into the crowd. An Asian couple approached, gesturing with their camera to take a photo of them next to the *Pont Neuf*. Jean forced himself to smile as he waited for them to pose and for his heartbeat to return to normal.

# CHAPTER 3

Chastity brooded over the unwelcome phone call while she waited for her son to come out of school. She hadn't been sure if she should tell Thomas about his father after he made contact, but in the end she did. When she asked her ex why he was calling after all this time, her question was met with silence. Then, "I don't know. When I moved to France it didn't seem right not to get in touch once I knew you were living here." He said he thought it was wrong not to be involved with his son. She curled her lip. *I can't say I feel the same way.*

She asked if he got her phone number from her parents, but no. Of course not. When Marc told her it was Caroline who spilled all the details about her move to France and her job at Fenley, Chastity rolled her eyes. *Didn't it occur to her to ask me first before she passed on personal details to someone who was such a jerk to me?* She wondered why she had bothered to keep in touch with Caroline when they had nothing in common, even if she didn't have many friends to choose from.

In the end she agreed to a meeting, unable to decide whether it was a good idea or not. Having worked so hard to overcome her anger over the way he had treated her, she didn't want to dismiss this chance to show forgiveness. Everything about this was unprecedented. Was it better for her son to know his father? *Deadbeat though he is?* She reluctantly admitted to herself that part of her 'yes' had to do with curiosity over what he looked like after eight years.

The school bell rang, and Thomas spotted her in the crowd. Running up to her, his backpack jostling on his back with each step, he held out a paper. "Mom, we got a ticket at school to go to the circus." Sunlight glinted off the blond hair that was parted to one side.

Chastity smiled at his enthusiasm. "Honey, that's not a ticket." She leaned over to kiss him on the cheek. "It's just a flyer, but—" when she saw his face fall, "we might still be able to go. It's in two weeks. I'll have to see what we have planned."

They started walking down the tree-lined street, and he looked up at her doubtfully. "Maybe we could see if my father wants to go with us." He spoke the words as if he were trying them out on his tongue.

Eyes ahead, she kept her voice neutral. "Yes, that might be a possibility."

When she didn't say anything more, he persisted. "Mom, why does he want to see me now after all this time?"

After a brief hesitation, she answered him honestly. "I think, at the beginning, he was just not interested in being a father. Maybe he thought he was too young. After that, he couldn't see you because he was in prison." She had never been one to hide anything from her son if she felt he had the right to know.

"My dad was in jail?" Thomas's eyes grew wide. "What did he do?"

"I'm not too sure," she replied. "I think he was selling drugs."

Thomas kicked a small stone off the sidewalk. "What are drugs?"

Chastity contemplated the clouds, waiting for inspiration. "Um... it's like a medicine you take. Only instead of making you healthy again, it makes you sick. Drugs also make you act foolish when you take them. And—" she added, "they're against the law."

Thomas, who had always been a precocious child, retorted, "You would have to be an idiot to take drugs."

"Yup." This was accompanied by a nod.

Her son sighed and shook his head. "My father's an idiot."

Chastity let out a peal of laughter that she cut short. "Perhaps you're right, my dear. But everyone deserves the chance to be recognized for their goodness and not their mistakes."

Thomas chewed on this information before saying, "He's not much of a father. He could have written to me while he was in jail. I'm sure they have pens and paper there. I would've sent him a drawing back."

"Yes, he could have," she answered in perfect seriousness, without any urge to smile. "Anyway, I think before doing something big together, like going to the circus, maybe we'll meet him for hot chocolate first. What do you say to that?"

"Okay." Her son slid his hand into hers as they turned towards the entrance to their apartment building.

On Friday, Chastity was no closer to knowing whether she was making the right decision to introduce her son to his father. As she came out of the classroom, she spotted the Math teacher ahead. *If there's anybody I can talk to about this, it's Maude*. She didn't easily invite people into her life, but Maude had managed to worm her way in, and so far she had proven trustworthy.

Maude was barely taller than her students, even in high heels, and Chastity eased past the teenagers who were lounging in the hallway to catch up to her. Her friend had thin, muscular arms and square shoulders that were visible through the light cardigan, and her hair was pulled back in a large bun. Originally from Martinique, her colleague had lived in France since junior high.

"Hey." Chastity smiled as soon as she was at her side.

"Ah. *Salut, toi*." Hi yourself. Maude could speak English but was more comfortable in French. "I need to stop in my office first." She veered off to the side, waving for her to follow.

Chastity imitated her abrupt turn and entered the office, which was decorated with candles, picture frames, and fresh flowers. She made a mental note to work on personalizing her own office space more. "You said you needed to come here 'first'? Where are you going after that?"

"Oh, you're coming with me." Maude grabbed her purse and hooked her arm through Chastity's. "Unless you need to get Thomas."

"No, no. He's in the after-school program today."

"Good. We're going to save Anne's job."

"Wait. Anne...Anne Meurier? The art teacher? What's up with her job? She's been here for years. And doesn't she volunteer at the museum as well?"

"No, she *works* there," Maude responded, emphasizing the word. "It's only part-time, but still. I've heard she's been let go in both places. I suspect the same person is responsible for both."

"Who? It must be a personal vendetta," Chastity cried out. "She's so sweet, and she seems really good at what she does. There's no way she deserves this."

"I know. That's why we're going. A bunch of parents are here to support her, and about half the teachers as well." Maude added, "Some don't like to go against the board and they're staying out of it."

Chastity shrugged, ever the idealist. "I don't care about that. Let's go."

When they reached the door to the community room, there was already a handful of people waiting on the landing and stairwell. Maude tapped the person in front of her and whispered, "What are we waiting for? Why don't we just go in?"

Chastity didn't recognize the woman and assumed it must be a parent. "We don't have the right to interrupt the board meeting, so we're waiting until it's finished," the woman answered. "We'll have to ask them to reopen the issue and hear us out."

Maude nodded her approval and turned back to Chastity. "You heard that?"

Chastity nodded back with a glimmer of a smile. "This hints at revolt. I hope they don't meet us with boiling oil."

Maude flashed her white teeth as she laughed noiselessly. "So what's new? You've been distracted lately."

Chastity sighed deeply and leaned on the railing. “Thomas’s father is in France, and he asked to meet us.”

“Oh. You’ve never mentioned him before. When’s the last time Tommy saw him?”

“Never.” Chastity’s smile was rueful, and Maude waited for her to continue. “He’s been in prison. But even before that he told me he wanted nothing to do with the baby. I was just a teenager, you know.” She darted a glance at Maude’s face and was relieved to see no judgment there. “He said he’d pay for an abortion. So nice of him,” she added.

Maude wrinkled her brows. “I’m afraid to ask how he was supposed to pay for the abortion. What did he go to prison for?”

“Selling drugs. But that wasn’t how he would have paid for it. In fact, I still can’t get over the fact that he would do something like sell drugs. He comes from a wealthy French family, and his dad is—or was—in New York on diplomatic business. I mean, tons of money and lots of snobbery to go with it.”

“In my years of teaching, I’ve seen a few privileged kids fall off the straight path like that. Sometimes the parents were too busy to give the attention and affection a kid needs. But sometimes it’s just bad luck. A good kid from a good, affectionate family will fall in with a bad crowd and make stupid choices. What were his parents like?”

“I think they were all right. His mom was maybe a bit cold, but it was clear they loved him. He was all they had, and they gave him all their attention.”

“Hm. Maybe too much. But let me stop analyzing. The truth is, you just never know. So when are you going to meet him? Or *are* you going to meet him?”

“Tomorrow. Do you think I’m doing the right thing, or should I run the other direction?”

“I can’t answer that for you.” Maude pursed her lips. “He left you to raise Thomas on your own. Then again, he was—what—seventeen? Eighteen? We are all stupid at that age.” Chastity laughed, and Maude continued in a more serious tone. “But then, what he did afterwards was not just stupid; it had serious consequences. I just don't know. I suppose everyone deserves at least one second chance, right?"

Chastity stole a glance at the others who were all involved in conversation. She answered quietly. "That's exactly what I told Thomas, but it doesn't bring me any closer to knowing what to do." She gave a small shrug. "The truth is, I'm lonely. It's not that I think he's going to be the answer to that, but it makes it harder for me to think clearly."

"How many men have you dated seriously since Thomas's father."

Chastity brought her thumb and forefinger together to make a zero.

"What? How is that possible? How are they not beating down your door?"

Chastity chewed her lip. "I don't know. A few tried, but there was always something missing. I suspected they didn't like kids—usually that was it. Sometimes there was no spark. Or I'm busy."

Maude grabbed her hand, which rested on the railing, and held it tightly. "Of course you're busy. You're a single mom. But I suspect with the right one, the obstacles would fade away. Don't you think?"

"The right one. Ha. If only I knew what I wanted. That's the problem. I don't know what I want." She tucked a curl behind her ear. "No, I *do* know, but I don't like to say the words because I'm afraid it will never come true."

Maude prodded her. "Now you have to tell me. You can't leave me hanging."

Chastity took a deep breath. "I want someone who loves both me and Thomas. Someone who's not afraid to commit and actually wants to *marry* me." She stretched out the word, then laughed and hid her face in her hands. "You know—what you and Michel have, and I'm afraid that just doesn't exist anymore. At least not for me."

"Oh, you want matching names?" Maude teased. "Let's see...what matches with Chastity?"

Just then the door to the community room opened, signaling the end of the board meeting. Maude was still staring at her and chuckling quietly, so Chastity whispered, "Nothing. Nothing matches with my name."

"Christophe." Maude whispered back. "Chandler." Then, as an afterthought, "Charles."

Chastity suppressed a smile and rolled her eyes. "Look ahead. The line's moving."

Chastity had no idea what to expect from this impromptu meeting with the board. She just knew it wasn't fair that they could get rid of someone for no apparent reason. This small group of supporters, about fifteen in all, would at least take a stand against the injustice. *Someone has to*, she huffed.

She was the last one to position herself on one end of the oval table that usually held student backpacks and cans of coke, but which now held espresso cups and a plate with nothing but crumbs. She studied the board members who were talking with one another and ignoring the crowd that had assembled the minute the meeting was over.

Chastity drew in a quick breath. Monsieur de Brase was here. Right in the center of the group of board members, talking and smiling as he shook the hand of someone she didn't know. Her eyes darted to the right and caught those of her principal, Elizabeth, who was sitting at the table, a stack of papers and notes in front of her.

Of course her principal would have to attend the board meeting. Chastity wondered if she would learn more details later but dismissed the idea immediately. Elizabeth was her boss and would never gossip. As if she knew what Chastity was thinking, Elizabeth smiled at her. Mr. de Brase, finishing his conversation, caught the silent exchange and glanced at Chastity. She thought she saw a flicker of recognition and was suddenly conscious of what she was wearing. Yet another bohemian skirt. She mentally shook herself.

Maude was looking around to see who was going to begin the dialogue. When no one stepped forward, she broke through the murmur. "Excuse me, ladies and gentlemen." The board members stopped talking and turned to face her.

"Thank you for your attention." Gesturing at the people around her, she said, "We've come to talk to you about your decision to replace Anne Meurier." She addressed Mr. de Brase who, Chastity was starting to suspect, had a principal role in the firing.

Mr. de Brase met her challenge with silence, which might have discomfited someone made of lesser stuff, but Maude just waited. Finally Mr. de Brase sighed. "You've come to talk. What is it you want to say?"

A couple of people in the crowd muttered under their breath, but Maude spoke over them. "Mademoiselle Meurier is good at what she does, and she adds value to the school and community. We represent staff and parents on this issue, and none of us are in agreement with her being let go. We would like to ask you to reconsider."

Mr. de Brase eyed her unflinchingly. "Madame...?"

"Madame Rosier," Maude answered.

"Madame Rosier. I appreciate your support of your colleague, and your interest in the board's decision. But that's just it. This isn't a democracy, and the decisions are the board's to make. We've made a ruling that we feel is best for Fenley, and that is to end Mademoiselle Meurier's contract early. We're not required to justify our decision to anyone."

Mr. de Brase turned to gather his coat and briefcase. The grumbling around them grew louder, and Maude attempted to speak once again. "Monsieur de Brase, we're just asking out of common courtesy to provide us with a reason..."

Mr. de Brase cut her off. "Excuse me, ladies and gentlemen, this meeting is adjourned. Christian, will you accompany me to my car?" The gentleman in question pulled on his coat and squeezed past the group of protesters that parted in the viscount's wake.

Elizabeth Mercer stood as well, looking self-conscious, if not embarrassed. Chastity decided she would see if an opportunity presented itself to approach her when some of the tension had died down. The crowd was now speaking more openly as the rest of the board filed out. Chastity glanced at Maude, who was staring at the doorframe where Mr. de Brase had just exited.

Maude looked back at Chastity. "Wow," she mouthed.

"I know." Chastity nodded, her eyes wide.

# CHAPTER 4

Chastity clipped the front of her hair in a barrette and let the rest fall freely in light-brown curls that turned red in the sunlight. She put on mascara and lip-gloss but kept the rest of her look natural, hating herself for wanting to impress him. *Why do I even care what he thinks of me?* Her movements were abrupt as she zipped her makeup bag and knocked the plastic cup off the sink. It clattered to the floor, and she absently picked it up and set it in its place. She wanted him to regret what he missed out on—to look at her and see that time had treated her well, like a fine wine, and pine away in misery for having thrown it all away. *No, not wine. I already feel old enough.* She wanted him to see her as bubbly and festive, like an out-of-reach champagne.

All her attempts at forgiveness seemed futile now, because she was too mad at how he had treated her to be even falsely festive. Chastity's eyes narrowed at the memory. She had become a despicable creature in her own eyes—and probably his—weeping and begging him in pleading whispers to reconsider. His parting words were, "I only went out with you because your name presented a challenge." He stalked over to the group of friends, for whose benefit he had rehearsed this line, and punched one of them in the arm, grinning. And she stayed behind and sobbed. *Like an idiot.*

Chastity forced herself to exhale and picked up the phone. "Hi, Mom." She smiled when she heard the familiar voice.

"Hi, Chassy." It was a name her mom only used in rare, affectionate moments. Why shorten a beautiful Victorian name? "How's my grandson?"

"He's good." Chastity paused, but there wasn't much time, so she plunged in headlong. "Mom, we're meeting Marc Bastien in a half-hour." She could hear her heart thump while she waited for her mom's reaction.

There was a beat before she got a response. "So he's back in France, is he? I suppose it's good for Tommy to meet his dad. It doesn't mean he has to be a regular part of his life, does it?"

"No." Chastity smiled to herself. Trust her mother to say something calm and sensible, and bring her back down to earth. "He said I'm the one to call the shots, and I intend to do just that." She didn't feel it necessary to mention the lip-gloss. "If it seems unhealthy for Thomas, I'll tell Marc he's not allowed to see him anymore."

"I wish you weren't living so far away." Her mother was uncharacteristically wistful.

"I'll be fine, Mom, I promise." Chastity was sure her anxiety was coming through and continued brightly. "We have to leave soon, but I just wanted to hear your voice. We can Skype tomorrow at our usual time, okay?"

After she hung up the phone, the tension eased in her shoulders. Pulling her hair off her neck, Chastity turned her face this way and that to check her appearance in the mirror. Then she couldn't put it off anymore. It was time to go. She peeked into Thomas's room, where he was working his way through a French book, although he was more comfortable reading in English. "Are you ready to go, sweetie?"

"Yes, Mom." He stood and tried to zip his sweatshirt, but it was old, and the zipper was not easy to get started at the bottom. She came over and knelt down to secure the bottom of the zipper before tugging it all the way up. She caught his glance and smiled.

"What if I don't like him?" Thomas's expression was worried.

"You never have to see him again," she answered, calmly.

After a pause, he said in a smaller voice. "What if he doesn't like me?"

Chastity breathed in and pressed her lips to crush the wave of feelings that started to rise. She managed a smile and said, "That, my dear, would be impossible."

She started walking towards the door, indicating for him to follow her out of the apartment. The furniture was mostly from Ikea, with a few old elegant chairs and side tables that she had recuperated from the neighborhood bulk trash collection. With these antique touches, a few large houseplants next to the window, and some abstract paintings she had done during one of her college courses, the place had a less bare-bones feeling to it than when she first moved in. She had recently added sheer white curtains and a dark burgundy living room rug.

Once in the hallway, she turned the large, modern skeleton key in the lock. As they walked to the elevator, she put her arm around his shoulder, pulling him close. "Don't forget that he asked to see you. We're the ones who decide whether we're going to let him into our lives or not."

Her son nodded once and ran ahead to push the elevator button, and Chastity smiled to herself. At times Thomas was so perceptive, and even sharp-tongued, she forgot how young he was. At other times, she was reminded of the fact that she had many years ahead of her before her son would be a grown man and no longer in need of her.

They were meeting in the town center, and it was a sunny, late October day so they decided to walk. Thomas was fully absorbed in the two riders ambling down the shady street near their apartment building. Maisons-Laffitte was an equestrian town, and the stables were located kitty-corner from the school.

They skirted past the Château of Maisons-Laffitte on their way to the café where they had planned to meet Marc. *I wonder what Mr. de Brase is doing now,* she thought—which annoyed her. *Who cares what he's doing?* She already had one irritating French male to deal with, and that was enough. But when her mind insisted on imagining bumping into him next to his home, her heart beat faster. *Oh no, you don't.* She groaned inwardly. *Even if he weren't so stuck up, he's totally out of my league. Leave it to me to have my first crush as a single mom be on someone who's so unavailable.*

They were in the busy part of town now, and she forced herself to focus as she faced the door to the Café Jerôme. Her switch in preoccupation happened so fast it made her head spin. As she opened the door, Chastity gritted her teeth. *I'm not a teenager. I'm a grown woman with a master's degree. And a job, which is more than I can say for him.* She scanned the tables inside the room, darkened by red curtains and mahogany tables, and her gaze fell on Marc. She knew at once it was him, but she couldn't believe the changes the past seven years had wrought.

He wore a hot pink dress shirt that gleamed against his olive skin and brown hair. He had on jeans and Converse sneakers to complete his look of youthful casual. Except he did not at all look young. His face showed premature lines, and there was a tiredness to his eyes, or perhaps a hardness. Even the way he sat looked less jaunty somehow. He slouched, and his fingers drummed the table. When he lifted his head and saw them, he got to his feet and shoved his hands in his pockets. He gave a nervous smile but made no move to walk towards them.

Chastity was shocked. *Has he really changed?* She couldn't believe it was true, but maybe prison had humbled him. He looked like he wasn't confident of his reception and didn't dare to push it. She felt the ice around her heart thaw. Putting an arm around Thomas, she walked towards him, attempting a smile.

"Marc," she said simply.

"Hi, Chastity." He moved to kiss her on the cheek, but she held out her hand, stopping him short. For a minute, he studied her hand, then he clasped it.

Thomas was examining his father openly, and Marc turned to him. "Thomas, do you know who I am?"

"Of course. My mother told me. You're my father."

"That's right. Here, I got you something." He reached over to the table and handed Thomas a small present, wrapped neatly in red paper with a ribbon and gold foil sticker. Thomas took it with two hands and carefully pulled off the wrapping paper, revealing a train engine, elaborately crafted, with a whistle that made noise when you pulled on it.

"I like it," Thomas said, with dignity. He set it down on the table.

"I asked the woman in the toy boutique what a seven-year-old boy would like, and she recommended this."

"Thomas, thank your father," his mother reminded him gently.

"*Merci.*" Thomas turned his face up to be kissed.

"Please sit down." Marc gestured to the two chairs next to him. Chastity took off her coat, helping Thomas with his, and placed the coats on the backs of their chairs before sitting down. The waiter came and took their orders—hot chocolate and a croissant for Thomas, an espresso for Marc and a *café crème* for Chastity.

"You take sugar?" When she nodded, Marc handed her two packets from the glass square in the center of the table.

"What grade are you in, Thomas?" Marc stirred a sugar cube into his espresso.

"I'm in first grade." Thomas took a bite of his croissant. His train sat untouched next to him, but he cast furtive glances at it as he spooned hot chocolate into his mouth.

"Thomas is an advanced reader," Chastity said. "He's already read the first Harry Potter book."

"Wow. That's amazing." Marc smiled encouragingly at him. "I was never much of a reader myself, but I did see all the movies."

Thomas nodded and continued to chew his croissant. He swung his leg underneath the table.

"So, Chastity, what have you been doing all these years?" Marc placed his hand on hers, which was lying on the table. She jerked her hand away as if he had burned it.

"Um." She tried to cover her confusion. "I got my degree at Columbia, which you probably knew. And I stayed on to get my master's. I got the connection to this job from Mrs. Hirtz at the *lycée*, and we've been here since August."

"That's great," he said. She didn't dare reciprocate the question so an awkward silence fell.

"So, where are you living and working?" Chastity asked, finding her voice.

"I'm living in Puteaux, near La Défense, and for now I'm working at the FNAC in the photography boutique."

"And your parents? They're still in New York?"

"Nah, they came back after, uh...afterwards. I think they were tired of living in Manhattan."

"I understand." Chastity fell silent. She imagined his demise caused too much embarrassment in their polite circle for them to remain there.

"So they know you're here and everything...?" She was hesitant to pry, but at the same time, was curious how he was getting along. She had a hard time imagining him—the golden boy—scraping by without his parents' help.

"They know." Marc shrugged. "I can't say they're too thrilled with the idea of having me over to see them, and I haven't pushed. I humiliated them."

"I see." Chastity studied the napkin folded on her lap.

Even when she had disappointed her own parents, they would never think of shutting her out. Thomas started to clink his empty chocolate mug in tune to his kicking feet. "Do you mind if we walk? It's hard for a boy his age to sit still for long."

"Of course." Marc stood, signaling for the check.

When they came out of the café, they turned left and started walking towards a playground she had seen in passing. They entered the fenced-in area, and Marc watched Thomas run towards the jungle gym, his feet flinging sand as he went. Chastity cleared her throat.

"I was thinking. Didn't you have to serve parole at all? Was there no problem for you to leave the country?"

"No," he said, shaking his head. "With the reduced time, it was as if I had served my whole sentence, so there was no parole. I was allowed to come back because this is my home country. I came back with a record, though. I'm no freer here than I was in America. I'll never have a career or anything like that."

"Don't say 'never'." Chastity frowned in sympathy.

He was quiet for a minute, then nodded towards his son. "What did you tell him about me?"

"I told him the truth. He deserves to know the truth."

Marc shook his head. "He must hate me. A father who was in prison."

His humiliation pained Chastity, even if she was wary of his own potential for inflicting pain. It caused her to speak with more gentleness than she had yet shown. "I've not made you out to be a villain, Marc. He'll judge you from what you are to him—not from anything I tell him."

Marc flashed her a quick smile before looking at his feet.

"But I do have to ask what role you hope to have in his life after seven years," she continued. "I mean, there hasn't been a word from you in all this time. I can't forget what you said to me when I first told you—or your parting words."

Marc cut her off with a groan, his face in his hands. "Please forget about anything I said back then. I mean, forget about it as much as you can. I was too cocky. I'm sorry—I know I was a jerk." His voice trembled, and he averted his eyes.

"Okay, fine," Chastity said, not unkindly. She chewed her lip. "But, so what role..." She trailed off, looking at Thomas.

"Whatever role you permit me." Marc shrugged and glanced at her with a hopeful smile. Their gaze met before they both turned to Thomas, who had climbed all the way to the top of the jungle gym and who was shyly watching them. The sun formed a halo around his straw-colored head as he straddled the top of the netted pyramid. He gave a small wave, and they both smiled and waved back.

"Let's just play it by ear, okay?"

# CHAPTER 5

Charles stepped off the Eurostar with his hand on Manon's back to guide her through the crowds. He signaled a porter to come and help with their bags and led the way to the taxi stand. Manon was relatively unknown in London, and it was a pleasure to be able to move about freely without fear of being recognized.

Nevertheless, she kept her sunglasses on and moved furtively, which drew more attention to her than if she had acted more naturally. They jumped in a taxi and headed to the newly opened Cambria hotel on St Thomas Street. Charles relaxed on the vinyl seat and meditated as they drove past the streets teeming with people.

When they arrived at the hotel, Charles contemplated the sparse pieces of artwork, bare marble floors, and isolated settees and decided the lobby was too austere for his taste. He was vaguely aware of the irony in his judgment since he lived in a rambling, drafty château. They walked up to the reception desk and asked for their suites. Manon Duprey was booked in the Kensington Suite, and Charles was staying in the smaller Cambria Suite. As they rode up in the elevator behind two bellhops, she leaned into him and whispered in his ear. "I don't know why we can't stay in the same suite."

He cracked a smile but only patted her arm draped around his waist by way of an answer. She was not used to men remaining immune to her charms, and he guessed this little gesture made her want to double up on the seduction. Or scratch his eyes out. Charles followed one of the bellhops out of the elevator and promised Manon he would be by to pick her up for dinner at eight. They were eating at Barney's Tavern and had reservations to dine there at nine o'clock.

Charles went into his suite and watched the bellhop place his suitcase on the folding stand with elastic bands across it. After he tipped the uniformed man, who let himself discreetly out, Charles was alone. He walked over to the window.

It had begun to rain outside and grow dark, and he watched the people below scurrying for shelter. His spirits sank as the rain fell from the somber, gray skies, and he couldn't help but wonder why he had bothered to come to London at all. He had been instantly attracted to Manon when he met her at a charity dinner several months ago, but sometimes it felt like the longer he spent in her company, the more he was aware of their differences.

A perfect example occurred on the way over. They had first class tickets on the Eurostar, but through a mix-up, another couple had been assigned the same seats on the fully-booked train. He was prepared to let it go, but she refused to be downgraded and made a quiet, but embarrassing, scene.

Charles had spent his entire life with a family who expected to be honored because of their title. More specifically, he walked in the shadow of a *mother* who expected to be recognized and given her due. He had had enough. The more Manon Duprey tasted the fame and glamor attached to her career, the more she was drawn to a pampered life. Charles de Brase, wealthy and titled, was aiming for simplicity in life. The actress, naturally simple, was climbing towards elegance. Their relationship seemed to be heading for a draw.

He wasn't used to indulging in such morose reflections, so he shook it off and walked over to his suitcase to take out a shirt for the evening. On his way across the room, he suddenly paused, struck by a thought. He picked up his cell phone and dialed.

"Bonsoir, Isabelle, it's your uncle," he said, when he heard a young woman answer the phone.

"*Oncle*," she squealed, dropping her heavily-accented English for her mother tongue. "Where are you calling me from?"

"I'm in London. Your mother asked me to look in on you to see what mischief you're getting up to."

"*Je suis sage comme une image*," she retorted pertly. "Innocent as you please."

"I thought I might come to Cambridge tomorrow afternoon for a visit if you're free."

"Oh." She was clearly taken aback. "I, um...I'm free, but I promised to work in the soup kitchen all afternoon. I don't suppose you want to join me for that?"

"That sounds like a perfect way to spend the afternoon, *ma filleule*. I'm pleased that you're getting involved in such a noble undertaking. I think I'll come." He smiled, waiting for more.

"*Oooh*. Uncle Charles, you called my bluff," she said, with her usual gaiety. "If you must know, I'm going along with a new...friend. We know each other from class, and he's invited me to go with him. To be perfectly frank, I don't wish to scare him off right from the beginning by having my imposing godfather come along."

"Ah, so I'm imposing, am I?" Charles laughed. "Don't worry. I won't come and frighten him away. He's English then, I'm assuming?"

"Actually, um, he's...Nigerian." It sounded like she was cringing over the phone. "I don't suppose you approve."

"Why do you need my approval? You're a grown woman—or nearly so—and you can make your own choices. Plus," he added, "I'm not nearly as archaic as you think."

"You don't let me call you Charlie," she retorted.

"No one is allowed to call me Charlie," he said calmly.

"Except *Maman*." He could hear the mischievous grin in her voice.

Charles said, "Your mother only thinks she can because she's older than me, but that doesn't make it true."

There was a pause and Isabelle's voice grew serious, "But Grand-mère *is* archaic, isn't she?"

"I'm afraid Grand-mère is."

"So you won't tell her or my mother just yet," she pleaded, "not until I'm more sure of my feelings?"

"Of course I won't, silly creature. When have I ever been a tattle-tale?" He always made her laugh when he used childhood slang. It was so strange coming out of his mouth.

"I suppose I should get going," he continued. "I just wanted to check in with you. I'll tell Louis you send kisses."

"If you want," she said. "But we text all the time, you know." He hadn't known, and was surprised, since he and his son never communicated that way. *In fact, we rarely communicate at all.*

"I'll send Grand-mère your kisses then." He paused, adding dryly, "Unless you text her too." Isabelle just giggled.

"Now I can tell your mother I have faithfully discharged my duty to look in on you."

"Of course you would never call me on your own volition," Isabelle said, teasing, but petulant.

"I'm hurt," Charles shot back. "How can you accuse me of such a thing when I was willing to come serve in the soup kitchen with you?" He thought for a minute before adding, "Come to think of it, this must be an exceptional young man to drive you to altruism."

Instead of retorting in jest as he expected, her voice turned pensive. "He is. Actually...before you go, there *is* a favor I'd like to ask of you, if you don't mind."

"Sure. Go ahead." Isabelle took a deep breath and began laying out her idea.

After they hung up, Charles selected a pink and white checked Alain Figaret shirt and a muted purple silk tie, and laid them on the bed. He began peeling off his jeans and shirt from the day's trip as he considered Isabelle's request. The phone on the nightstand rang, interrupting his thoughts, and he went over to pick it up.

"Hello, chéri." Manon's animated voice spilled out of the receiver. "I just wanted to let you know that Bruce is also dining at Barney's Tavern with the director, and he arranged to have us all seated together. I hope you don't mind."

"Not at all," Charles answered. It was widely rumored that British actor Bruce Richards had been smitten with Manon ever since he met her, and it was he who pushed the director to give her this first starring role in an international film. If this was a ploy to get him jealous, it was not going to work. "We can meet them in the lounge."

"That's precisely what I told him. I knew you wouldn't mind."

When they arrived, Bruce Richards and Guy Moss, the director, were already seated at the bar. Both of them had a whisky in front of them, and Bruce stood. "Manon," he cried out, his fair skin already flushed from the alcohol. "It's great to see you again." He kissed her on one cheek.

"Hello, Bruce. Hello, Guy." She tilted her cheek to be kissed and spoke in awkward English. "I present Charles."

"It's an honor." Bruce shook his hand, and Guy gave a nod and extended his hand.

"So you've made it." Bruce switched his attention back to Manon. "I hope you find the Kensington Suite to your satisfaction. I haven't seen it myself yet, but I'm told it's very comfortable."

"It's lovely." Manon smiled graciously. "It will be hard to leave the bed in the morning for our five o'clock call."

"That won't start until Monday and will only last for two weeks," Guy interjected, with a strong Glaswegian accent. "This is the last location before we wrap things up, and I find it's best to get through the difficult scenes first." He smiled in his crooked way that was easy to mistake for a grimace. He was not known for being an easy person to work with.

"How long are you staying?" Bruce addressed Charles, before lifting his drink to his lips.

"Only until Sunday," Charles answered. "I'll have to begin work again."

"He has to oversee the upcoming races, too. He owns the racetrack *and* the château at Maisons-Laffitte." Manon tapped her escort's arm.

"Not to mention my real work," Charles muttered inaudibly.

"Oh—where's that then?" Bruce's pale eyes didn't waver from Manon.

"It's not far from Paris." Charles took a sip of the whisky, which had just been set down in front of him.

"I'll have to come and visit the château sometime," Bruce said, not realizing he was inviting himself over to the viscount's principal residence.

"Certainly," Charles replied, without missing a beat.

At that moment, the hostess came over to tell them their table was ready, and a fan walked up at the same time to get Bruce Richards's autograph. Manon tensed up when he headed their way but looked comical when she realized the young man had no idea who she was. Charles put his arm around her slender waist and pulled her close. Bruce caught the gesture and put his brows together, but immediately handed the signed napkin back to the gentleman with a large smile.

The dinner did not interest Charles, and it took all his good breeding to hide just how bored he was. The talk centered around the industry, actor gossip, details of the scenes in the movie, with Guy giving directions to both Manon and Bruce in a sonorous voice, and no one apart from Manon making an attempt to include Charles in the conversation. When they finally stood to leave, and Charles was signaling for a taxi on the corner, Manon leaned in and said in a small voice, "I'm afraid you found the evening to be terribly boring."

"Not at all," he responded, politely. But when they reached her suite at the hotel and she invited him in, he surprised even himself by saying he was tired and would see her in the morning. The pretty blond actress was unable to cover her chagrin, and her smile glittered. She shut the door loudly behind him as Charles walked away, which made him chuckle. When he entered the blessed silence of his own room, he found he didn't regret his decision.

# CHAPTER 6

Thomas tugged on Chastity's hand then ran up the grassy steps ahead of her. Up and up without seeming to tire at all. Each small footstep spun off the old wooden beams that were pegged into the earth to make stairs.

Chastity made her way up more calmly, preserving her energy for the long climb. They were at Etretat—the beach in Normandy, famous for its cliffs, with long arches carved out by centuries of water flowing through. She rounded the bend in the rustic staircase, and her son was sitting calmly on a boulder waiting for her. As soon as she appeared, he darted off again, running up the hillside.

Nearing the top, Chastity saw the edge of the cliff on her left, but the path was distant enough from the edge that she didn't fear for Thomas's safety. On the right was a small hill where cows grazed. The solid and wooly white creatures munched on long, lush grass, almost silver in its shininess. Perhaps the cows needed that extra layer on their hides against the wind that must blow fiercely on the cliffs in the wintertime. Even now, at the end of October, she and Thomas wore scarves and jackets zipped tightly to their necks.

The two of them reached the highest spot on this side of the cliff, the best view for the rock formation that Monet had made famous across the bay. Chastity stood at the top, her hands on Thomas's shoulders, both of them looking over the horizon into the soft autumn sun. The water crashed against the cliff below, and the wind blew steadily against her face, filling her lungs with cold air.

*This is my life!* She wanted to shout in the joy of that moment—alive, with her beloved son, breathing in the age-old, glorious surroundings. But later that night in the hotel room, she sat next to her sleeping son and brushed a lock of hair off his forehead with her hand. *This is my life*, she thought again, quietly.

She got up and walked over to the little desk. They were spending the All Saints holiday at a Bed & Breakfast in Trouville, which was cheaper than Deauville, but not far. Their room—papered in light, flowered wallpaper—was on the top floor with a sloped ceiling and dormer windows. A candle she had bought at a small boutique in Etretat caused flickering shadows to dance on the faded walls. Leaning her head in her hands, Chastity let out her breath.

*I'm lonely*. She picked up her phone and turned it over in her hands, tracing the red poppy decal on the white background. She had no one to call. It had never bothered her much that she never had anyone to turn to, apart from her parents. But here, with all this beauty around her, she found she wanted to share it with someone. She missed intimacy.

Passing the phone from hand to hand, she turned her thoughts to Marc, remembering the way he stared at her on their recent outing after that first date—the baby steps in their relationship of two plus one. His gaze never left her face when she spoke, and he looked at her the way he used to. He put his arm on the small of her back as they crossed the street together, Thomas on his scooter sailing across in a way she had told him countless times not to do. Marc's touch distracted her, but it didn't weaken her. She wasn't ready to go back to that place. *I'm not sure I ever will be.*

She put the phone down on the desk and touched the switch on the lamp cord. The flickering shadows on the wall entranced her, but only for another minute. She got up, blew out the candle, and went to bed.

Charles walked briskly down the broad sidewalk in the noonday sun, his face a perfect scowl. He had seen the morning paper. *If she thinks she can play me for a fool, she doesn't know who she's dealing with*...He grit his teeth, and his pace quickened.

With the package his trainer had forgotten in the hotel tucked under his arm, he made his way with sure steps towards the racetrack. The whole town was filled with spectators, trainers, and managers who were here for the race. He walked past a drum of roasting chestnuts and was instantly transported to his childhood.

"Will I be able to ride in this race one day, Papa?" he had asked, looking up at the person he loved and trusted most in the world. The man who was Viscount de Brase to everyone else, but Papa to him.

His father leaned against the railing at the racetrack, watching his groom handle the favored horse, cigarette smoke curling around his dark sideburns. He was distracted by the mounting excitement but always had attention to give to his son.

"I'm afraid to tell you this, Charles, but you're likely to be too tall and heavy to race." He watched his son's shoulders droop, and he poked him, smiling. "It's good to be tall, isn't it?"

Charles moped. "You can kiss the tall girls?" His father nudged him and winked, but Charles's continued sulk showed what he thought of that notion.

"It's Dancer," Charles called out, all pouting forgotten by his glee at getting such a close glimpse of the famed horse.

He could still see the way the horse rounded the track, always a head further than every other horse. His father had tried to buy him, but the owner refused to sell. So they were doomed to watch his success from a distance, along with everyone else, and regret not owning such a fine specimen.

Charles came back to his surroundings when his cell phone pinged. It was a text from his manager. He stopped and pulled off to the side of the street, against the wrought iron fence, and told him he was on his way. No sooner had he started walking again than his phone chimed once more. He glanced at it, and the corners of his mouth turned up.

He answered. "Jef."

"Charlie. You weren't there last night at the reunion. I didn't call ahead of time because I was sure I'd see you there. Too good for your old friends, are you?" Charles could hear the grin in his oldest friend's voice.

"You forgot—I'm at the race."

"Ah right. I did forget," Jean-François said. "Good for you. You need more fun in your life. You work too hard."

Charles gave a dry laugh. "Okay. If you can call this fun. Truthfully, it's just another thing I have to do."

"If that's true, it's too bad," his friend answered. "You used to love racing when you were growing up. You can't let all your hobbies go... " His voice trailed away, knowing that any hint of Miriam left him treading on dangerous ground.

Charles ignored the reference. "Sorry I didn't call. I meant to—I did want to see everyone. But I had back-to-back committee meetings before coming here."

"How many committees are you on?" Jef asked.

"Outside of the hospital? Three. And that doesn't include the racetrack."

"And you're working part-time?" His friend's voice let him know what he thought of that idea.

Truthfully, he was starting to feel the strain. "I consult more than anything. But basically—yes, I work part-time. Don't worry. I'm fine,"

Charles replied. "Look, I'll call you when I get back, and we'll have a drink together, okay?"

"That'll be good." Jef sounded distracted. "Before you go, um...just wanted to make sure you're following the news and all? You know, current events, society pages?"

Charles felt a stab in his chest—annoyance? Pain? He put his friend out of his misery. "Yeah, I saw about Manon, if that's what you're asking. She hasn't called yet, but I'm sure she will eventually."

"Okay, good. Good." Jef seemed relieved he didn't have to be the one to break the news to his best friend concerning the rumors about her and Bruce Richards. "Okay, so then, ah...talk to you soon."

"See you." Charles ended the call. He leaned against the iron bars of the gated property, ignoring the bustle around him. He was anonymous here so most people left him alone, although there were always the women who flirted based on his looks, not his title.

The phone rang again. At this rate, he wasn't going to be on time. He was about to put the phone on mute when he saw who it was. He checked his watch, then clicked the answer button as he started to walk briskly.

"*Allô?*"

"Charles, chéri." Manon's voice was hopeful. "I hope this is not a bad time."

"I've only a minute. I'm on my way to meet Grégoire to give him some supplies for my horse."

"Okay, I won't keep you." Manon sounded breathless. "The thing is, I don't know if you saw the pictures in the paper?"

Charles didn't know how to reply, so he gave a clipped, "*oui.*"

Manon rushed on. "I don't want you to get any ideas. This was a scene from the movie that the journalists misinterpreted. There's nothing going on between us." When he didn't respond right away, she persisted. "I hope you believe me."

*I really don't want to be having this conversation.* He knew he had to say something. "You can do whatever you want with your life. Just don't think I will sit here and wait." Charles regretted the words the instant they left his mouth. He sounded like a teenager.

"Yes, but you have to believe me. I'd never be unfaithful," she said, with a rising hysteria that Charles had no patience for. "I'd be crazy to when I have you...I'm not about to start now."

When he was silent, she added, "I'm supposed to come back in a month for the holiday break. Let's just not make any decisions before then. Okay?"

Charles didn't feel like committing, but he found himself agreeing. "Fine," and added, "I need to go. I have to meet Grégoire."

"Call me soon, okay?" she pleaded. He had never heard her sound so desperate, but he found he was unmoved by it. After Charles ended the call, he shut the phone off completely. He didn't want to be disturbed, and since his son was at the racetrack, he decided everyone else could wait.

He couldn't identify what he was feeling. Manon wasn't anything more than a passing fling, but he hated looking foolish. He hated being betrayed, something he never had to worry about with Miriam.

Charles picked up his pace again. Although he worked hard to smooth his features, his mouth was set in hard lines.

"Mom, Mom," Thomas shouted as he chased seagulls on the empty beach. She waved back at him, smiling broadly. Her sober reflections from last night were chased away by the fresh air and the sound of waves. They had already explored the old Normandy hotel, *Deauville Barrière*, looking at the photos of famous guests who had stayed there. Thomas was bored.

Now they were on the other side of the busy street, and she was standing on the sidewalk that bordered the beach, watching him as he ran in circles. It was almost time for them to drive home, but she thought they might walk through the town center one more time and find a place that served a hot meal. By the time she had convinced him to go, she was more than ready to get some warm food in her.

They walked down the cobblestone street together that served as a pedestrian walkway, and she was drawn to the cozily-lit restaurants that lined it. They were all too expensive. She had not chosen a cheap place to vacation.

Thomas's steps started to flag and his mood to sour when she finally gave up on the idea that they would be able to sit somewhere nice. She spotted a sandwich shop that had a seated area indoors. "Do you want to eat a sandwich?"

Her son's eyes lit up, and he nodded. They walked around the corner to where the entrance was and took their place in line. Fifteen minutes later they left with their sandwiches and a bottle of water. At least they were grilled Panini sandwiches, which would feel warm going down.

"Look Mom," Thomas said with his mouth full. "There are horses over there." She focused on where he was indicating. It was on the opposite end of where the car was parked, and she could feel a fatigue set in through to her bones.

"I see, honey." Her son didn't say anything else, but started to inch in that direction. She figured they could turn down the next street without going too far out of their way, so she followed.

"Mom. It's *Victoire Absolue*!" He ran straight down the street without looking behind to see if his mother was following, and she was grateful it was a pedestrian area where she need not worry about cars. Thomas slowed when he reached a fence, behind which a brown horse stood at some small distance, and he slipped easily through the barrier.

Chastity's heart beat faster at his proximity to such a massive animal, and she tried to speak calmly. "Tommy. Come here for a minute." He reached up to touch the horse's side with the hand that wasn't holding his sandwich.

"It's *Victoire Absolue*, Mom," he said, caressing the horse's flanks. The horse turned and lowered his head towards Thomas. He blew his breath out in brisk snorts, sniffing at the sandwich.

"It's all right, miss," said a gruff voice. "He doesn't hurt anyone." An older gentleman in a tailored tweed coat poked his head around from the other side of the horse where he had been hidden from view. "Hello, young man."

"This horse is enormous." Chastity said, attempting a smile. "You're sure my son's okay?"

"Aw, Mickey's as gentle as they come."

"Mickey?" Chastity turned towards Thomas. "Why did you call him *Victoire Absolue?*"

"The young man is correct. His proper name is *Victoire Absolue*, but in the stable, we call him Mickey."

Thomas moved to the other side of the horse, and Chastity asked the gentleman, "Where does this horse come from? Who owns him?"

"This is the champion horse of the Viscount de Brase. He took first place in the race today, even though he was not a favorite." The gentleman caressed the horse between the ears and continued with gruff pride. "He's from Maisons-Laffitte, just outside of Paris." The blood drained from Chastity's face. She stared at her sandwich.

"Ah. There he is. I was expecting him."

Chastity turned, just as the viscount strode up to the older gentleman. Mr. de Brase barely glanced at her, and his face looked thunderous.

"Grégoire, here are the leg wraps you needed. I have somewhere I need to be." He handed a soft bundle of fabric to the older gentleman and walked off in the direction of the racetrack.

Chastity's face grew hot. She was sure he had seen her, and that his snub was on purpose. *He probably wanted to humiliate me for daring to mingle with his world. Oh my God. He probably thought I was just hanging around his horse so I could talk to him or something*. She glanced at her son and tried to think of something to say.

The older gentleman, Grégoire, seemed nonplussed. "Mr. de Brase usually has a bit more time to spare than that, but that's him in any case." Then he addressed Thomas, eyes alight. "So you know Mickey, do you? How so?"

"I go to Fenley Academy, and I see him walking by in the mornings." Thomas continued to stroke the horse's side. "He's so much finer than the other horses."

"You seem to know a thing or two. You know the stables are right across the street from your school?" Thomas nodded eagerly. "Why don't you come by and say hello sometime."

"That would be great," Thomas cried out with boyish enthusiasm. "I can—can't I, Mom?"

Chastity was trembling, but she managed a smile. "That's kind of you, monsieur." She addressed the trainer before turning to her son. "It's time to say goodbye now. We need to go, okay, sweetie?"

Thomas patted the horse one last time. "Goodbye, Mickey," he said. "See you soon."

"*Au revoir*, monsieur."

They started walking down the street, and Chastity spotted a trash can on the side of the road. She chucked her half-eaten sandwich in it. *No way,* she thought. *We will not be visiting your stable.*

Ever.

# CHAPTER 7

Louis sat in the kitchen, eating the steak and French fries the cook had set out for him. Paltier came in and asked how his lunch was, and he grunted in reply. *He's only nice to me because he's an employee*. Even as the uncharitable thought crossed his mind, he knew it wasn't fair. Paltier had always been kind to him.

Louis knew he wasn't overly friendly. He used to talk too much—could say "Papa" forty times in the space of an hour. Now he never had anything worth saying. He wondered if he ever would. The phone buzzed next to him.

*Hi L. Talked to ur dad in London.*

*Ya. Was there w/ Manon.*

*Have u met her yet?*

*RU kidding? Then he'd have to spend time w/me.*

*Come on. U know he only pretends 2b tuff.*

*Whatevs. How's ur bf?*

*Good. Ull meet him soon.*

*Really? Ur bringing him to France?*

*Ull see. TTYL – have class. Stay off the drugs.*

After a minute, Louis received another text:

*I mean it.*

Louis deleted the conversation and speared a French fry with his fork. He was nervous. Jumpy. He wished he hadn't told Isabelle about the pot. He liked her and trusted her—probably more than anyone. However, he liked to keep his own counsel, and only told her one night in a moment of weakness when he thought he was smoking too much. Now that it was daytime, and sunny and cheerful outside, he realized he had been exaggerating the problem.

He took his last bite and drank an entire glass of water. Then he jumped up, wiped his mouth on the cloth napkin, and slung his sack over his shoulder. It was a quick walk to the school, but he was early and didn't go straight there. He lit a cigarette, and started smoking as he headed towards the old fountain. Walking past the smaller family houses, ones that most people would find majestic, he imagined the people's lives there, filled with the warmth his own household lacked. Maybe it was simply because there were fewer echoing rooms to fill. He hitched his bag higher on his shoulder and scowled.

Louis hadn't gone out of town with his father in years. He always stayed behind with Paltier or one of the other staff members. He had looked forward to their trip to Deauville but had found his father distant and testy, asking too many questions about how Louis spent his time. *He knows about the drugs,* he thought. *Probably the only reason he invited me.*

When he arrived at his destination, Jean was already there. He was an older man—Louis guessed in his mid-twenties or thirties—and he always dressed well, but young. Today he was wearing designer jeans, an Oxford, and a padded designer vest. Louis liked the guy because he didn't treat him like a stupid kid. Jean was seated on a bench facing the fountain, and Louis reached down and shook his hand before sitting next to him.

They both faced forward, and Louis took out his textbook so it looked like they were discussing his studies together. This had been Jean's idea. Louis spoke first. "So there are five people who want to buy."

“That’s good,” Jean said. “Up from last week, which means there’ll be more for you.”

“Yeah.” Louis’s mouth turned downwards. “The two extra people are from word of mouth because I’m not friends with a lot of people.”

Jean responded with a shrug. “You will be. You’ll be the most sought-after guy in school. Don’t you worry about it. People love the guy who can provide the entertainment.”

Louis nodded and pulled out the euros stuck in the pages of his textbook. He slid them discreetly to Jean underneath the book. Jean took the money and slid a couple small bags of marijuana back.

“Do you know of any parties coming up where they might want more?”

“I’ll ask around,” Louis answered. “I don’t wanna draw a lot of attention to myself, especially since no one really knows me.”

“Don’t worry,” Jean soothed. “Take it slow." He held out his fist, and Louis bumped it with his own.

"If I don’t hear from you before then, I’ll see you next Monday. You know how to reach me if there’s a problem." Jean stood and stretched, and when he did that, he looked like someone Louis’s age. “By the way, there’s a little surprise for you in your bag to help you get through the rest of the day.” With a wink, Jean sauntered down the street, his hands in his pockets.

As soon as Jean was gone, Louis peeked inside the bag of marijuana that he supposed to be his own. There was a little red pill inside. He was surprised because he had never taken anything that didn’t require smoking. He sat for a moment, considering. It must be safe to take now if Jean had told him he could get through the day like that. The more he thought about it, the more appealing the idea was. There was an additional benefit—he would have no telltale smell of marijuana. *I’ll just try it.* His pulse quickened.

Chastity was crossing the street towards the school entrance when someone called her name. It was Marc.

"Oh, hey." A blush stole over her features. "What are you doing here?"

"I'm not stalking you, don't worry." Marc laughed. "I had to meet a friend in the area."

"Really?" She raised her eyebrows. "You know people in Maisons-Laffitte besides us?"

"I really do." He grinned disarmingly. "I still have a few friends from my summer visits home who are willing to be seen with me. One of them has moved out here."

"Oh, good." Chastity was distracted. She didn't expect to meet Marc here, and she wasn't sure how she looked. Plus, her class was about to start in fifteen minutes. *Yikes. I forgot to get the handouts I need for the next class.*

Marc studied her face. "I can see I caught you off-guard. Sorry about that. When I saw you, I didn't want to keep walking without saying hello." He scratched his chin, which had a tiny bit of stubble on it. *He looks cute*—the thought distracted her even more.

"Anyway," Marc continued. "We never set up another coffee date. Do you have time this weekend? Unless—did you want to have dinner with me instead?"

"Um..." Chastity was trying to sort out what she wanted. "You know what? Let's stick to coffee dates for now. I don't want to have to worry about finding a babysitter." *Or about explaining to Thomas why I'd be going out with his father without him.*

"Okay, so then Saturday?" Marc leaned in. "I'll call you."

"That sounds fine," Chastity said, evading his kiss aimed at her cheek. "See you."

When she arrived in the building, she found her heart was beating fast. She tried to decipher what that meant, and whether she could possibly be falling for Marc again. *That, my dear girl, would be the height of folly.*

She ran up the stairs, and after a quick detour in her office, walked into the small classroom, which sat sixteen at most. This was her largest class for the day, and no one was there yet. She went over to the whiteboard and wrote at the top.

*Reflective Essay*

*What cultural elements of the Colombian fishing village played into Santiago Nasar's death?*

As she was writing the other questions, the crowd of students that had congregated outside the doorway began to enter the room noisily, throwing their book bags down and talking over one another.

"Take a seat, everyone," Chastity commanded over the bustle. "We've got a lot to cover this afternoon, and you have a homework assignment. The more we have time to discuss in class, the easier the assignment is going to be for you."

Everyone settled into their chairs, got out their laptops—or in some cases—their notebooks and pens. A few took out the book.

"I hope everyone had a good lunch." Chastity gave a friendly smile and continued, "but not so good that you're falling asleep." She wrinkled her nose, and a few laughed. The students generally liked her, but they didn't want to break the secret teenage code and make her life any easier by showing it.

"You were supposed to have finished reading the book by now. How many of you really did that?" Almost everyone raised their hands, but a few made her doubt their veracity.

"Good," she said brightly. "Then it should be no problem for you—"

She was interrupted by Louis's entrance.

"Sorry, Miss Whitmore." His words tumbled out. "I didn't mean to be late. I was in the library trying to finish the book and then a class came in, so I went down to the computer room, but there was a class there too. So I went outside and read on the bench and didn't notice the time. As soon as I saw I was late for class, I rushed right in. I'm here now, though. Prepared to work. Ah. Here's a seat."

He dropped his bag on the table and hooked the chair with his foot, pulling it out with a loud scrape so he could sit. He pulled the contents out of his bag and put them on the table noisily, opening his computer and squinting at the board to read the words before typing them on a new document. He did all this with precise movements and loud alacrity.

"Okaaay," Chastity said. If she were not so alarmed by his behavior, she would have wanted to laugh. He had not spoken that many words in the entire semester so far, and this..."Energizer Bunny" was a far cry from his usual state of sullen lassitude. A few of the students were giggling, and others were looking at Louis curiously.

With practiced deftness, she took control of the situation. "So let's take a look at the first question. What are the cultural elements in the story?"

The hand of the brightest student in the class shot up. "One of the cultural elements is religious piety, which would cause an entire town to rush to the dock to meet the bishop, giving opportunity for a murder."

"Great point, Samantha," Louis interjected before Chastity could comment. "I hadn't thought about that aspect of it. I was more focused on machismo and family honor." He put his head back down and began to type madly again.

At this, the whole class erupted in laughter. Samantha was offended.

"Yes," Chastity said evenly. "Samantha, you're absolutely right. Religious piety is often overlooked as a contributing factor, but it's true that it provided an opportunity for the murder. It also affected the way the people viewed the murder, as the priest did not publicly condemn it."

"And you're right too, Louis," she continued smoothly. "Family honor and machismo are perhaps the two dominant cultural elements that contribute to Santiago Nasar's death." She turned to the class. "Now. Someone tell me—how is that so? How do they contribute?"

A student named Justin raised his hand casually. "The Vicario brothers couldn't let Bayardo send their sister home because she wasn't a virgin without going after the guy who did that to her."

"She wasn't a *viiirgin*." Louis played with the words dreamily, biting his lip on the V sound and then puckering his lips out for the rest. He said suddenly. “Hey. We don’t know whether she was a virgin or not. We don’t know whether Santiago did it. Whether *they* did it.”

People in the class started laughing again. “That’s half-true, Louis,” Chastity said, raising her voice over the noise. “It’s pretty well accepted that Angela was not a virgin, but it’s never sure whether Santiago was involved or whether it was someone else.”

“What are some of the other cultural elements?” Chastity prompted, trying to turn the teenagers from the runaway subject of virginity. Some of the kids in the class launched into a discussion, in which Louis didn’t participate. After having typed every word that had just been discussed, he stopped suddenly and scrutinized a spot on the wall near the ceiling. He stared, immobile, barely blinking.

Chastity kept the discussion going, and only glanced at him discreetly from time to time to see how he was doing. Her mind was turning over what should be done. Should she talk to his father again? *Ugh.* She didn't want to do that. She definitely needed to speak with the principal about this because his behavior was uncharacteristic. Should she offer student counseling in hopes it might encourage him to open up? She was worried and unnerved by his behavior.

Towards the end of the class, Louis snapped out of his trance and seemed to come to life again. He didn’t participate. However, he took furious notes and flipped through the pages of the book whenever the teacher referenced a passage. She had never seen anyone so assiduous in class, much less Louis.

When the bell rang, everyone shoved their books back into their bags and stood, talking.

"Wait. Not so fast." Chastity gestured for everyone to sit back down. "You should’ve all noted the questions. I want you to write a one-page reflective essay on how your perspective changed on at least two of these issues following our class discussion. It's due next class. Got it?"

A few students muttered their assent, and the rest of the class began walking towards the door. Louis did the same, making a beeline for Max and slapping him on the shoulder. "So. Max. Do you know of any parties going on this weekend?"

Max frowned at him. "Ah, sure. I'll be sure and let you know." He and his friend exchanged a look.

Louis followed them out of the classroom, waving to people in the hallway he barely ever spoke to, much to their amazement. "Hi, Tiphaine. Hi, Vincent." They offered him tentative smiles and turned away.

There was not another class scheduled for the next period, so Chastity did not immediately gather her materials. She erased the board mechanically and chewed her lip. Setting the eraser on the metal ledge, she sat back down again. Suddenly she shuddered. *I do not want to have to call that man back in here, but I don't see how I'm going to avoid it.*

# CHAPTER 8

Charles sat at a broad table that filled the conference room in the Town Hall—the *Mairie*. He was following the committee members' discussion, while simultaneously reviewing some research he had brought home for the weekend.

He looked up from his papers and unscrewed the cap from the water bottle before filling the crystal glass in front of him. He drank and didn't look up again until they began talking about the art collection in the local museum.

"We haven't found anything suitable for the main gallery starting in March," the director said, tackling the subject frankly. "This is not the end of the world because we have the possibility of keeping Lenny Malinski's work up until April." The gallery director stopped speaking and tapped her notepad with a pen.

The assistant director, sitting to her right, had been overlooked for the title of director and had to content herself with replacing Anne Meurier, whom the board had decided to let go for unknown reasons. She tossed her silvery blond hair over her shoulder and turned to Charles coquettishly. "We usually have everything in place, and I'm not sure how it happened this time. We've always known what our next exhibit would be months in advance. That way we can plan a harmonious transition from one artist to the next."

The director was too old to flirt with the viscount, and she put her colleague back in her place. "You know, as well as I do, that this wouldn't have happened if our scheduled artist hadn't pulled out."

The silvery-haired Venus dropped her carefully controlled façade and snapped back. "Yes but if you had taken my advice and booked someone more dependable..."

Charles had no patience for internal squabbles. "I think I may have a solution for your next exhibit, and that's something I wanted to talk to you about." He reached into his briefcase and pulled out some glossy photos. "I've discovered an artist, some of whose work I've already purchased for myself. His name is Randall Mooers, and he lives in New York. I've asked him if he's willing to lend us additional paintings for an exhibition here, and he's agreed to it. There'll be plenty of time to get them sent over before March."

He caught the director's eye. "He's good. I like his work a lot—it's reminiscent of Cézanne. In addition to what we borrow, I'd be willing to lend the ones I've purchased from him for the exhibit. And I can also lend three Cézannes for the smaller room, adjacent to the main gallery."

He waited for their reaction but was not worried about their refusal. His family had stood on the committee for two generations, and without their financial support, the museum would not be able to afford an exhibit at all. He was also confident about his ability to judge art.

"That's excellent news." The director smiled smugly at her assistant. "I knew we'd be able to come up with a solution to our dilemma." She turned towards Charles. "When shall we begin the paperwork?"

"You'll have to speak with my business manager to arrange all that, I'm afraid." He stood and collected his papers and notepad, sliding them into a soft briefcase. "I need to get to the hospital."

"Of course," the director replied in a placating voice. "I have his number, and I'll give him a call."

As Charles headed towards the main entrance, he had a moment's appreciation for how lucky he was to be able to orchestrate the parts of the museum committee he enjoyed—namely the art selection—but not get mired down in paperwork. He was the one, however, who had had to fire Anne. Given the circumstances, he couldn't delegate that responsibility to anyone else. Between the school and the museum, they'd had a warm working relationship. In fact, with time and under different circumstances, it might have grown into something else.

He remembered the day it had come to his attention that she was not who she said she was. The information had come to him anonymously, but there was too much proof of its veracity to ignore. He asked his manager to check into a few details, and sure enough, she had none of the degrees her resumé claimed she did.

She'd come into the conference room that day, wreathed in smiles, ignorant of the hard blow her life was about to receive. Charles couldn't hide the strain in his greeting, and she sensed it immediately.

"What's wrong?" She had seemed concerned, as if he were the one who was suffering.

"Anne..." When he couldn't think of anything else to say, he silently handed her the letter he had received. As soon as she read the first couple of lines, she reached for the table with a trembling hand, before her feet gave way and she fell into the chair. Her eyes filled with tears. "I'm sorry."

"How did it happen?" Charles asked her. "How did you get mixed up in all this?" When she didn't answer, he pressed her. "How did you even pull it off?"

Anne began to weep silently, and he was grateful for the lack of windows in the conference room that would keep her humiliation private. She dug through her purse and pulled out a Kleenex, and when she had a reasonable control over her voice, said, "I was young when I needed that first job, and they didn't seem to have their act together so I took a risk and applied. I lied about the schooling. They took me in on a temporary basis and were pleased with my work, so they kept me. One thing led to another and I got the job at the school, and this one at the museum. And—it was too late to go and get the degree my CV claimed I had. It would've gotten out somehow. All these years, and I've been waiting for the ball to drop."

Her lips trembled, and she held the Kleenex up to them as more tears fell on to her splotched face. Charles took a breath and dealt the unpleasant blow. "We have to let you go. You know that. I'll talk to Elizabeth at the school and spare you from having to deal with her directly if you wish." She nodded.

"I've appreciated working with you." He allowed a moment for that to sink in. "As I'm sure you know, there're a couple of universities in the South of France that offer art degrees. Why not try to get a degree now? You already have the experience, and I'm willing to give you a recommendation." She shot her head up in surprise, which made him smile.

"I don't deserve—" she began.

"It's nothing." He cut her off before she could show her gratitude. "I'll ask Elizabeth to keep this between the three of us so you'll have a chance at a fresh beginning." He reached out to shake her hand, but she showed him the mangled tissue by way of protest and gave that wry smile he had come to appreciate. He hadn't had news from her since.

When the meeting with the art committee was over, he pushed open the heavy iron doors, and the bright, cold sunlight shook his thoughts back to the present. As he jogged down the stairs, he heard his phone ring. It was the school.

*"Oui, allô?"*

"Charles, this is Elizabeth Mercer. I hope I'm not disturbing you."

"As a matter of fact, I'm on my way to work. What can I help you with?" He walked towards his car and pressed the alarm. His tan Mini Cooper chirped.

"I'm here with Louis's English teacher, Chastity Whitmore," she began. Charles inwardly groaned. *What does she want now?* "I'm afraid we need to talk to you as soon as possible about Louis. When might you be able to come in?"

Charles glanced at his watch, and thought for a second before replying. "If we can have a short meeting now, I can come in right away. I won't be able to stay longer than fifteen minutes. Is that possible?"

"That sounds fine."

Charles climbed into his car and slammed the door shut. He put his car in reverse and pulled out of the parking spot, going in the opposite direction from where he had intended, and in a dark mood.

The doorbell to the front gate rang, and Elizabeth peeked out the window before ringing Charles in. She went to the front door to meet him and shook his hand.

Students bustled past them in the passageway, as the principal led him to her office. When he entered, the English teacher fixed her light green eyes on him then stood to grasp his hand before motioning towards the other seat. He couldn't shake the ridiculous feeling he was in trouble.

"I think Louis was on drugs during Tuesday's class," she said, getting right to the point. "In fact, I'm almost sure of it." She frowned, waiting for his response.

*Good grief, woman. Lighten up a little. Or do you just have it out for me in particular?* He couldn't explain to himself why he reacted so irrationally when he was around her or why she irritated him so much.

Charles knew he should have postponed this discussion. Now he was sure he'd be late for the staff meeting. *Maybe she's attracted to me and that's why she puts in all these parent-teacher requests.* He checked himself.

*I'm too old for that. I'm losing it.* He inhaled deeply and caught the scent of lavender.

After what seemed to him an interminable amount of time, he found his words. "What makes you think so?"

Chastity seemed to consider before speaking. "At times I suspect he's on marijuana because his clothes sometimes smell like that. Although it's subtle, and that makes me wonder whether I've imagined it. He's often laid back to the point of being almost. . .comatose." She laughed self-consciously, and without humor. "Again, I'm not sure because that could be his personality. I don't know him well enough." Frowning, she added, "I've told you this already in our last meeting."

"Some of it," he acquiesced, remembering how he had practically stormed out because it was more than he wanted to hear. A curl from her chignon fell onto her collarbone and his eyes gravitated towards it.

"Well, this last class was different," she said. "He came in late and was so talkative. He actually had some good ideas, and it seemed as if he'd read the book, which was different from any other class discussion he's participated in."

She shook her head. "I can't put my finger on it. I might be wrong. There were no outward signs, like red eyes or the smell of drugs. Something was. . .off. It was like he was a different person."

Charles's muscles twitched, but his face and posture remained impassive from years of breeding. He stared at the teacher, unseeing. *What am I going to do about this?* He couldn't bear to think of his son going down such a path, and at the same time, he couldn't believe it. His son was an awkward teenager. That was all. He never saw any signs of this at home. After meditating speedily, he decided it couldn't hurt to be open to seeking advice. It didn't mean he had to follow it.

"What course of action do you recommend?"

The English teacher relaxed, as if she had been expecting a fight. She shrugged imperceptibly and turned her attention to the principal.

Elizabeth answered. "I think he should speak to the counselor who's associated with the school, unless you have someone else you're connected to." Charles shook his head.

"And then—Mr. de Brase, do you talk to your son? Spend time together?"

"Of course," he answered in irritation. "We went away together during the *Toussaint*."

Chastity broke in. "I think what she means is, do you talk about the things he's worried about, or how he's feeling?"

Charles tried not to glare at her as he searched for the best way to answer. Sweat pooled under his shirt. "I don't believe this is the place to discuss how I parent my son. I give you my consent to let him meet with the counselor, and I'll make sure his private life is well taken care of."

This time he didn't rush out, but looked at each of them to make sure they all understood each other. Finally Elizabeth stood and gave him her hand. "Thank you for your time." The teacher stayed seated, and he gave an infinitesimal pause as he wondered if he should offer his hand. In the end, he just left.

Charles strode from the school. He could see Mademoiselle Whitmore staring at him critically, as if he were a terrible father. *Just like my mother*, he shuddered, gritting his teeth.

*There's no way he takes drugs. He can't even muster enough energy to rebel in that way*. He tried to recall the last time he had kissed his son in greeting, and whether or not he had noticed the smell of smoke. He couldn't even remember the last time he had been that close to his son, even in Deauville where they spent three days together.

As a boy, Louis was different. A vision flashed before Charles—the memory of chubby little legs running ahead to the man who sold pinwheels near the port for the Seine River Cruises. He smiled as he remembered his son at this age, back when he still laughed with enthusiasm. It was not just his son who had changed, Charles had to admit. He didn't delight in spending time with his son like he had when Louis was little. *I don't even know what to talk about.*

There was no specific reason to pinpoint for this metamorphosis—no trauma occurring in the last couple years between his son's boyhood and his adolescence. No, the trauma happened much earlier at the time of Louis's birth.

His wife, Miriam, had died two days after the birth of their son from complications resulting from placenta accreta. They had made it through the birth successfully, and he was sure she would recover, but the scheduled operation to discover the source of bleeding resulted in her losing her life.

He remembered holding her hand and looking at her tiny smile as she was in the gurney ready to be wheeled in. She had been a frail thing with cropped blond hair and the large brown eyes she bequeathed to her son. He brushed the locks off her forehead and allowed the nurse to slip a cap over her hair. Leaning down, he whispered, "Don't be too long in there. Your son and I will be waiting."

"Use the waiting time to get some diaper-changing lessons while I'm under. I won't be able to pick Louis up for a while, and I don't want him to be soggy."

"I'll have him swaddled like a pro." Charles had forced down the lump in his throat and grinned.

"I'll see you after." They began to wheel her away, but her gaze didn't leave his until the swinging doors hid her from his sight.

He couldn't go to the nursery, not while he was waiting. Instead, he went to the waiting room and sat on one of the hard plastic chairs to begin those long hours that would eventually end in anguish. "There were just too much blood loss," the doctor had said. "There was nothing we could do." Charles hadn't thought about that moment in a long time. He frowned.

In those early years, Louis was the only connection Charles had to his young bride. As his son began to grow and lose some of that innocence that causes a child to blurt out the first thing on his mind—that causes a child to reach out for his father without any fear of rejection—Charles began finding excuses for why his son didn't need him much anymore.

. . .

As Charles pulled off the exit on the highway, his thoughts turned again to the English teacher. *The viper*, he thought with quickened breath, as he remembered her green eyes and the way she slammed the file on the desk at their first meeting. He thought about her ugly American clothing and aggression. Her accusations.

He was annoyed. He was also bothered. For the first time in many years, he began to wonder if he had done well to leave his son to his own devices as much as he had. *I'm not going to browbeat my kid the way* I *was raised*. He would not meddle in even the smallest affair the way his mother had done to him. At the same time, he couldn't be easy.

And he reflected on how unusual it was for him to question himself in this way.

# CHAPTER 9

Paltier walked down the smooth stone steps that led to the basement. The stairway was lined with dim light fixtures, which flickered next to the large windows at the landing. The stone walls held centuries-old deer heads, mounted on green felt-covered wood. The air was chilly.

His shoes echoed on the stone floor as he made his way towards the old kitchen, with its brick fireplace that took up most of the wall, and the wine room that was just off to the side. Entering the damp room, he selected a bottle without hesitation, dusted it off with the chamois cloth he had brought with him, and tucked it under his arm.

At the landing, Paltier hesitated before taking the stairs to go back up. Following his internal prompting, he continued walking through the corridor into another unlit stone room. This one had small windows placed high where above ground was. He walked over and routinely pulled on the gate to a tunnel that led nowhere. It had been condemned before his time and no one had the key to the iron gate. It was the only alcove the previous viscount hadn't had filled in. Something about not wanting to ruin the history of the place.

He scrutinized the room to see that everything was in place and opened a closet to make sure nothing had been moved there either. The château was set on a hill, and this part of the basement was ground level, decorated simply with worn armchairs, old frames, a chest and bureau, and a few of the inferior artifacts. He swiped his finger on the tabletops and made a mental note to talk to the housekeeping staff about not neglecting the basement.

With one last sweeping glance around the room, he retraced his steps down the corridor. Just as he was about to exit the narrow walkway and enter the landing at the foot of the stairs, Paltier heard the sounds of a heavy door being scraped open. The wood had swollen and was being shoved against the tiles, and he could hear the door opening in short bursts as someone heaved his body against it.

It occurred to Paltier that no one would hear him if he yelled for help, and that he had no weapon on hand with which to defend himself. What never occurred to him was to save his own skin and go hide while the interloper helped himself to whatever treasures the château had. He stepped out in plain view in the alcove that held the door. Standing with his back turned as he closed the door, was the gardener—André.

"What are you doing here?" Paltier was indignant, and out of breath from a fear he didn't realize he was feeling. "Your work is outside."

André seemed embarrassed at being caught, and his mumbled reply was barely audible in the echoing room. "I left my shears in the lower kitchen."

"What were you doing in the kitchen?" Paltier glared at him, suspecting the attraction of the wine cellar.

André cleared his throat and spoke louder. "The ivy that was growing along the base of the house grew through the cracks in the kitchen windows, and I couldn't access it from the outside because the windows were closed."

Paltier couldn't think of anything to respond to that, so he dismissed André. "You can go after you shut that door the rest of the way. In the future I want you to tell me first before you enter the house for any reason."

"Even when I'm to come in and water the houseplants?" André responded with an innocence, Paltier suspected, was false.

"If you enter the house on any day, apart from your set day to care for the houseplants, please let me know." Paltier was no fool.

André went to the kitchen and came back with the tool in hand. Without looking at Paltier, he tugged the heavy door shut. Paltier closed the deadbolt from inside, thinking that the door needed to be fixed so it closed more smoothly. He couldn't bear to let any part of the château remain unkempt, even if it was just the basement. He then walked into the kitchen to verify André's story, and when he examined the kitchen windows, noted the pockmarks left behind by ivy recently removed. He nodded at the observation. *He was telling the truth.*

Suddenly, Paltier's legs gave way, and he sat on the edge of the stone sink that had been used in centuries past. He exhaled and contemplated the shrubbery out the low windows on his left side. A cat leaped up to the sill and picked its way carefully across, en route to who knew what adventure.

It took him a minute to gather his strength. *I'm not getting any younger*, he thought.

It was cold enough without the wind, but a freezing gale whipped the leaves into a frenzy, causing Louis to hunker down further into his coat. There was little sun for mid-morning, making the atmosphere bleak. The community service every student was obliged to do was always a pain, but with this wind, it was even less pleasurable to babysit the younger kids on the playground. Louis had hoped to be able to skip the volunteer work now that he was forced to see the counselor (whom he'd already decided he wouldn't tell a thing). He had had no such luck and was told he'd need to manage both.

He straddled the end of the cold, stone bench, turning to his left to watch the younger children run and scream on the playground. He was supposed to be interacting with these kids, but he had absolutely nothing to say and was one of the few bigger kids that elicited no cheering squad when he entered the school grounds each morning. From his seat, Louis turned his head furtively to the right to watch the part of the street that wasn't obscured by evergreens.

A slender kid with blond hair walked up to him and sat, which was a first. As if he sensed where Louis's curiosity lay, the kid sat on the part of the bench facing the street. Louis glanced at him, and then, grateful for the excuse to be looking in the direction that concerned him, turned fully to face the street as well.

"You're supposed to be talking to us, you know."

The kid spoke with a clear voice and didn't seem to be self-conscious carrying on a conversation with an older kid. In some ways, the kid was more sure of himself than Louis was. Louis shot him another glance, and then looked back at the street, feeling edgy. "I know."

"So why are you just sitting here?" came the next question.

Louis didn't know how to answer him, which was stupid since he was just a kid. "I'm tired," he finally said.

"What's out there? What are you looking for?"

Louis pinched his eyebrows together in irritation. *Why is this kid bugging me?* "What makes you think I'm looking for something?"

Suddenly the boy shifted focus. "My name is Thomas." He held out his hand to shake.

Not knowing what else to do, he gave his own hand in return. "Louis." Then as an afterthought, he added, "Do you, uh, need help with your homework or something?"

"Nah, I'm good." Thomas started to swing his legs back and forth on the stone bench, causing his rear end to jump off the seat with each swing. There was some movement on the street beyond the evergreens that caught Louis's attention. He stood, as if unsure of what he had seen, then reached down to grab his bag.

"Where are you going?"

"I'll be right back."

Having nothing better to do, Thomas leaped off the seat and walked towards the school building until Louis had gone out the front gate and was rounding the sidewalk outside the fence. Doubling back under the cover of the evergreens, Thomas walked close to the sidewalk and stood in front of the hedge that blocked the street view. He bent down and pretended to tie his shoe.

"Jean." He heard Louis from the other side of the hedge. Then he heard a muffled sound in reply that he guessed was a handshake or a clap on the back. There was a sound of a lighter flaring up and a sharp intake of breath.

"So why did you need to see me so urgently?" The words came out on an exhale and the voice sounded familiar, though Thomas couldn't place it.

"Un... Deux... Trois..." One of the kids counted noisily while the others scurried to hide.

"Um. I lost the, uh, the money for the stash you gave me. The whole thing." The fence rattled as someone—probably Louis—kicked it. "Or, it got stolen by one of my new friends."

Even at the age of seven, Thomas could hear the irony in his voice.

"Louis...that's not good news. Not good at all." There was the slightest pause before the man asked, "So how are you going to pay me back?"

Louis's voice rose slightly in pitch. "How am I supposed to pay you back? I don't have that kind of money."

There was another silence before the guy said, "Your dad does."

This caused Louis to retort indignantly, "There's no way I can ask my father for that amount without explaining why. And...I'm not going to steal from him."

"Look, kid." The man's voice was so low it was hard to hear. "You don't seem to understand a business transaction. In a business transaction, one person supplies the goods and the other person supplies the money." He spoke with exaggerated patience, as if he were explaining a simple concept to a child. "The minute the goods pass over into the other person's hands, he's responsible. If you think there's a risk you can't be responsible for the merchandise, you need to get yourself insured. Are you insured Louis?"

"Am I insured for my drug collection?" A flash of spirit—of rebellion—showed in Louis's voice.

There was another pause, and in a voice so light it made his neck tingle, Thomas heard, "If you can't find a way to pay me back, I can always introduce you to the gentleman you stole it from. He knows how to get what he's owed."

"I didn't steal it. Someone stole it from me."

"It's all the same to him. You took goods without paying for them."

Louis's voice sounded defeated. "Just...give me more time. I'll figure it out somehow."

*Why doesn't he just tell his dad?* Thomas thought. *Drugs are illegal, and his dad could throw the guy in prison just like what happened to my dad.* He chewed his lip for a minute. *He's probably afraid he'll get into trouble.*

"We're good then." The man's tone was too cheerful for what they had just been discussing. After a moment when neither spoke, he went on. "Listen, if you're open to a fair exchange—more than fair considering what you owe me—I would be willing to forget the money in exchange for a favor at a time when I need it."

"What favor?" Louis's mistrust was unmistakable.

"We'll get to that soon enough," was the answer. A girl shrieked as someone chased her by Thomas, swallowing up what he said afterwards. When Thomas turned back to listen, he caught the last words as their voices moved away, "—and as a sign of good faith, this should tide you over."

Thomas tried to follow them on the parallel path that lay on his side of the hedge, but his teacher was calling the children to order, and he had no choice but to run and get in line. That big kid seemed to be in some kind of trouble.

# CHAPTER 10

You could hear the throngs of people through the wall of plywood cabins that lined the grounds. Thomas ran ahead to where the opening was and turned back to smile at his mom, beckoning. Then he was gone.

"Thomas, wait." It was half-hearted. She was already letting the bright atmosphere of the *marché de noël* pull her in from the cold darkness that lay outside the enclosed festivities.

The open-faced cabins were set up in a large square with aisles connecting the two ends, forming a labyrinth. The aisles were carpeted in red, vibrant with Christmas colors and bustling with people, and each stall was brightly lit on the outside with the interior of each stall muted in soft lighting. You could spend hours in the market, going down one edge and examining the goods, then going up the other side and catching the stalls you missed. Chastity smelled the hot, spiced wine from the entrance, its fragrance mixing with the smoky scent of roasting chestnuts.

Thomas was in front of one of the first stalls, his attention already fixated on a stand with wooden toys. There was a chess set, wooden puppets in various sizes and positions, and complicated puzzles that

Chastity had no interest in even beginning to attempt. Thomas gingerly took one of them in his hands.

Chastity bit her lip to keep from admonishing him to put it back and simply watched him instead. He turned the puzzle this way and that, his brows pulled together in concentration. The vendor studied him, then gently took the puzzle from his hands and gave an unexpected series of twists and pulls, which freed the wooden loop from its prison. Then he winked at Thomas and handed it back to him. Thomas's eyes shone with delight as he flashed a grin at the vendor. She made a mental note to come back and get the puzzle for a Christmas gift.

"Come," she said. "Let's get a waffle first and then we can visit all the stands. We won't be eating dinner until after we get home, and I don't want you to get grouchy."

"I never get grouchy," was his indignant reply.

"You're right, honey." She gave his shoulder a soft squeeze. The woman at the confection stand was waiting, so she gestured "two," pointing at the waffles, before leaning down to kiss her son's head.

Charles walked next to Manon, her arm woven through his. She made a pretty picture with her blond hair set against a red wool coat, tied at the waist. The actress was home for the holidays, and as promised, he did not end their relationship before they had a chance to see if they could make it work in person—to see if there was something there.

However, Charles was beginning to regret his decision to bring her to his city's Christmas market, and it was not helping their relationship. For one thing, she was wearing her sunglasses, although night had fallen early. And her permanent reflex of moving furtively called attention to herself just as it had in London. As he watched her, he couldn't help but feel that her gestures were theatrical. Nothing seemed genuine. No expression of delight, no pleading for him to offer her a "darling little trinket" seemed natural to him. He was polite, but his heart wasn't in it.

She stopped at one of the stands and squealed over the Belgian lace. The silk threads were woven so daintily, it seemed like they would fall apart at the touch, but the salesperson assured them the pastoral image was stronger than it looked.

"May I offer you one?" He scanned the various designs.

"Oh Charles, would you? Of course I can afford it, but it's nicer to receive it as a gift than buy it with my own money. It makes me feel cherished." Charles felt a twinge of guilt as he opened his wallet.

Handing her the paper bag containing the expensive token wrapped in tissue paper, Charles indicated the stand in front of them. "Shall we get something to eat?" He could see her hesitate as she scanned the menu of fried dough and candy apples.

"Sure." Manon hesitated. "I'll have a crèpe with jam." Charles went over to pay, knowing that most of it would end up in the garbage. Manon made her way to the only wooden bench that was left, looking down, and fiddling with the tassels on her camel-colored purse with gold buckles.

Chastity thought the woman facing her seemed familiar as she took a bite of her waffle, and she only caught the end of Thomas's sentence. "...too bad my father couldn't come." She snapped back to attention. "Yes it is, sweetie. I think he had to work."

To tell the truth, she was surprised that Marc had given up the chance to accompany them to the market, in what would have been their first public outing surrounded by people she might know. She'd tensed up when Thomas invited him, breathing a sigh of relief when he turned it down.

She squeezed his hand. "I have to say, buddy, I'm glad it's just the two of us."

Chastity glanced up as Mr. de Brase walked towards her, easily managing two glasses of spiced wine and plates of food. For a minute she thought he was coming to sit with her and she felt her face grow hot. He stared right through her, though, then sat with his back to her, a short distance from where her son was sitting across from her. She looked down and discovered powdered sugar all over the front of her sweater. She brushed it off as her heart raced wildly. *Oh right. That's the viscount's girlfriend—the famous Manon Duprey in the flesh.*

"—but can we invite him for Christmas?" she heard Thomas asking. He was almost done with his waffle and hadn't noticed anything with her was amiss. She caught his last words and was able to reply smoothly. "Um. Perhaps not for Christmas. But maybe we can invite him for New Year's."

"Oh, yes. He can stay up with us until midnight." Chastity immediately regretted having offered even this intimate part of their lives. She wasn't ready for the holidays yet.

Manon took a dainty bite of her crèpe and chewed it thoughtfully. She took a sip of wine, before saying, "So, are we okay, you and me? We haven't talked since I got back."

Charles looked up in surprise that she would bring it up in a public place. "We're fine," he said shortly. "Unless there's something you haven't told me." He examined her quizzically, but she didn't take the bait.

When he had taken another bite of his baguette and sausage, she spoke. "You're trying to turn this back on me, but I've given you every reassurance I can think of, and it's like talking to a brick wall."

He watched her blink away tears and realized that for once she was being sincere. He felt guilty for the second time this evening for having kept her at arm's length. Maybe it was hasty to think about breaking up with her this soon. It wasn't like he was ever going to have what he had with Miriam again. Surely this was as good as it was ever going to get.

Charles reached out and touched her hand, giving her a genuine smile for the first time all day. "You're right. I haven't been very giving. But we're fine." He gave her hand a pat, then picked up his plastic glass of hot wine and drank what was left.

She pushed her plate away. "I can't finish this. Shall we get out of here?" He noted the crèpe, which had exactly one bite taken out of it, just as he had expected.

"Of course. You know I can't leave here yet. I need to stay and support this event a bit longer since it's the grand opening."

"I knew that," she lied.

Chastity watched as Mr. de Brase stood and put his black wool coat back on. It was warm enough in the food stall to take it off, but the cold air crept into the rest of the *marché* and made the outerwear indispensable. She noticed how nice his red scarf looked against his matte complexion, and how well it matched the actress's coat. He put his arm around her as they walked out, tilting his ear to catch what she was saying while they turned the corner. *Just perfect*. Chastity sighed.

"Are you finished, Thomas?" She forced herself to be cheerful.

"Yup, Mom. You're the one who's not." He pointed at her forgotten waffle on the plate and grinned.

"Ah, silly me. I must have had too big of a lunch." She scooted her plate towards him. "Want it?"

"No thanks, Mom. I'm full." Thomas was silent, spinning the paper plate in front of him. Chastity's mind was filled with the image of the viscount's unsmiling face as he walked towards her.

"Mom?" Thomas's voice was tinged with a worry she didn't pick up on.

"Hm?" she murmured absently.

"You said I could talk to you about anything, right?"

"Sure thing, sweetie." She was not looking at him, but at the crowd walking by. "Oh look." She pointed. "There's Maude. Shall we go catch her?" With the eagerness only a child could possess, Thomas forgot the subject and raced after her friend, grabbing the back of her coat.

"Tommee," Maude squealed, picking him up and twirling him around. "You know, in a year or two I won't be able to do that."

"I know." Thomas grinned as his mom walked up.

"Hey," Chastity greeted Maude with the *bises* on each cheek. "Have you seen anything you liked?"

"Well, yeah," Maude said. "I'm interested in the knitted hats and scarves because I'm willing to bet I could make something like that and it would sell."

"Wait. You knit?" Chastity raised an eyebrow.

"Every scarf and sweater Michel owns."

"I can't believe you find the time." She thought of her own life and how busy it was.

"We don't have kids, for one thing," Maude reflected comfortably. "I find it relaxing. It's orderly, just like Math. Every stitch has its place."

"Maybe you could teach knitting to your Math students," Chastity teased. "The boys would love that. Anyway, show me. I want to see what kinds of things you can make. Thomas, let's go see if we can find some other stands with toys in them too, okay?"

He ran ahead by way of answer, even though he didn't know where he was supposed to go. Chastity admired his energy and laughed. "Don't go too far, Thomas." He stopped suddenly and darted over to a stall that had stickers and pens, and small desk toys that were propped up on little wires.

"Oh perfect," said Maude. "He's stopped just in the right place. There's the knitted-wear stand."

Chastity fingered a tomato-red scarf. "Oh, this one is nice." She sighed. "Too bad I can never wear it."

"But this one you totally could." Maude pulled out a forest green hat with pale green trim. She whispered, "Don't buy it though. I'll make you one just like it."

Manon pulled on Charles's arm and headed towards a stand with soaps from Provence. He extricated himself, saying, "I see the mayor over there. I'll be right back." Her eyes grew wide, probably at the thought of being left alone, but she schooled her features to hide it.

"Okay, chéri."

"Bertrand." Charles extended his hand to an older man in an expensive suit that pulled at the waist.

"Ah, Charles." The mayor returned the handshake. "Are you here on your own?"

"No. Manon Duprey came with me. She's over there." The gleam in the mayor's eye meant he would be expecting an introduction. "I'll introduce you to her," Charles promised with a wry smile.

"In good time, Charles. You know I have to ask you again this year if you'll consider opening your home for a spring ball." Charles started to shake his head, but the mayor went on. "Now think about it, Charles, before you say no. Your father agreed to it in the past, and it did such good for the community."

"My father agreed to it until the artwork went missing. I just can't take that risk again."

"I understand that. I do. But some of the townspeople are pressuring me on this one. The château is no longer a patrimony that belongs to the town, and the people want something in return. If you agreed to this, we would have every available officer on call to keep an eye on things. Think about it, okay, Charles? Everyone is hoping for this."

"I'll...think about it," was the most Charles could manage, although he was sure he would not change his mind.

"Now, let's see about that introduction." The mayor clapped him on the back and steered him towards the soap stand where Manon was accepting a brown paper bag with her fragrant collection inside.

"I got almond, green tea, and lemon—" She stopped when she noticed the mayor walking next to Charles.

"Mademoiselle Duprey." He took both her hands in his own and kissed them, before pulling her in and kissing her on both cheeks.

"Let me introduce you to Bertrand Le Neveu, the mayor of Maisons-Laffitte," Charles said drily. The mayor already had his arm around Manon's waist and was walking forward with her, pointing out a stand that boasted chocolates made in France. He whispered something in her ear.

"You rogue," she said, laughing and blushing. She was used to this kind of attention—an older gentleman of position and wealth favoring her with his notice. These gentlemen could be useful to her career, and it wasn't hard to please them.

"Charles, I'm just going to buy Mlle Duprey some chocolate. You can catch up with us further on." The mayor dismissed him with a wink.

Charles nodded, unthreatened. He wasn't unhappy to be alone and continued down the aisle of the *marché*. His main goal was to make an appearance and let everyone know he was supporting the town. He didn't need anything in particular among the goods that were displayed. To kill time, he paused at one of the stands on the corner of the aisle to examine the collection of fountain pens.

"Mommy, it's starting to snow." Thomas ran forward again. Sure enough, fat snowflakes were visible against the overhead lights, although they were hidden in the night beyond that.

Chastity and Maude began to walk behind him. "We'll just follow this row down to the exit and then be on our way. I don't want to get Thomas home too late."

"Oh. Guess what," Maude said. "I saw the actress here—Manon Duprey. She must be here with Mr. de Brase."

Thomas had stopped at the corner stand, which contained horse paraphernalia, so they stood in the aisle just next to him.

"I know," said Chastity. "I saw them eating at the next table. He didn't look happy to be here." Her dimples showed as she lowered her voice. "Mixing with the commoners."

"His father had more of a reputation for interacting with the people of the town than our Mr. de Brase does," Maude said in a wry voice. "Apparently the older viscount even put on an elegant ball in the château and opened it for the community to come and dance. The mayor has been begging the current viscount to do the same, but so far he's refused."

"Thomas, wait." Chastity said, as her son darted forward again.

The two women followed him, and as they crossed the intersection of stalls, she said in a voice louder than intended, "Ha. The *current* viscount."

A gentleman in a black wool coat at a nearby stall turned his head slightly at her words. Though she lowered her voice, he caught the rest before the women were out of sight. "No surprise that he refuses to host a ball. Why should he lift a finger to do something nice for the town when he clearly has nothing personal to gain from it?"

# CHAPTER 11

Paltier absently rubbed a dusty bottle of champagne in the wine cellar. It was only six o'clock in the morning, but he had a train to catch in the direction of Montpellier, where he would be visiting his brother for the New Year's celebration. He took his annual vacation this time of year but wouldn't dream of leaving without having personally selected the wines for the viscount's intimate dinner with Mlle Duprey.

He thought about how stark the house seemed when she was there as opposed to the lively warmth the viscount's young wife had brought. She was nice, but not friendly—polite, but cold. It just wasn't the same. Paltier carefully placed the champagne bottle in the leather bag he had carried down with him and set about searching for just the right wines that would accompany both the smoked salmon and the thinly-sliced roast beef.

Christmas had been a family affair. Paltier opened the door to the viscount's niece as Isabelle barreled past him to give her uncle and cousin a hug. Adelaide followed more sedately and held out her hand to Paltier with a warm smile. She walked over to her brother and kissed both his cheeks, her eyes bright with mischief. "England has ruined Isabelle's manners."

Isabelle's cheeks turned pink, and she turned to address Paltier with a charming, "How do you do?" She then kissed her uncle and cousin, murmuring, "How good it is to see you again." Her exuberance could not be hushed for long, and she threw her arm around Louis. "Show me the speakers you got."

Adelaide watched the pair of them run up the marble staircase and was reminded of how many times the same scene had unfolded before her, but with two sets of shorter, chubbier legs. She turned to follow Charles who headed up the other marble staircase towards a spacious room with wood floors. He strolled over to a table by the fireplace and took a cigar out of the drawer, which he lit.

"Ugh. The annual holiday cigar." Adelaide wrinkled her nose. "That's one habit from our father I wish you had not acquired."

"At least it's only once a year and not every evening," he answered with a puff. He sat on one of the settees and gestured for her to do the same.

"Where's Maman?" she asked suddenly.

"I believe they've run into traffic."

His sister smoothed out her skirt and said with an air of innocence, "It's too bad Eléonore and Raphael were otherwise engaged."

Charles let out a quiet chuckle but then fell silent. Adelaide observed him shrewdly. "Okay Charles, what gives? You're not one to share much of what's going on in your life, but this is melancholic even for you."

Charles considered her for a moment, then turned to the small round table by the settee and tapped ashes onto an ashtray. "The school suspects that Louis is using drugs."

Her lack of reaction made him think that somehow she already knew, until he noticed her expression, which was stunned. After a short silence, she found her voice. "Have you spoken to him about it?"

"No." He flicked some imaginary ash from his brown corduroy pants. Adelaide knew her brother well, so she waited in silence for him to continue. At length, he did. "My own son is like a stranger to me. He tells me nothing, and I find I don't have it in me to pry. He knows I'm here for him. I think he'll open up when he's ready."

Adelaide understood men enough to pause before uttering hasty words, which would only alienate her brother (and which threatened to include "idiot" among them). She spoke carefully. "Still, it would not be a bad idea to let him know what the school told you and remind him that you're there for him. Teenagers can sometimes forget that."

She could see her normally proud brother was not opposed to her advice, but that it would not do to push. "Shall we—" Her words were interrupted by the doorbell.

"Ah. Maman." Charles stood. Paltier was already hurrying past him to welcome the dowager in from the cold.

"Good evening, Paltier." His mother stood regally in the doorway. Her children walked over to the stairwell and descended the marble stairs to greet her.

"Merry Christmas, Maman." They each kissed her dutifully. Charles took her arm, accompanying her back up the staircase.

"I see you decided to put your tree here this year," his mother observed, immediately upon entering the room. Adelaide raised one eyebrow at her brother behind their mother's back, her eyes twinkling. Charles clamped his lips shut and turned towards Paltier who was hovering discreetly near the entrance. "Let the children know their grandmother is here, please, and then you may bring in the appetizers."

Paltier didn't hear the rest of the conversation. He hadn't intended to hear what the viscount revealed concerning his son, but he had been sorting through the crystal in the adjoining room to be used during dinner. He would never discuss this with another soul, but in his own private council, he felt it would explain a lot about Louis's behavior. He sincerely hoped the viscount would heed his sister's advice.

When Paltier arrived at Louis's door, he tapped lightly and

announced their grandmother's arrival. "Oh, I suppose we'll have to go down," he heard Louis say.

"Savage," Isabelle teased. Paltier smiled to himself as he walked back down the stairs. Louis's cousin was a good influence on him.

When Paltier brought the tray of champagne in, serving the dowager first, he witnessed Isabelle's affectionate greeting and Louis's more sullen one. Carrying the tray around to each family member, he was just in time to hear Isabelle squeezing her uncle's arm, and saying in a low-pitched voice, "Thank you, Uncle Charles." He gave her an answering smile.

When they had been seated at the table, and served, Paltier took his place in the back of the room to await the change of plates. Presently, the viscount spoke up with news that did not surprise Paltier, for they had already discussed it a few days earlier. "I've decided to hold a spring ball in the château this year."

His mother's fork did not exactly clatter on the plate, but she lost some of her poise. "Charles, I am astonished."

The viscount, who must have been expecting opposition, was prepared. "The mayor has promised every available officer to be present the night of the gala. I don't expect a second theft to occur."

The dowager enunciated with asperity. "It's that actress of yours. You're holding this ball to impress her."

"Maman," Adelaide couldn't resist crying out.

The viscount pressed his lips together for a moment before replying. "There will be significant tax benefits to my doing this. I am motivated purely by financial reasons—and the duty someone in my position has to the town. Surely you understand that, Maman."

That was all Paltier heard because the viscount signaled for him to remove the first course and bring the second. He had brought the under-waiters in to assist but decided on his way down to the kitchen that he would be bringing the food in himself while the family was discussing such confidential matters.

. . .

He remembered all this in the dusty wine room, and wondered if the château would once again see some of its former glory—the days when the young viscount's father had held the seat. He picked his leather bag up from the wooden shelf, carefully shielding his selections and made his way up the stairs.

As he disappeared from view, a shadowed figure crept from one of the side rooms. He looked both ways to make sure he was unobserved, although he did not expect to be. He stuffed his roll of bedding in the closed space underneath the ancient unused heater where he knew it would not be discovered. Then he went to the door leading to the garden, took out his key and noiselessly slipped it in the lock, stepping out. The air was biting and it was dark, but he knew of a place where he could get a cup of hot coffee this early, even on New Year's Eve.

Thomas was eating handfuls of popcorn, allowing stray kernels to fall on the floor. Nat King Cole's Christmas album was playing in the background, although Christmas was over. It made the ambiance in Chastity's apartment that much more cheerful. The decorations were still up, and the white lights on the tree emitted a soft, cozy light.

Thomas took a break from eating popcorn. "Papa, what did you do to celebrate New Year's when you were in prison?"

Marc was sitting on the couch with Thomas settled at his feet. He glanced down at his son. "There wasn't much of a celebration. Christmas was better because we had good food to eat, and even a couple of gifts if we were lucky. The guards weren't exactly going to let us stay up late and have a party on New Year's. That would get too rowdy." He grinned and tousled the boy's hair.

"I bet you're glad to be here celebrating with us, aren't you?" Thomas smiled up at him, and put his hand back into the popcorn.

Chastity went towards the kitchen, bringing the dessert dishes with her. She wasn't precisely nervous, but she wasn't completely comfortable either. She checked her reflection in the mirror that hung in the small dining room. The black cardigan she wore, with shiny black sequins sewn into it, caught the light and set off her auburn hair.

Satisfied, she went into the kitchen and set the dishes down, exhaling as she leaned against the counter. Marc appeared in the doorway. "Can I help with the dishes?"

"No, no, that's fine," she protested.

"I insist." He grabbed the heavy meat platter and set it in the sink. She wasn't exactly a maniac about cleanliness, but even she could see that the cold water wasn't going to cut through the grease. She would have to wash the dishes again.

She busied herself with putting the plates in the dishwasher, and they worked in silence.

"Chassy," Marc said, using the old nickname. "Thanks so much for allowing me to be part of your evening. It means a lot to me."

"I'm glad you could come," Chastity replied, not quite lying. Her own feelings were a mystery to her. Marc picked up the ceramic bowl that had held the potatoes and began drying it with a towel. He stared at her, and when he set the bowl down, she finally looked up at him. "What?"

His expression was intent. "Do you think there's any chance of us..." He trailed away uncertainly.

Her mouth opened in surprise. She should have noticed his feelings had shifted, but she hadn't been paying attention. She had only been trying to figure out what her own feelings were.

"Marc, I don't know." She shook her head. "It's been a long time and we have both changed a lot."

"What I want," he responded, "is to start fresh—as the people we have become. Create a new story."

"I still don't feel like I know you." She laughed without humor. "Honestly, I'm not even sure I know myself."

"Maybe we could start by spending more time together," he said. "I think nothing would make Thomas happier."

Chastity, flushing at what she viewed as presumption on his part, walked over to peek into the living room. Thomas was now lying on the couch, and though he was awake, his eyes were glazed and he seemed to be just about to drop off. The clock showed three minutes to midnight.

Marc sensed her anger and folded his arms. "I'm sorry. I don't know the right thing to say here."

Chastity turned back towards him, softened by his admission. "I'm sorry too. I need time. There's just no way to rush this—there's too much history between us."

He stood silently, facing her, and nodded. The mood shifted and Chastity was able to breathe. She was about to propose they go in to celebrate the countdown when Marc grabbed her by the arms and planted a soft kiss on her lips.

"Happy New Year, Chassy." He gave her a small smile then walked into the living room.

# CHAPTER 12

"It's nice to be here." Paltier gave a contented sigh as he shifted his feet on the stool next to the fire. He sipped the brandy and shook his head. "We're getting older, but I guess God will grant us a few more years of this."

His brother leaned back in his worn armchair and lifted his own glass in reply. "To our health." This was met with an answering salute before they both sipped and relapsed into silence.

"What time does your train leave in the morning?"

Paltier answered promptly. "Seven o'clock. I wanted to get an early start as I'll be going straight to work from there."

"I've no doubt," his sibling answered in a rallying tone. "Gus, I wouldn't know you if you didn't rush to get back to work. Heaven forbid you should sleep in."

"I've had two weeks to sleep in, thank you very much. Work is good. One never feels as alive when one's hands are idle." His brother, a diligent vintner with a solid label, simply nodded in agreement. The fire snapped, and Gaston stood and reached for the iron tongs to turn the burning log.

The two brothers were unalike in appearance—Gustave was tall and slim with a stately bearing that suited him to his life's work.

Gaston was ruddier and shorter with a stocky build that kept him closer to the grapes, as he liked to joke. There was an easy understanding between them, and they looked forward to the two weeks of annual company out of their generally staid bachelor existence. Gus had never been interested in marriage; Gaston had married, had two children who had no interest in inheriting the vineyard (although they did not despise the money), and had lost his wife younger than he would have liked. He bore it all with fortitude.

Maybe it was the mellowing effects of the brandy and the fire, or the knowledge that the morrow would take him back north where he wouldn't see his brother for another year, but Paltier opened up. "The young viscount will be holding a spring ball at the château this year."

Gaston raised his eyebrows at that. "When was the last time? It was when the late viscount was still alive, wasn't it?"

Paltier stared off in the distance. "It was the year before he died. We'll have to go through storage and pull out all the glasses, cutlery, dishes—have everything washed. It hasn't been used in twenty years."

"Will it be a sit-down affair?"

"Yes, and the viscount mentioned he'll take some of your red. I'll fill out an order form and send it to you as soon as I have a better idea of the quantities. We won't invite the entire town to the dinner, of course, but the idea is to open the gates to anyone with a purchased ticket for the dancing."

Gaston pursed his lips. "There was something funny about that last ball, wasn't there? Some scandal? I seem to remember the late viscount's death was in some way related to it, and honestly I didn't pay much attention. Penelope died that same year, you know."

Paltier cast him a sympathetic glance and lifted his glass again. "You are correct. There was a burglary. Stolen art."

"Ah. I seem to remember something about that. What was it?"

"It was a Manet. The self-portrait."

Gaston whistled through his teeth. "I'm not at all surprised at his having such a painting, but how someone managed to steal it, I can't imagine."

"It was a strange affair." Paltier sighed heavily. "You know, the family is used to money. They don't count the silver." He turned to his brother with uncharacteristic energy and pointed at him to emphasize his words. "But you can bet I do." His brother murmured what was appropriate before Paltier continued.

"Anyway, they have a few paintings. They have a couple of Cézannes, a Van Gogh, a Monet, and then they had this Manet. The viscount's father was quite the collector. They never thought this private collection could be at risk in such an open setting with so many people around." He broke off vehemently. "I should have thought of it."

His brother shook his head with a quiet *tsk tsk*. He knew it was no use to try and persuade his brother that he put too much blame on himself. "So how did they pull it off?"

"I'm sure they took advantage of when there was a performance in the Italian Apartment because the room went dark and a light show was part of it. That would have have blinded everyone to any suspicious activity. I imagine the person slipped into the King's Chamber and took the painting from there down a side staircase, which no one would have been using just then. The stairs lead straight to the basement where they must have escaped into the garden."

"That's too easy," his brother protested. "Why, aren't there alarms in the château? Weren't there guards?"

"Normally, yes," Paltier answered. "But it was during a strange period when they were doing some work down there to repair some of the stone walls and fill in the empty alcoves, and the alarm must have been cut. Or—the gardener, Pierre Maçon and his under-gardener were supposed to be watching it or some such thing. And, now, that's what is strange. Pierre disappeared that night."

"Oh, I do remember that," his brother intercepted. "A friend of yours, wasn't he?"

"He was. And I'll never believe it." Paltier shook his head firmly. "I don't care that he wasn't around to explain his disappearance. Something must have happened to him."

Gaston sucked his teeth thoughtfully. "Doesn't look good though."

"No," his brother answered simply.

"What about the under-gardener? What was the fellow's name? What did he have to say?"

"I don't remember his name, but he was there that night. Said he hadn't seen anything. He was standing in front of the door when a few officers came rushing down. Said Pierre told him to keep an eye out and prevent anyone from accessing the lower levels."

Gaston snorted. "As if any of the guests would do that. But, so then, the thief could not have left that way."

"No. Except the under-gardener had not been in service more than a couple of months, and even he disappeared after a day. No one has seen him since."

"Hmph."

"The evil in it," Paltier continued, "is that the late viscount was blamed for insurance fraud, and I know the shock of it caused his death."

"How could they blame him when the signs pointed to the missing gardeners?"

"Because he had the misfortune to adjust the value on the Manet to a higher amount a week before the theft."

Gaston turned in surprise. "If it were him, he would have to be an idiot to do something so stupid. Anyone can see that."

"That's why the charges were cleared—that and the missing gardeners. There was no proof. But I have a feeling the late viscount made a few enemies when he bought the château and the racetrack, and these enemies encouraged the investigation. He was cleared, but the damage was done, and his fatal stroke occurred less than a year later."

"The art was never found, hm?"

"No, and I have to say I'm surprised the young viscount agreed to hold another ball after the pain the family went through. I'm sure he felt my disapproval, much though I try to conceal whatever I'm feeling on the issue." Paltier sniffed.

Gaston chuckled in reply. He knew his brother was able to communicate exactly what he thought with just a look. "Ah well," he said. "It's just as well he's bringing some life back to that castle again. Mind that there are guards in every part of the château this time."

"Never you fear," Paltier replied with determination.

Chastity and Thomas picked their way through the clumps of melting snow on the sidewalk. The snow that had started during the *marché de noël* continued intermittently throughout Christmas then remained frozen and cold past the New Year. Now the winter sun caused the edges to soften, then liquefy. Soon there would be sparse traces of white on muddy grass bordering the sidewalk, and then none at all.

"Can I have a croissant?" Thomas jumped over clumps of brown snow when a simple step would have sufficed.

"No, honey. We're just going to get some baguettes. I'll give you a small piece, but I don't want you to ruin your appetite since we're going to be eating lunch soon."

Thomas absorbed the news diplomatically. He continued hopping even when there was no snow, his boots making tiny splashes in the mud. "Mom, do you love my father?"

Chastity was startled because he asked her the very question she was wrestling with at that moment. "Ah." She gave a tiny laugh, but her smile vanished quickly. "I don't know, sweetie. I like him. I love you." She emphasized the word. "Would that make you glad, or...feel bad if I loved him?"

"Glad, I guess." Hop. Hop.

"We have all the time in the world to see about that, my baby." She smiled at him. They were approaching the corner where they would turn and walk down the busy street towards the *boulangerie*.

"Here, kitty, kitty." Thomas coaxed a starved-looking cat that was sitting at the crosswalk. When the cat did not come, he gave up and changed the subject. "Mom, if I thought a kid was in trouble—"

"Hold on, sweetie." Chastity dug in her bag for the phone, which had started to ring. She pulled it out and looked up as she went to press the talk button. Suddenly she gasped.

"Tommy, NO!" She couldn't stop him. She was just in time to see the cat dart into traffic and her son leap after him. The next was all a blur. His small body was tossed to the side of the road as a blue car screeched to a halt.

"*Madame, Madame, je l'ai pas vu.*" A woman stumbled out of her car, crying.

Chastity was already kneeling on the pavement, next to the parked cars, traffic piling up beside her. Her voice was caught in her throat as she looked at her pale, prostrate son. Trembling violently, she tried to scream, but it was stuck in her ribs. "No," she whispered.

# CHAPTER 13

The ambulance screeched to a halt in front of CHI Poissy hospital. The driver leaped down and opened the back door while the attendant inside unsecured the gurney and pushed the end forward so it could be carried down. Chastity jumped down from the ambulance and promptly fell to the pavement. She had no strength in her knees, and it was only by sheer will that she got up again and ran after them.

The first responders pushed the gurney between them, shoving the swinging doors open with a bang as they brought their charge through. A triage nurse met them.

"Seven-year-old boy with a severe concussion. He's unconscious."

"What happened?"

"He was hit by a car."

"Get Docteur Bellamy in here," the triage nurse yelled to an aide that was stationed nearby. She began cutting off Thomas's clothes as the team rushed in to draw blood and prep him for scanning. The neurologist was not long in appearing.

"What do we have here?" The details were repeated to him as the triage nurse inserted an IV. Another nurse placed the monitors on the boy's chest and forehead. After a brief glance at his vitals, the doctor said. "CT his head. Now."

They pushed the gurney through another set of doors, and one of the nurses finally turned to Chastity, kindly. "I'm afraid you'll have to wait in the waiting room over there. You're not allowed in this section, but we'll give you news as soon as we have some." The nurse pressed Chastity's arm and went through the swinging doors. Chastity nodded dumbly but remained rooted to the spot.

The doctor examined the screens as the inert patient was pulled through the hollow white tunnel. "We'll need to relieve that cranial pressure," he said, shaking his head. "I'd be more comfortable getting a pediatric neurologist in here since he's so young." Then, speaking decisively, "Page Docteur Toussaint."

The triage nurse replied, "Docteur Toussaint is at a conference this whole week. There's another doctor who's covering for him while he's away. He's normally on leave—"

"Has he retained his hospital privileges?" Upon being assured that he had, the doctor barked, "Get him in here."

Chastity walked numbly over to where the waiting room was indicated and searched for a seat. The floor was blue, and the chairs were orange plastic. The fluorescent lighting was garish and made a soft buzzing sound. An older couple sat across from her, the wife's hand tucked into the husband's arm. She gave Chastity a sympathetic glance but didn't say anything. A teenager bounced his knee up and down, absorbed in a video game. Chastity sat stiffly on the chair nearest to the door.

She couldn't cry. It wasn't the lack of privacy that prevented her. It was the horror. She was conscious of a sensation of icy cold in her limbs while her chest was burning hot. A lump in her throat prevented her from swallowing or speaking. She raced through the scene, again and again.

Here, kitty, kitty...

Mom, if I thought a kid was in trouble...

Hold on, sweetie.

*Oh, if only I could go back and get his attention away from the cat. He wouldn't have run into the street.* Over and over her thoughts turned. The cat. Tommy, *no!* The screech. His lifeless form.

The winter sun began to set outside, making the fluorescent lights seem even more harsh. The short wait was already interminable.

Early in the morning, Charles strode through the corridors on his way to the pediatric ward. He stopped at the nurse's station to pull the chart and ran his finger down the notes from yesterday's surgery, taking in the patient's post-operative condition.

"*Bonjour, docteur.*" An attractive nurse smiled up at him, and he frowned at her, muttering a reply before walking over to the ICU recovery area. The progress for his young patient was far from certain, and not all the cranial pressure had been alleviated.

"Ah. You're here. Bonjour, docteur." He looked up at the sound of Martine Garcia's voice, a dynamic, middle-aged woman, and his favorite nurse in the hospital.

"Hello, Martine," he replied, his eyes twinkling. "I see everyone is keeping you busy."

"Aw, now that my own children are grown and out of the house, I need some other ones to look after." She flashed him a grin.

"On top of the pediatric cases," he teased. She had a reputation for being no-nonsense with the more belligerent patients, and they were always the older ones.

"Right you are." She laughed heartily. "When will we have you back full-time at the hospital?"

"I'm halfway through my year-and-a-half sabbatical, so not for another nine months."

"We sure miss you around here. Docteur Toussaint is great, of course, but you know he's married. And old," she added with a glimmer of a smile.

Charles couldn't help but laugh. Martine was only fifteen years his senior, but she treated him to just enough informality to put him at ease, and nothing missed her sharp observation. It was impossible to escape the lures cast out at him with—as Martine would say—his inebriating combination of looks, wealth, medical degree, and a title.

"I've been meaning to stop by to ask how my intern is doing," Charles said.

Martine smiled and sighed as she reached for the boxes she had pulled from the supply closet. "I wish there were more like him. He doesn't put on any airs, and you can tell his concern for the patients is genuine. Too bad he's only here for a few months."

"Hm. I'm glad to hear he's doing well. If he continues to be a good fit, perhaps he'll apply here." Charles spoke briskly, ready to move on. "Now, for our young patient in Room A. I see your notes here. I'll take a look at the ICP and see if we need to schedule a decompressive craniotomy. Who's been with him?"

"His mother hasn't left his side. I don't have the sense she gets much support. One visitor, no family."

"I'm on my way there now." He closed the chart with a snap and walked down the corridor past two open rooms, one of which was empty, before reaching the correct room. He entered it, his eyes on his young patient's still form.

A slender woman, with long auburn curls that hid her face, leaned on the bed, her forehead resting on hands clasped in prayer. Almost immediately she turned towards him, lifting a tear-stained face, and wiping her nose on her sleeve. He stopped short in surprise, but she was the first to speak.

"You." She leaped to her feet, her voice incredulous. He was unable to reply for a moment.

Of course. Thomas Whitmore was this woman's son. How did he not make the connection as soon as he saw the name? There couldn't be that many Whitmores in the suburbs of Paris. She looked different than she did at the school, though—vulnerable, young. In the morning sunlight that filtered through the half-closed blinds, he could see that, though her nose was an unattractive red from crying, her eyes were a brilliant green.

He collected himself. "Good morning, Mademoiselle Whitmore. I apologize for being unable to brief you on your son's progress last night, but I was called into another emergency. Did you understand everything Docteur Bellamy said?"

"Um yes. Yes...I understand that the pressure in his skull..." Here she choked a bit, and seemed to be trying to master her emotions. She cleared her throat and continued.

"I understand that the pressure has been alleviated, and that I shouldn't expect him to wake up right away. And, but...that I can't be certain he will wake up?"

Charles did not respond immediately. His eyes on her, he finally gestured to the chair she had just been occupying. "Please. Sit down." He went to the neighboring room and pulled a chair from there.

Before he could take a seat, her words came tumbling out. "I'm sorry, Mr. de Brase. I don't understand how you came to be here. You're a doctor?"

"Is that so surprising?" The corner of his lip quirked upwards. People were always surprised by that fact.

"No, it's just that I didn't think you...you *did* anything," she blurted out.

Charles hesitated before replying, the whisp of amusement now gone. "It's reassuring to know you have such a high opinion of me." He perused the patient's chart, hiding a rueful sigh. He hadn't given her any reason to think he was anything but a profligate.

"No, no. I mean...I thought owning a château was a full-time job, and that if you did anything, it would be to manage your estate. I just have a hard time seeing you here—it's all so unexpected." She reached over to the bedside table and whisked a tissue out of the generic box, wiping her face and blowing her nose.

"I don't know why I'm bringing all this up. Of course it doesn't matter. I'm sorry. I'm not myself," she added in a watery voice.

"You're doing well, considering the circumstances," Charles

replied. "Docteur Bellamy was correct, but I think it's too soon to look at the worst-case scenario."

At those words, tears trickled down her cheeks again. "He's all I have." Chastity spoke in little more than a whisper. Charles had thought himself immune to the emotions of his patients' families, and he was surprised when his throat tightened. He looked ahead into the corridor, giving her time to collect herself. She blew her nose and stood abruptly. Charles read the agitation in her gesture and followed suit.

"Let me have a look at his catheter." He went over and examined that and the ICP, his face unreadable. He scanned his notes again and pressed his lips together before speaking. "There's a possibility we'll have to temporarily remove part of the skull to allow the brain tissue to expand." He shot her a glance. "I know such a procedure sounds terrifying, but if the pressure in his skull becomes too great, it will be the best course of action."

"Oh, oh...okay. I didn't know this could—" Chastity seemed to have trouble forming the words to match her patent horror at the idea of such a procedure. Finally she looked up, her eyes troubled. "Is this what the other doctors recommend?"

Charles overlooked any potential for insult and answered gently. "It's simply the standard procedure for patients with severe brain trauma where the cranial pressure seems to build rather than decrease." He leaned over and put his hand on the boys arm.

"What's his first language?"

"English," she answered.

He brought the chair up to the side of the bed and sat, laying his hand on Thomas's arm again. "Good morning, Thomas." He knew his English was nearly perfect. "You've had a car accident, and you're in the hospital where we're taking good care of you. My name is Docteur de Brase, and your mother's here too. You can rest as long as you need. The important thing is for you to get better."

He didn't expect a response, but he stayed for a minute longer before standing and turning to face Chastity. She offered him a tremulous smile in return. "Thank you for taking such good care of my son."

"Don't lose hope," he replied. "Do you have anyone here who can support you?"

"Um. I have a couple of colleagues...I think you know Elizabeth Mercer?" Charles nodded. "She stopped by early this morning."

"I'll be back tomorrow morning then, unless there's a change in his—"

There was a bustle in the corridor as a young man—well-dressed, but with dissipated features, and smelling strongly of smoke—rushed into the room. "Chassy. You should have called me immediately. Oh my God. Thomas. How is he? Oh—*bonjour Docteur. Comment va-t'il?*" He switched to French when he saw the doctor standing there.

"And you are?" Charles felt the frown forming.

"I'm the boy's father." The man stepped back and put his arm around Chastity's waist. Her face was drained of color, but otherwise remained expressionless.

"I see. A catheter has been inserted to relieve pressure from the swelling of his brain, and we're monitoring it." Charles knew there was no trace of the previous warmth in his face.

"Mademoiselle." He nodded towards her. "I'll come back tomorrow."

He strode out of the room, and as he was leaving, heard the man say, "He's not very friendly, is he?" Without waiting for an answer, "So. What happened?"

# CHAPTER 14

There was the man, who went by the name of Cyril, standing by the stone wall that overlooked the Seine. The same scene, but this time it was a different wall, a different part of the Seine. He waited in the bright sunlight, and having finished his cigarette, tossed it below onto the cobblestone walkway that directly bordered the river.

Cyril scanned the area impatiently, and at this cue, Jean didn't waste any time jogging across the street to join him. "You kept me waiting," was all the man said.

"I'm sorry. There was a delay in the train schedule. So do you have news on the buyer?"

"Yes, I'm in touch with him. Come, let's walk." Cyril surged forward without waiting to see if Jean followed. "The buyer's a Russian, and he'll be ready to receive the package when his cargo ship has been reloaded and is ready to return. That's going to be some time towards the beginning of April. I've got the driver in place, but you need to let me know now if you're sure of your end of the deal."

"I'm getting there, and I'll be ready by then," Jean reassured him. "I'm working on getting through the point of entry so I can come and go without detection. Once I'm through, all that'll be left is for me to choose the right moment when no one's around."

"The place is more fully guarded than it was twenty years ago," Cyril warned. "I hope you have a better plan than breaking a window or picking a lock. If that were the case, I'd use one of my own men."

Gaining confidence, Jean shook his head. "It's all about relationships, and I have two in place that'll allow me to gain access when I need it."

Cyril dodged some tourists and walked back next to Jean. "I'll need to have more specific details before long to make sure there aren't any screw-ups."

"As soon as I get a few more items in place—namely figuring out when it's going to happen—I'll let you know everything."

"I'm counting on that." Cyril nodded in Jean's direction before taking abrupt leave of him again. This time Jean was less disconcerted by the encounter. It didn't matter how much more cunning or dangerous Cyril was. Jean knew he had something Cyril did not—the map.

Chastity fluttered around the hospital room, picking dead leaves off the plant that had been brought in by Maude, tucking the teddy bear sent by her parents next to her son's arm, only to remove it and put it back next to the window where he would see it when he opened his eyes. She walked back to his side and sat, kissing his cheek with great care and taking hold of his hand.

"Hi, baby," she murmured. "Now that the room's in order, shall we continue with our story of Harry Potter?"

She reached over and grabbed her reading glasses mechanically, but she didn't pull the book out right away. In the week that her son had been in a coma, she hadn't left his side except to shower. She knew that French law permitted her to extend her paid leave of absence because her son was gravely injured, but she was beginning to accept that her son might be in this state for some time. Then what would she do? She had no family here, and she couldn't imagine ever leaving him to go back to work. If his coma were of long duration, she would have to—

*Oh, I can't think about that now.*

Mr. de Brase—Docteur de Brase—had been in every day since the accident and, almost without realizing it, she had begun to look forward to his visits. He spared those few extra minutes after examining Thomas to provide subtle reassurance. He dropped comments like how the body used the coma to allow itself to heal, and it was by no means a sign he wouldn't wake up. Or he would tell her of a case he handled a few years back where the child was hit in exactly the same way as Thomas, and how the end-result had been better than anyone had hoped. She would have been hard-put to explain exactly why, but her spirits always lifted by the time he left.

"Bonjour, Madame." A handsome young man with a large smile walked into the room. He came over and shook her hand, speaking in perfect English. "I'm an intern in this hospital, and my name is Dr. Okonkwo. Docteur de Brase charged me with keeping a special eye on your son." His broad smile caused her own to appear.

"Are you studying to be a neurosurgeon too then?"

"It's my plan," he replied. "This is my sub-internship so it's not too late to decide on a different specialty, but if I can get a residency here, this is the field I would choose."

"You're not French," Chastity observed.

"No, I'm Nigerian. I was studying in Cambridge with Docteur de Brase's niece, and she made the introductions that allowed me to intern here."

"Oh, that was kind of him to bring you in," she said, politely. "You must be fluent in French then."

"Yes. I went to the Lycée Français in Lagos."

"I went to the Lycée Français in New York." Chastity smiled. "I guess learning to be fluent in French has its uses after all, since we both ended up here."

The intern went over to Thomas and checked the catheter and the stitches, making notes in the patient's file. "Has he shown any movement that's new?"

"No." She shook her head. "He sometimes jerks suddenly, but he did that right from the beginning. The doctor said it's not necessarily a sign of awareness."

"That's tr—" The intern was interrupted.

"Bonjour, Mademoiselle." The viscount strode into the room and clasped Chastity's hand warmly, before shaking the intern's. "Samuel."

"So you were able to come earlier than expected," the intern observed.

"Yes. My estate manager is quickly getting up to speed, and I'm able to extricate myself more easily these days." Dr. de Brase smiled at Chastity as he said this. "So, you've been introduced to our intern then."

"I have."

"Has he reviewed your son's progress with you?" Dr. de Brase caught her gaze, and Chastity felt her heart spark to life. She was able to breathe again when he lowered his eyes and studied the patient's chart.

The intern spoke up. "We were just going through the exam. No new movement. His ICP is down to sixteen." He turned to Chastity, "This is good news. It's within the normal range."

"So it was the right decision to avoid the craniotomy then?" She looked back and forth between the two of them, but it was Dr. de Brase who answered.

"It was a risk, but one worth taking. If his intra-cranial pressure had gone higher than twenty at any point, we would have rushed him into emergency surgery. I'm glad it didn't because the surgery can engender other issues, even if it can also save a patient's life. All in all, I'd say that, given the circumstances, we had the best possible outcome. Now we need to keep waiting. Patiently." He turned to the intern.

"Samuel have you done rounds with Docteur Bellamy yet?"

"Yes I have, but I wanted to come and see Thomas as you suggested."

"I'm glad you did." Dr. de Brase turned to Chastity. "I asked Samuel to start checking in on Thomas regularly to see how he's doing. That way he can keep me in the loop. I'll be off after this week because the in-house doctor is returning from his conference." He added, "I'll still come in to check on Thomas, though."

She smiled softly at him, touched. "Thank you."

Dr. de Brase gestured the intern towards the door. "Shall we?" The intern nodded his assent and gave his hand to Chastity. "I'll come as often as I can. Have me paged if you need anything, or if you want to reach Docteur de Brase directly. I'll make sure he gets the message."

As soon as they left, it felt as if the room was closing in. Chastity walked over to the window and looked out over the parking lot. The gray winter weather made it seem late afternoon rather than mid-morning. She didn't dare call and ask, but she hoped Maude, or even Elizabeth, would come and visit her. She was so lonely. Completely forgetting her plans to read to Thomas, she stared forlornly out the window and watched as tiny snowflakes began to fall. Tiny desolate snowflakes that tainted an icy world with bleakness.

It was the scent of freshly ground coffee that hit her first. Chastity spun around, brushing the tears that had pooled in her eyes, but had not fallen. Dr. de Brase had returned quietly, carrying two porcelain cups, and he gave a tentative smile. "The coffee here is awful, but we have a machine in the back that's better." And in timing that could not have been more auspicious, as soon as the words left his mouth, the sun pierced a hole through the clouds and brightened the room.

Chastity smiled up at him even as tears threatened to form again from this sweet gesture. She almost didn't trust herself to speak, but managed a "thank you." After he handed her a coffee, he stood awkwardly with his own cup until she gathered her wits and asked him to sit down.

"I wasn't sure if you took sugar," he said.

"Actually, I usually take sugar and milk." She gave a crooked grin.

"Sacrilege for a French person, I know. The black coffee is actually better than the café au lait in the machine here, so I'm getting accustomed to it without milk. And even sometimes without sugar, but yes, I usually take it." *Stop rambling*, she scolded herself, and sat.

The silence was not uncomfortable as each one sipped the coffee. Dr. de Brase stretched his legs forward and examined his shoes.

"Tell me how you came to be a neurosurgeon." Her voice squeaked on the last word, which made her blush. She had forgotten how to be sociable. Dr. de Brase had nothing to set his cup on, and was sitting in a folding chair, but he managed to look elegant.

"My wife—she died when she was young—was interested in medicine from a young age. We sort of grew up together. Went to the same bilingual school in St Germain-en-Laye, and even after my family moved to Maisons-Laffitte, I continued to go there. We were best friends before we even thought about a romantic relationship. She was definitely the one who influenced me to choose medicine.

"She was smart, you see. And I have a competitive nature. If she was going to do something, I was going to do it better." He chuckled—"although I rarely succeeded. She was completely focused on medicine and wanted to work in South America in one of the poorer communities. At the time, I thought it was what I wanted to do as well. But—"

Dr. de Brase stood and reached over to set his cup on the windowsill before resuming his place. "First, my father died, and I inherited the château when I was still in university. Then Miriam and I married young, and she got pregnant with Louis while we were medical residents. She died as a result of a complication from childbirth, so I continued in the medical field alone."

Chastity scanned his face compassionately. "What happened to Louis while you finished studying and started working?"

"My sister brought my niece over to spend time with Louis, and I had a live-in nanny, of course. I spent every minute that I wasn't working with him."

Chastity nodded as she processed this. "How did you choose neurosurgery?"

The doctor inhaled, then gave a shrug. "Part of it was chance. I happened to secure an internship in the field. But I was drawn to neurosurgery—probably because my father died of a stroke. Although...if we're going with that reasoning, I should be in obstetrics to save future husbands from becoming widowers." He laughed without humor. "The psychologists would be able to explain it all, I'm sure."

"It does seem logical enough," Chastity replied in a low tone. "I mean, that you would go into medicine. You're saving lives no matter what field you've chosen." She finished the last of her coffee and held the cup in her lap. "I just wanted to say thank you—for treating Thomas so gently, and for taking the time to explain things to me. I think that somehow...it has kept the panic at bay. It kept me from going over the edge." She didn't dare say anything else, but smiled at him through the lump in her throat.

Dr. de Brase nodded in response and the ensuing silence gave her some peace that allowed the crippling emotions to ebb away.

After the doctor had gathered the espresso cups with a promise to see her the next day, she went back over to the window and peered out. The sun had disappeared again, but the weather seemed less sinister. The snowflakes fell playfully, darting suddenly to one side in a gust of wind. Chastity drew in a deep breath, and with it—strength.

She turned to her son and felt hopeful for the first time, even though there had been no change in his condition. "Tommy." She kissed his nose playfully. "Let's read The Chamber of Secrets."

# CHAPTER 15

"How is he tonight?" The words were uttered breathlessly, not from panic, but simply from having rushed into the room an hour later than he had promised. Chastity looked up, reverie broken.

"Hi, Marc. He's pretty much the same." Her voice was flat. "The swelling is down, both inside the skull and also on the outside. You can even see his head is less swollen." She went on talking, more from a desire to fill the silence than a desire to share. "He's been moving more. He jerks his feet suddenly, or pulls at his tubes—we have to be careful of that—but the doctor said it doesn't necessarily mean he's gaining consciousness."

Marc peeled off his scarf and leather jacket—with the gesture came a strong smell of smoke—and pulled up a chair beside her. He sat, designer jean-clad legs apart, elbows resting on his knees. He searched her face. "I wish you would let me spend more time here. I wish I could be here when the doctors come and visit him so you don't have to handle it alone."

She gave him a fleeting look and an imperceptible smile. "It's fine. That's sweet, but the doctor is clear in what he says, and he seems to care about Thomas. He takes the time to answer all my questions. It helps me to meet with him alone so I can absorb everything he's saying without being distracted. I need to be able to communicate any changes in Tommy's state."

Marc leaned back against the folding chair suddenly and examined the ceiling with nonchalance. "So. I heard Docteur de Brase is none other than *le Vicomte de Maisons-Laffitte*."

"Yes, I was surprised." Chastity fiddled with the hospital blanket at her side. "I teach his son, and our interactions had not led me to believe he would have a profession like this. To be honest, I thought he was rude and unconcerned about his own son. But now I know it can't be true—not with the care he gives his patients here."

Marc paused before replying. "Yes, I can see why you might have thought that. He didn't strike me as being someone who cares about anyone else."

"I suppose you can't be a doctor, and particularly one who works with children, without caring somewhat." Chastity shrugged.

Marc gave a forced laugh. "He seems to have everything going for him, doesn't he? Rich, owns a château, and now a neurosurgeon—and he's nice, on top of it all."

Perhaps he expected Chastity to laugh at his attempt at a jest, but she responded absently. "That's true."

Marc's expression twisted into a grimace. "Chassy," he commanded, and her eyes focused on his. "Have you given any thought to us?"

When the shock and anger flashed in her eyes, he leaned forward. "I'd like to take my place with you at the hospital as more than just the person who fathered your child. I want to spend more time here and be with you as you talk to the doctors—be a support to you."

"You have to work," she answered feebly, looking at her hands clasped on her lap.

He mistook this for weakening on her part and pressed on. "I'll take time off work. I'll ask my parents for some financial support. I know they'll give it to me if they understand why I'm asking. I want to make this work, Chassy. I still have feelings for you—"

"Shh." Chastity cut him off sharply, glancing at her son. "Not in front of Thomas." She stood and walked over to the door, beckoning him to follow. After checking that no one was passing by in the corridor, she lowered her voice. "Seriously, Marc. I can't believe you're talking about this now. I can't think about anything other than Thomas. Surely you understand that. I'm allowing you to be here for his sake, but that's where it ends. I don't have room in my thoughts or my heart for anything else."

Marc put his hand on the doorframe and leaned his forehead on his arm. He exhaled loudly then faced her. "Can't I at least spend more time here? Come during the day? I can take the relay so you can go outside, or go home for a bit."

Chastity chewed her lip. "I can't imagine leaving him. Maude brings me changes of clothes and anything else I need and even stays while I run and shower or take a quick walk outside. I don't need anything else."

When he gave a pained expression, she relented. "Don't quit your job, okay? You can come on your days off, and maybe you can stay with him for a half-hour while I take a walk or something. That will be...helpful."

"Okay. I guess that's better than nothing," Marc replied gracelessly and returned to take his seat at the bedside.

"Tommy," Chastity said, following Marc to his side and attempting cheerfulness. "It's time for your favorite show." She clicked the TV on, and as the sounds filled the room, she and Marc turned towards it in silence.

Charles drove on the autoroute, the dark road lit by headlights in both directions. He was listening to a classical radio station, but his thoughts were elsewhere, jumping from one issue to another. He wondered how Louis was doing since he had seen him even less than usual the week before. He had looked haggard. He also remembered he needed to follow up regarding the paintings he had borrowed for the exhibition that was to open in just a few weeks. He was irritated with himself for forgetting to bring it to his business manager's attention.

Then Mademoiselle Whitmore flashed before his eyes. He considered the difficulty of her situation and the minimal support she had compared to the other parents he dealt with. He remembered how green her eyes were whenever they turned towards him and how her gaze had changed in the months since he had first met her. She had gone from the stern, judgmental teacher to a vulnerable woman, terrified when faced with the severity of her son's condition. Now she was changing yet again and becoming softer. Confiding.

By now he had driven through the streets of Maisons-Laffitte, and was turning through his tall iron gates, driving over the small pebbles that led to the front entrance. Charles strode into the marble foyer and jogged up the steps onto the first landing. Paltier came running as soon as he heard the front door open.

"Monsieur." Paltier was slightly out of breath.

"Paltier," Charles addressed him with a smile, "how many times have I told you you don't need to greet me when I come home?"

"But of course I do." The worthy gentleman divested Charles of his wool coat, and took his scarf and leather gloves.

"How is Louis? Is he here?" Paltier carried the viscount's coat over to a large armoire set against the wall and hung the coat on a wooden hanger before replying. "Louis is upstairs, and from what I can tell, he seems to be his usual self." Charles did not have time to ask him to explain these cryptic words because Paltier went on. "Monsieur, I should warn you that Mademoiselle Duprey is in the Italian apartment."

Charles stopped short and turned to Paltier with a raised eyebrow. "I was not expecting her."

Paltier replied in a wooden tone, "I apologize if I've done wrong, but she was visibly upset and quite unlike herself. She demanded to see you and wouldn't take 'no' for an answer, insisting she would wait. And considering she is your..." He coughed discreetly.

Charles sucked in his breath and said, "No, you did well. Please let her know I'll be with her in a moment, but I want to see Louis first. Oh, and bring her some refreshments."

"I've already offered." Paltier's spine was perfectly straight as he added, "but she refused."

"Of course you did," Charles soothed. "I won't be long." He walked up the steps to his son's room and tapped on the door.

"*Entre*," His son yelled from inside above the loud music. Charles opened the door and was met with a strong cloud of smoke, dim lighting, and clothes strewn all over the floor. His son was lying on the bed playing, what appeared to be, a video game on his iPad.

When his father came in, he started up. "Papa. I didn't expect you." He managed to snub out the burning end of his cigarette and stand in one movement.

His father took in the room with quiet irony. "I see I should visit you more often. Since when have you started smoking?"

"Oh, that." Louis had recovered, and his defensiveness returned. "It's not all that big of a deal."

His father returned no answer but leaned against the messy desk near the entrance and stared at his son. Louis squirmed under his searching gaze.

"I was just wondering how you were doing, and if you needed anything." Charles reached down and pulled something that poked at him from where he was sitting. It was the screwdriver from a Swiss army knife.

"I'm fine."

Charles reined in his exasperation. "Louis, you say you're fine, but it doesn't seem like you are. I'm here to talk, you know. Are you sure there's not something you want to talk about, or something you need?"

Louis jabbed his toe against the wood floor, sending a sock skidding across the room, and looking at that moment much younger than his teenage self. "Well, uh. I was thinking I would like to buy a moped. Can I have one?" He glanced up, frowning.

Shifting position, Charles said, "Sure. But why don't we discuss it once you get your grades back up."

Louis flushed and crossed his arms. "I've been working on them. But some of the classes are really hard."

"Maybe we could get you some tutoring."

"Yeah, whatever." Louis turned back to his iPad. "Forget about the moped. It's not that big of a deal."

Charles struggled to find something to say that wouldn't harp on his son's grades but couldn't think of anything. "Okay, we can talk about it another time. Paltier told me that Manon paid me a surprise visit, so I'm going to see what she wants." Louis just nodded. As Charles reached the door, he suddenly turned back. "Who's your English teacher now?"

His son looked up in surprise. "Miss Whitmore."

"Yes, but I mean now that she's in the hospital with her son and not teaching classes."

"Oh. Uh. I can't remember her name. Mz. Mercer taught one class, and then this other teacher came in."

"Do you like her as well as Mademoiselle Whitmore?"

"I don't know." Louis shrugged. "I suppose not. You can tell Miss Whitmore cares about the kids." He looked embarrassed to have revealed as much and scowled.

"Okay. Well...good night." Charles went into the hallway and shut the door with a soft click.

He found Manon curled up on one of the hard-backed sofas, her shoes off and feet tucked underneath her, and her coat serving as a blanket. Her face was tear-stained, her eyes tired. "Charles." There was no trace of her usual animation.

He walked over to where she sat. "What is it, Manon?"

She leaned her face into her hands and sobbed quietly. He had never seen her so distraught. "My grandmother died suddenly. That's why I've come back from London."

Charles knew how close Manon was to her grandmother so he just sat on the couch and put his arm around her curled-up legs. "I didn't know where else to go." She sniffled. "I didn't want to go back to my empty apartment."

Rubbing her leg, he asked, "What happened? When we saw her at Christmas, she seemed to be in great health."

"Aneurism," Manon choked out through her sobs, which were growing louder. Charles pulled her up next to him and put his arm around her, hugging her close.

"My grandmother raised me. She's the only family I have."

"I know," he said. This was only slightly inaccurate. Charles knew that though her parents had been killed in a drunk driving accident when she was a baby, her narcissistic extended family had wanted nothing to do with her until she became famous. Her grandmother, alone, had given her a loving and orderly—if bourgeois—childhood.

After a period of crying, while Charles waited, Manon finally pulled out a tissue and blew her nose. She spoke numbly. "The funeral is on Wednesday. I was given time off to attend it until Thursday. Could I stay here?"

Charles cleared his throat and looked down at the top of her blond curls. He was not thrilled at having her stay in the same house as his son, but he was not a monster either and could see she needed him. She felt small in his arms, and her perfume was familiar, even if it had stronger overtones than he generally liked. After a minute he perceived he had not yet answered.

"Of course."

# CHAPTER 16

The music was audible as soon as Louis entered the iron gates and turned down the lane towards the house, a somewhat crumbling old manor that was set far back from the street and encased in tall oak trees. This was probably how the party was able to carry on in full force without incurring a neighborly call to the police.

There were a few people outside the house, and one or two of them nodded at Louis. As soon as he walked through the door, Mitchell and Sandeep hailed him in an inebriated pitch. "Louis. You made it, man." He gave a small wave and walked over to Max and shook his hand.

"You got here just in time," Max said. "I was starting to run out."

"My dad wanted me to have dinner with Manon Duprey. I couldn't leave until we were finished."

Max whistled. "Is she just as hot in person? You're a lucky dude."

"Yeah, but she's dating my father, so—"

A girl fell into Louis, laughing as she was pulled to her feet again. He tugged his beer-soaked shirt away from his bare skin and tried to wring it out.

"Hi, Louis." Another girl with straight blond hair walked up to him, her skin tanned from makeup, her voice flirty. "I've never seen you at any of these parties before." He didn't recognize her.

"I've been to one or two," he mumbled, torn between surprise and annoyance.

"What?" she yelled over the music. She fell forward into him.

"I've been to a few," he said more loudly. He glanced around, desperate to leave her company and find a place where he could get his hands on a drink, anything that would give him something to do. He didn't see the bar from where he stood, so he stayed put.

"So," she said with a glinting smile, her breath a combination of beer and cigarettes. "What do you say you and I head upstairs and find someplace to talk and get to know each other better?" She linked her arm through his, and added, unnecessarily, "If you know what I mean."

Louis looked her over. He was sure she didn't attend Fenley, though she seemed to know a lot of people at the party. Even in the muted lighting, there was something repellent about her. He realized with dim surprise that he wasn't even interested in a one-night fling with her. He shook his head and pulled his arm away.

"He may be the son of a viscount," she said to no one in particular as she walked away, "but he's still a loser."

Sandeep jerked his head towards the departing figure. "She's from Sartrouville. I have no idea who invited her. Come on," he said. "Let's get you a drink."

Louis turned to Max. "I'll be right back."

Max had a satellite of girls around him, but he didn't seem interested in any of them. He was watching what happened at the party with a keen eye. To anyone but a casual observer, it was obvious he was the one who kept all the plates spinning. "Make it quick," he said.

When Louis returned moments later, one drink downed, the other in hand, Max immediately disengaged from the girls and signaled with two fingers for Louis to follow. They walked up the winding staircase, carpeted with a faded oriental rug, and continued down a hallway decorated in shabby chic, with old wallpaper and well-chosen frames. Max stopped, and rapped on the door in front of him.

"*Entre*." a voice called from within, but Max was blocked from pushing the door open by a meaty hand. "It's just me," he said with a tinge of impatience.

Inside, the room was dark with a red lava lamp in motion, which was strangely compelling to Louis in his altered state. He hadn't taken anything strong, but he smoked some pot on his way to the party to calm his nerves. He had been tempted to use the little red pill that now made a regular appearance in his stash, and which he had learned was speed, but he wanted to save it for next week when the exams would start. He was just starting to understand how to use the drugs properly, and the knowledge made him feel wordly and grown up. The speed helped him to maintain good grades and get things done, and the pot—or hash, whichever he had on hand—kept him mellow and cool so he could talk to people without fear.

"Louis is here with the supply," Max said, crisply. "Move over. And you—give me that scale. Let's bring it out and weigh it."

Louis opened the backpack full of various packets, wrapped in plastic. His supply had increased, as had his acceptance in the crowd, just as Jean had predicted. Now that he had promised that favor to Jean—still didn't know what it was, but he was assured it was nothing illegal—he was able to get a certain amount of drugs for free. This had become necessary since his father didn't exactly give him an unlimited allowance, Louis thought with disgust. *As if he didn't have it.*

Max watched with an eagle eye as Louis brought the packets out, one by one. He said, more to himself than to Louis, "I don't know why the dealer insists on using you to bring the supply when I'm the one with all the contacts. He could save himself time and money." Louis only shrugged, mellowed by the combination of vodka and pot.

When the money had been counted and tucked in the inside pocket of his bag, Louis had the vague idea he should head straight home and put the money in a safe place. He started walking down the stairs, taking his time to stop and look at the paintings with a fixed interest.

"Good evening, Louis," he heard someone say. "Louis." The voice was now lilting, brimming with laughter. He turned and faced a girl he recognized from his history class. Her dark brown hair was cut short to frame her face, and he had never seen such beautiful, large brown eyes as the ones that were raised to his at that instant.

"Eloise," he managed.

"Ah, good. You're not completely stoned then." She smiled at him, and he continued to stare at her face, fascinated by the multitude of colors reflected in her eyes.

Her dimples peeped out at this, and she concluded with slightly raised eyebrows. "All right, then. Take care, Louis." She turned to walk up the stairs and only glanced back at him once before walking down the hallway. He was relieved to see she headed into the bathroom instead of going into the room where Max was. He thought hazily that he would wait for her to come back down. In any case, it was so pleasant on the stairwell, he saw no reason to move.

Charles marched through the hospital doors. He was unable to explain, even to himself, why he was at the hospital again when his week of filling in was over. He had already handed all his patients over to Docteur Toussaint, except young Whitmore. He told himself he was particularly interested in how this case was progressing from a medical point of view, curious as to how the young boy would fare cognitively once he woke up. He found himself anxiously hoping for the best—for the mother's sake, as well as the boy's.

"Bonjour, Samuel." Charles smiled at the intern as he walked by.

"Bonjour, monsieur." The young man didn't dare jump to a first-name basis though his mentor had assured him it was fine. Samuel ran to catch up. "I didn't expect to see you so soon, but I'm glad you came in. I have a progress report for you to sign if you have a minute?"

Charles glanced at the door just ahead where his patient was and stopped in his tracks. "Sure. Let's go do that now." They walked side by side in the direction of the small office Charles had borrowed during his short stay, and turned into it. Charles skirted the desk and gestured to the chair in front of it. Taking the paper that was handed to him, he pulled a pen out of the square holder full of blue glass pebbles and skimmed its contents.

"How's it going for you here?" He kept the question purposefully open-ended.

"Good," Samuel answered firmly. "I feel less hassled and...ignorant"—here he chuckled—"than I did the first week or two."

"Have you given more thought to a specialty?" His mentor ran his finger down the page of ratings, and skimmed the questions at the bottom.

"I'm definitely interested in pursuing neurology, although I'm not yet sure whether I want to pursue pediatric." Samuel paused, looking down. "This may make me sound weak, but I'm not sure I have it in me. The sight of the children suffering is harder than I expected. Or—there's something about a parent's fear and grief that's magnified compared to other patients' family members. You know, Thomas, for instance. Every time I go into his room, I see this despair on his mother's face, even though she attempts to remain cheerful. It's hard to see."

Charles didn't answer as he checked off several ratings and scribbled notes in answer to each of the questions. He paused over the last one, wrote something, then capped the pen and put it back. "You'll be a good doctor," he said. "You have a heart. However, you're wise to know your limits. Not everyone can handle pediatrics. We all have a cap to our effectiveness that's linked to our personality and, I suppose, our level of humanity." He gave a crooked smile— "of which some seem to think I have none."

"Isabelle would not agree to that," Samuel said, roundly, with an unaccustomed allusion to their personal connection. Charles simply smiled, and handed him the report.

When he walked into Thomas's room, Chastity was occupying her usual spot. She looked surprised to see him, but pleased. "Any changes?" He walked over to take a look at the chart.

"It seems so," she said. "Docteur Toussaint is encouraged—and so am I—that Thomas seems to be opening his eyes for longer stretches of time. There seems to be more of a deliberateness to his movements too." Her eyes twinkled. "I think he's bent on getting the IV tubes out."

Charles read the patient's chart, noting the same progress recorded that she spoke of. "This is good news. I'm pleased to hear it. I hope, of course, that we might start to see some changes now, but it's impossible to predict when these will happen, and what the final outcome will be."

"I know," Chastity said, "but I cannot give up hope."

"And you should not," he replied, firmly. He studied her closely now, something he didn't often let himself do. Her already slim frame was thinner than it was weeks ago, but she was starting to have some bloom to her cheeks again. He was distracted by the curly locks that were always falling from her loose chignon, and how she tucked them behind her ear. She wore the same frail pendant earrings every day that swung back and forth as she talked.

Realizing he'd been staring, Charles shuffled the papers in his hands. "You look well."

"I am well." Her smile brightened and lit up her face. "I have good news." Charles drew his eyebrows together, wondering if the good news had something to do with this father of Thomas's that he had met only once—who had not left him with a favorable impression.

His expression must have been forbidding because she flushed suddenly and looked down. "I don't know why I'm telling you this. It's only that my mother is coming to France." When he heard this, the pressure in his chest eased.

"I never thought she'd be able to get away because she works with my father in the dry cleaning business. She handles all the accounting aspects, and my dad can't function without her. But one of his retired friends, who's a whiz at numbers, offered to take her place." Her voice was tremulous, despite her grin.

"I'm glad to hear it. This kind of support is just what you need."

"It's true." Her voice throbbed with suppressed emotion. "I've been trying to keep my strength up for Thomas, you know, and even though I'm grateful to Maude and Elizabeth—" Chastity smiled at him, "—and to you, I would love not to have to be so strong all the time." Charles nodded thoughtfully, mesmerized by the delicate angle of her chin. She tilted her face when she was saying something vulnerable.

He realized he was staring again. "When does she arrive?"

"Next week." In a burst of good humor, Chastity walked over and kissed Thomas on the cheek. He fluttered his eyelids and both of them watched him intently, but he didn't move again after that.

"Can I bring you a coffee?" Charles offered, as he had done the few times since he brought her that first delicious espresso.

"I would love one," she answered, warmly. Her smile was reflected in her expressive eyes, and when she looked at him like that, he couldn't see any resemblance between this woman and the one who taught his son—the one he had thought of as a shrew.

When Charles returned, he handed her one of the tiny white porcelain cups but stopped short. "I'm sorry. I forgot the sugar."

"Oh, stay—I'll run and get one from the nurse's station." Chastity's voice was almost merry. "They keep a stash there and have always encouraged me to help myself. They are so good to me."

She walked off lightly, coffee in hand, and Charles went over to Thomas and set his cup down on the bedside table. "Thomas." He jostled the small arm carefully. "Thomas. Your mother wants to see you."

There was no response. He nudged him again more firmly, but his words were caressing. "Thomas. Open your eyes."

There was a sigh, and Thomas opened his eyes; but he stared, unfocused, at the ceiling. "That's better, Thomas. Can you see me? I'm Docteur de Brase."

The boy's eyes seemed to focus for a second, but then stared ahead, unseeing. Charles sat on the side of his bed, and held his hand. "Thomas, if you can hear me, squeeze my hand."

There was a pause, and then, "Very good, Thomas. You did it. That was a strong squeeze too." He grinned.

He heard the crash and turned towards the noise, Thomas's hand still in his. Chastity stood in the doorway in mute astonishment, her gaze going from Charles to her son, the porcelain cup shattered at her feet.

# CHAPTER 17

Charles gazed steadily at Thomas's mother and in a quiet voice, said, "Come." He turned to the slim figure lying on the bed. "Thomas, your mom is here. Can you squeeze again for her?"

She darted to his side and took his hand in hers. "Hi, sweetie, I'm here. Can you squeeze my hand too?" There was no responsive pressure. The machines continued their calm and steady beeps.

"He's out again," Charles said. "I think that effort exhausted him. But it was a significant leap. He was able to comprehend what I was saying and command a physical response in answer."

Miss Whitmore's cheeks were flushed, and the quick breaths betrayed her agitation. "I wish I could have felt him squeeze my hand. I wish he would wake up."

"I'm pretty confident he will wake up in the next few days. But with brain injuries, it's impossible to predict with accuracy because we don't know if the neurons have been damaged or just bruised. You have to be prepared that even if he does wake up, his will probably not be a fast recovery, and we're unlikely to know straight away the extent of his injuries." Charles resisted the urge to take hold of her hand. "I encourage you to hope for the best outcome, and let Thomas sense your hope."

Their gazes locked, and Charles felt something flash through him. Awareness. Longing. He could see she was trembling.

"I cannot thank you enough," she said.

Charles returned the smile, but shook his head. "I was just in the right place at the right time."

"I know it was a coincidence for you to be here when Thomas regained some awareness." There was a crease between Miss Whitmore's brows. "But I want to thank you for...what I can only describe as your friendship these past two weeks." She blushed. "I'm sorry. I don't want to presume too much."

"You're not," he answered quickly, anxious to reassure her on that point. "I hope you'll come to me if you need anything." Leaving the bedside, Charles went over to the door to pick up the pieces of porcelain that lay shattered, and he threw them in the garbage.

"I'll ask the cleaning staff to come mop this up," he said, wrapping his scarf around his neck. "Here's my card, which has my cell phone on it if you need to reach me." Handing her a cream-colored card with gold lettering, he hesitated, strangely nervous. "My friends call me Charles."

Her eyes darted to his, and she took the card. "Chastity."

"Okay, then." He snapped his leather gloves against his hand, almost reluctant to set out. "I'll check in on Thomas tomorrow."

He left the room, a spring in his step. *Chastity*.

When the doctor was gone, all the emotions Chastity had held in check seemed to crash at once, leaving her exhausted. She was grateful for the steady beeps and the silence behind them that blanketed the room and the ward. She had too much to think about and desperately hoped Marc would not choose this moment to make an appearance. Wiping her palms on her jeans, she rested her forearms on the bed, her two hands touching her son. She laid her head on her arms.

Tommy. Her eyes welled with tears when she thought about him regaining consciousness. She took his hand and squeezed it, but his hand was limp in hers. If he was on his way to getting better...she would give anything for that to be so.

And then—the viscount. Mr. de Brase, *Dr.* de Brase—*Charles*. Her thoughts were a confused jumble when it came to this man. He had appeared so indifferent and cold as a father, and it seemed he acted out of sheer disregard for anyone else in his role at the school and the town. Yet he was so clearly warm and caring as a doctor, going beyond the duties required of him—even continuing to watch over her son when his week was over. She had noticed he was there today in casual clothes, not his doctor's jacket. Why would he make the effort?

Chastity lifted her head and breathed out a sigh. It was like he had a split personality when she compared the two versions of him, but his behavior towards her since Tommy was injured was unmistakably sincere. Perhaps she had misjudged him initially. Did she dare ask him about his son? Ask if he had taken the time to seek help for him? She found that she wanted to reconcile the two personalities into one, and hoped the result would be one she liked.

Restless, Chastity stood suddenly and started walking across the small room. She yanked some paper towels out of the dispenser and began to wipe the coffee off the door, absent-mindedly. No, she couldn't ask him about Louis—couldn't think about work. She would have to return to it eventually, and in some ways even wanted to. A few of her students had sent her cards at the hospital on their own initiative, which brought tears to her eyes. There was just not enough room in her mind and heart to think about that now. As much as Charles de Brase was starting to treat her like a friend, she felt she could not ask him such a question just yet. The two worlds had to stay separate for the time being. As such, the viscount-doctor would remain a mystery.

Having settled that, however unsatisfactorily, Chastity resumed her seat by Thomas's side. Her mother's visit could not get here quickly enough. The silence, although sometimes welcome, often threatened to drown her when she connected it with the absence of

Thomas's chatter. And she was discovering that Marc's presence was not the remedy.

If Charles, returning home, had been privy to Chastity's reflections and questions regarding his inconsistency, he would have been surprised. Already the image of his son's slightly annoying teacher of a few months ago was replaced by the woman he had spent time with every day for the past couple of weeks. If he thought about her role in his son's life at all, it was to admire her tenacity in trying to help him. In this, he was reminded of someone. A young bride...

He liked the way the creases in her brow gave way to smiles when he entered the room. He appreciated how Chastity looked him in the eye when he gave his medical opinion—and her regard was free of the predatory look he usually got from other single, beautiful women.

And she was beautiful, especially with her hair down that way. *Mon dieu*.

He was not in the habit of questioning his own motivations or actions except, perhaps, when it pertained to his son. He had inherited enough of his father's character to be sure of his actions, and enough of his mother's to think no one had a right to question them. In all areas this served—except for Louis.

Charles thought about the last time he had seen his son. It was around noon a couple days prior, and Louis had only just rolled out of bed. He was in the kitchen, having a piece of baguette smothered with butter and raspberry jam and a cup of black coffee. Louis had showered and was wearing clean clothes, but it was a set of weary eyes that he turned to his father.

Charles, who had only gone into the kitchen to discuss with his chef which catering companies they would use for the spring ball, was taken aback to see him there.

"Louis, it's noon. Is that your breakfast? Why aren't you...out?" He was chagrined to discover he didn't know what his son generally did on

Saturdays ever since Louis had declared himself finished with riding lessons. In fact, he didn't even know who Louis's friends were. Louis examined his plate and shrugged.

"Where were you last night?" Charles had frowned then, and realizing the chef, who was new, was listening to the conversation with undue interest, dropped the subject. "Never mind. We'll talk about it later. Don't forget to call Grand-mère. You missed last week and she was upset."

"I won't," muttered his offspring.

And that was it. Charles had not spoken to, or even seen, Louis since. It had been some time now that they had fallen into the habit of living completely separate lives, brought on, perhaps, by the troubles in the estate management, which eventually forced Charles to take the longest sabbatical the hospital would allow.

Before he could notice the shift soon enough to remedy it, his son stopped asking for him and kept to himself. Even now, it didn't help that Manon had only just returned to England the day before, after having extended her stay. Since she showed no interest in getting to know Louis, he hadn't tried to throw them together.

Ah. That was complicated. The more he thought about it, the more he was certain things could not continue with Manon. It was ill-timed that she was in too fragile a state for him to end things with her now.

He put that out of his mind and punched one of the saved numbers into his phone, putting it on speaker. After a few rings, he heard the laughter in the deep voice.

"Charles. So soon?"

"It's been a few months already, Jef," Charles rallied. "When are we going to have our drink?"

"At your place, as soon as you can find time for me," Jef shot back, adding, "as long as your sister will be there."

"What, still have a crush on her after all these years? She'll never have you, you know. She said you're too much of a babe." He couldn't resist adding, "even though you look like you're fifty with all the smoking you do."

"Now that I'm a gray-beard, maybe you'll start heeding my advice." Jef chuckled.

"Whatever you say," Charles said. "Listen, we need to meet. Why not join me for the art gallery opening in two-weeks' time. I want to talk to you about the spring ball."

"Charles—" Jef protested, disapprovingly. "You're not going to open up your home again to the public after what happened last time."

"Let's just say I was persuaded too," returned Charles cryptically. "There is little risk a second theft could occur, and even so, there will be heavy security. I want to run a few ideas by you."

"Okay." His friend was thoughtful. "I see why you want my help. You want to have someone you can trust."

"Exactly. My own security detail, if you will. So can I count on you for the opening?"

"Send me the details." Then just before hanging up, his friend quizzed, "And see that Adelaide is there too so I can get her to accompany me to this ball."

André Robin pulled his gardening coat over his shoulders and stretched on the makeshift bed that protected his body from the cold stone floor. It was five in the morning, and he didn't have the luxury of staying here much longer before the old man was going to be awake and bustling about. In the year that André had been employed at the château, he never knew a day to go by when he didn't spot Paltier walking about by six o'clock at the latest.

It was nearing the end of January, and unseasonably cold outside, and he wasn't looking forward to going out there. He knew of a café a few streets over that opened early enough to receive him for breakfast, and by now they knew his face. He could stake out a table there until it was time to report to work.

Hiding out in the basement with its cavernous rooms was the only solution that presented itself to André when he lost everything in disastrous gambling debts. He could no longer afford to pay his rent and had to give up his apartment. With no family in the vicinity, and none he could confide his troubles to—and a girlfriend who had recently discovered a preference for a trainer at the gym where she worked—there was no option left to him. He crept in close to midnight each night, washed himself in the kitchen basin that was downstairs, and huddled in one of the dark passages close to the wine cellar. Each morning, he crept out the same way, only to return for work.

André stretched. The sounds had stopped some hours since—noises that had begun a few weeks earlier, and which started to take on a familiar rhythm. The first time he heard them was at two in the morning, and there was a scraping sound coming from inside the wall on the far room of the basement. It wasn't the scraping that drew him towards the noise because that—he had assumed—was rats. It was only when he heard a soft banging, as if someone were hitting the stone with a chisel from the inside, that he went to investigate. He located the spot next to an old, locked gate set into a tunnel that it seemed no one had a key to. At least he had never seen anyone open it. When he was assured that no one was around, he put his ear close to the wall and listened more carefully. He was, by no means, certain of what he was hearing, but he understood enough to nod once in satisfaction and move off quietly to where he was sleeping.

Ever since that first time, he heard the muted noises almost every night, which ceased long before dawn. He got up decisively and rolled his bedding into a bundle, which he stowed, along with a few of his essentials, in a long-unused cupboard. He had had a close call with his previous hiding place when he heard talk of dismantling the old furnace, but this spot was not likely to be discovered. He stretched, and tied his boots, before putting on his coat and beret.

The door there led to the lower grounds, and he slipped out silently, locking the door behind him. He walked off to the side of the property where there was a copse of trees that would lead him to the gate and the warmth of the café. As soon as the trees obscured his profile, he lit a cigarette and crunched on the snow in meditative rhythm. André Robin had an idea about these noises, and he considered how he might turn the situation to his advantage.

# CHAPTER 18

Louis spotted Eloise through the school doors, and raced outside after her. "Eloise, hi."

She turned to face him, poised and with a pleasant smile. "Hi, Louis." When he stared at her without speaking, her smile grew broader and her eyes twinkled. "Did you want to say something?"

He shifted uncomfortably. "I was, uh, wondering how late you stayed at that party."

"Oh, so you remember that, do you? I wasn't sure you had any memory of meeting me because by the time I came back downstairs, you were sitting on the steps, passed out."

"Yeah. Someone woke me up before Christoph's parents came home, and everyone was gone. To tell you the truth, I don't know why I passed out. It's the second time it's happened to me after only drinking a little bit. And—" he added conscientiously, "after smoking some pot."

"Hm." She chewed her lip. "Did you ever think that maybe someone was slipping something into your drink? Do you know anyone who would do that to you?" Eloise added, "You know, since it happened twice?"

A teacher, leading a line of elementary students towards the gate, passed them, crunching over the pebbles in the courtyard and instructing them to keep to their line of two-by-two.

"Hey, Eloise." A tall, lanky boy called out to her at the same time, causing her to break off and smile at him. "Do you want me to walk over to class with you?" He indicated the outlying buildings across the street.

"Hey, Pierce. No thanks. I want to finish talking to Louis, and we still have time." Pierce shrugged and loped off, and Louis smiled at that, his cheeks stiff and unused to turning up. When they were alone again, Eloise turned her attention back to him. "So, we were saying...?"

"You were asking if someone could have slipped something in my drink, but I can't see why anyone would do that."

"I don't know." She shrugged. "To humiliate you? To steal from you?" Louis flinched.

"Did someone steal from you? I hope you weren't carrying anything valuable."

"No, no, it was nothing." Louis hid from her the realization that for the second time, the money he had collected for drugs had been taken from him while he was passed out at a party. For the past week, he had been racking his brains trying to figure out what he was going to tell Jean about not having the money, and he hadn't given much thought to how odd it was that he would be robbed twice.

"—and so, because of that, I never drink or eat anything at parties. Unfortunately, I have a friend who lost consciousness at a party after only having had one drink."

Louis snapped to attention. "Was she okay?"

"Yeah. Luckily her friends were there and they took her home. She reported it and the police are looking into it. I wouldn't think they would target a guy, which is what makes me think they either thought to steal from you, or—" She reached her hand out and touched his arm, "humiliate you. I'm sorry it happened," she added.

Louis seethed as he remembered the sequence of events that night. Someone was definitely working against him. When he didn't respond right away, Eloise spoke up again with obvious reluctance. "I know you're friends with Max, but I can't help but think he goes with a bad bunch."

"We're not friends," Louis said firmly. "And he doesn't go with a bad bunch. He *leads* it."

"Okay, so you know your own mind then. That's good," Eloise said.

"Not as well as I should. I can't believe some of the situations I've gotten myself into," he said with uncharacteristic candor. "That's going to change."

"Hm." She smiled, pulled her bag on her shoulder, and started to walk away.

"Eloise," he couldn't resist calling out. She turned back. "I just didn't want you to have the wrong impression of me. You know—after what you saw at the party."

"I don't think I do." Her serene reply and twinkling eyes warmed Louis's heart and stayed with him after she left.

"Mom," Thomas whispered. It had been the first word he spoke, and that was three days before her mother arrived. In those three days, he had impressed the doctors with his improvement, establishing set periods of sleep and wake. He wasn't talkative, but he had been able to answer every simple question they asked him, except for what had happened the days leading up to the accident. He had been able to communicate his desire to drink some water almost right away—in French. It was more than Chastity could have hoped for.

Marc accompanied her to pick her mother up at the airport. It seemed like an easy way to lure him away from staying with Thomas while she was gone. She couldn't quite place why, but she would rather have Maude or Elizabeth at Tommy's side than Marc. "I'll stay out of your way," Marc said as he drove. "I know you need lots of private time with your mom. It's going to be good for you to have her here."

She turned to him in grateful surprise. "That's sweet of you. I agree. It will be good—for both Thomas and me to have her here."

After a moment's silence, she added, "I'm sorry you don't have this. I wish you still had a good relationship with your parents."

"Actually, there is something I've been meaning to tell you." She looked at his profile expectantly. "My mother made contact with me."

Chastity gasped. "You're kidding me. That's great."

"Yeah." Marc nodded. "Apparently she heard through some mutual friends that I was showing interest in my son and that pleased her enough to forget some of her anger. She's hoping to be able to meet Thomas."

"Oh." Chastity was caught off-guard. "It's not possible right now, obviously."

"You don't think she could come visit him in the hospital and bring him a gift?"

"No, Marc. He just woke up from a *coma* and needs as little stimuli as possible." She peered out the window on her right, hiding the red spots of anger on her cheeks.

"Yes, but your mother is coming to see him," he argued back.

"Thomas already knows my mother. She's not a stranger. So please forget the idea. It's not going to work."

"I'm sorry for asking." Marc huffed and stuck his lip out.

A silence fell over them, and Chastity sighed. Here were some signs of his old self surfacing, the things that made her more and more certain their relationship could not work.

They began to see billboards for the airport, and her spirits lifted at the thought of seeing her mother again. That's when Marc broached the subject in a kinder tone. "Do you think it might be possible at least for you to come and see my parents in Paris? Perhaps after your mom has been here for a while and is familiar with everything, she could stay with Thomas while you come with me. I think the whole reason my parents are interested in a reconciliation is because of you and Thomas."

Chastity struggled internally, afraid he was trying to gain ground. If she said yes, it would move them closer to a relationship she wasn't sure she wanted—even platonically—but she also suspected it would help heal some of the anger from the past and allow her to be free from those shackles. When he added, “I want to do anything I can to reconcile with them,” her compassion won over. “Of course, Marc. Anything I can do to help restore your relationship with your parents.”

They didn’t say much else before arriving at the circular airport where they drove down the ramps leading to the parking garage. At the Arrivals gate, she could see her mother yanking a heavy suitcase off the conveyor belt through the glass walls. Chastity tried to signal to her but wasn't able to catch her attention. When her mom finally exited Customs, Chastity threw herself in her mother’s arms, and Marc had the decency to stay back against the wall.

If her mom felt any surprise at being picked up by Marc, she hid it. “Hello Marc,” she said, placidly. “You look well. I'm glad to see your life has taken a turn for the better.”

“Thank you, ma'am,” he replied. “May I push the cart?”

Marc remained true to his word, and for the following week he held back from visiting the hospital so they could have their time together. Now Chastity, her mom, and Thomas had formed a ritual of playing, eating, and watching TV each day in his hospital room. This was the picture they presented when Dr. de Brase finally came to visit. Chastity was sitting on one side of Thomas's bed, and her mother on the other, with her back to him. They were playing Go Fish—a simple card game chosen so it wouldn’t tax Thomas.

“Grandma, give me your kings.”

“I have only one.” She laid it on the table that spun over his bed, and he reached for it but flinched in pain and lay back against the pillows.

“Are you all right, Tommy?” His grandmother pushed the table closer to him.

“Dr. de Brase,” Chastity exclaimed, jumping up when he entered the room. “We haven’t seen you in a while.” She walked over to him, her eyes alight.

"Charles," he reminded her with a smile. "I'm sorry for it. I had to turn Thomas's case back over to Dr. Toussaint while I took care of some personal things. Are he and Dr. Okonkwo taking good care of you?"

"They're both great. And, here's my...I'd like to introduce my mother, Sherri Whitmore." She turned towards her mom, who stood at Thomas's bedside.

"It's a pleasure." Charles took two steps forward and shook Sherri's hand. Her mother assessed him frankly, and Chastity smiled to herself. Surely, her mother would notice how handsome he was.

Charles moved over to the bedside. "Hi, Thomas. How are you feeling?"

Thomas had his arms crossed, but his expression was doubtful. "Sometimes I get mad. I'm not used to feeling mad a lot of the time."

The doctor sat carefully on the bed next to him and took his hand. "That, I'm afraid, is normal after a head injury. Some of your anger is happening because the part of your brain that usually keeps you in a good mood was hurt, and so you get mad more often. And you also feel frustrated at not being able to do what you're used to doing. Does that make sense?"

Thomas yawned. He didn't answer and just picked at the blanket with his fingers. "I'm tired."

"Here, let's lower the bed," Charles said, quietly. When he finished, he gestured to Chastity to follow him out to the hallway. Her mother remained by the bedside.

"I'm getting the updates from Samuel—Dr. Okonkwo—so I'm following his progress from the medical end, but I'm curious. Does he act like himself when he's awake?"

"In some ways, very much so." Chastity was happy to share the progress with him after a few days' absence. "He seems just as sharp as ever. He gets frustrated much more easily, though. He used to be such an easy-going kid, so this is a pretty big change for him."

Charles nodded and leaned against the doorframe. He was wearing a cable-knit sweater with a V-neck under his winter coat, and Chastity was struck by how much she wanted to lean against him and have him put his arms around her. She mentally shook herself.

"... this can change, actually," he was saying. "There's no guarantee that this is his new personality. It could be part of the healing process. I have to say both Dr. Toussaint and I are encouraged by his cognitive progress. His is the best we could hope for."

"That is so good to hear." Chastity broke out into a smile, and Charles went still, holding her gaze a second longer than someone who was interested from merely a professional regard. At least that was what her wildly-beating heart told her.

Pulling his gaze off Chastity's face, Charles stood upright, glancing at her mother. "I was, uh, wondering if you and your mother would like to come to an art gallery opening this Friday? It's a painter from New York, actually, so your mother might have heard of him."

"Mom?" She beckoned her mother over and indicated for Charles to continue. He addressed the tall, older woman in front of him.

"Have you heard of a New York painter called Randall Mooers?" Chastity's mom shook her head and he continued. "We're having an opening at the art gallery featuring his work. I thought it might be fun for you to visit the museum if you're ready for a night out."

"That sounds nice." She turned to her daughter. "We don't leave the hospital 'til about 7:30 or so, right?"

"That's right," her daughter confirmed, unsuccessfully trying to hide her eagerness. "So we could do that after Tommy goes to sleep, couldn't we?"

"It doesn't start until 8:00," offered Charles. "And it goes on until 11. So whenever you get there will be fine."

"Thank you very much for the invitation," Sherri replied. "We'd love to come."

"It's kind of you to think of us," Chastity added.

After Charles's short visit, Chastity lifted her arms in a stretch and removed the pins from her hair then rolled onto the balls of her feet. She dropped her head down and swung her hair back and forth. As she stood and twisted from side to side, her mother leaned back in her chair. “So, he’s another one of Tommy’s doctors?” Her tone was casually inquisitive.

“Mmhmm.” Chastity walked over to the windowsill and fiddled with the toys there, stacking the books and putting the pieces to a game in a more orderly fashion. “He was the first doctor who treated him, but he’s on sabbatical so he handed the case back to Dr. Toussaint.”

“And it’s the strangest thing,” she added, turning around swiftly. “He owns the château at Maisons-Laffitte, and I teach his son at the school."

“What a coincidence.” Her mom raised an eyebrow. “He seems like a nice man.”

“Oh.” Chastity shrugged one shoulder. “He’s nice—at least here in the hospital. Honestly it came as a surprise to me. When I met him at the school to talk about his son, I never could have imagined him being this warm. Believe me, his expression is not always that friendly.” Restless, she straightened the blanket over her son and sat, crossing one leg over the other.

“Hm.” Her mother picked up her Sudoku puzzle and pencil. When her daughter turned to stare out the window, the older woman allowed herself a small smile.

# CHAPTER 19

Max showed up at the café fifteen minutes late. He stood at the entrance, his eyes blinking in the poor lighting. Jean sat to the right of the small round table with an empty espresso cup, hooded eyes fixed on Max and a lit cigarette poised in his hand.

Max finally spotted him. He moved unhurriedly to the chair at the left of the table and threw his book-bag on the floor. With deliberate movements, he took out a cigarette, tapped it on the package and lit up, exhaling before he spoke.

"Okay, I'm here."

Jean stared at him until he penetrated Max's armor of confidence—the chink that was his youth. "Don't be late again," was all Jean said.

He stood, threw a couple of euro coins on the table and said, "Come," without a backwards glance. Max slammed down the menu, grabbed his bag, and followed his dubious mentor. When they were on the street, Jean led the way over the crosswalk into the *Jardin des Tuilieries*, where there were plenty of people, and just as many empty spaces to talk.

Climbing onto a park bench, Jean sat on the back of it, his feet planted on the seat. Max did likewise. "So? What happened." Jean lit another cigarette.

"I was able to get the money again, so he won't have it. What are you going to do to him?"

Jean ignored the question. "Did he ask you about it?"

"No, why would he?" Max answered with hostility. "He doesn't suspect me. I mean, the guy doesn't have a clue. I don't know why you insist on using him when I would do a much better job."

Jean took a drag on his cigarette. When he spoke, Max felt the hair stand up on the back of his neck. "Drop the attitude, kid. I know all about your ambition. I was you not all that long ago. Now. Give me half of what you stole like we agreed."

Max played with the strap on his bag while staring at the ground. Finally, he reached into the side-pocket of his jacket and took out a wad of cash, handing it over without looking. "It's all there."

Jean counted it. "I'm sure it is." When he flicked the last bill, his gaze went to Max. "I need Louis for a little longer to serve my own purposes. When I'm done with him, I'll need someone with more balls. If you drop the attitude, it'll be you. If not, I'll find someone else."

Max exhaled, and contemplated the blue sky. He thought about where he would be if he were no longer able to provide the other kids the drugs he had promised. He swallowed his bile and nodded. "I'll wait to hear from you."

"Smart kid." Jean climbed off the park bench, dusted the seat of his pants, and sauntered off. Max waited until he was sure he wasn't looking, then gave him the finger.

❧

Chastity didn't know why she was so nervous to go to the museum exhibit. She put on neutral lip-gloss and leaned close to the mirror, puckering her lips. "Your lips are kissable"—words that came back to her unbidden. Marc had told her that before he kissed her for the first time, and it was one of the few good memories she had of that time.

The front of her hair was clipped back, and the rest fell in large ringlets to the middle of her back, partially covering the royal-blue, low-backed dress she was wearing. Swiveling to the side, she admired the way the pleats of the dress accentuated her curves. She shook her hands nervously and padded out of the bathroom in stocking feet.

Her mother wore a modest beige dress with a blazer. Her face was unadorned, but her eyes were merry. "You look lovely, Chastity. It's so nice to see you dressed up."

"Thanks, Mom. I guess we should go." Chastity bent down to slip into her high heels. "I'm glad the car's fixed so we can drive. There's a parking lot there." She reached for her navy wool coat, which belted in the middle, and grabbed her car keys and clutch. "Do you think Tommy is all right?"

"Thomas is fine, dear. He's sleeping, and the nurses are there." Her mother walked to the elevator at a sedate pace.

The air was crisp and cold under the starless night sky. As Chastity parked the car, they could see streams of people pouring into the lit museum, and they were greeted at the door with live jazz music.

The museum was built with old stones and bricks, its tall windows comprising small, irregular squares of hand-blown glass. There were exposed wooden beams on the ceilings, and worn squares of stone on the floor. Music floated from one of the rooms upstairs, and people were milling through the large gallery graced with elegant paintings. All the canvases were of still life, with the exception of two portraits.

There was a series of paintings of comice pears, and next to that were arrangements of fruit and vegetables—watermelon ripped apart with red jagged edges, and onions shedding their outer layers onto a shiny tabletop. Chastity crossed to the adjacent wall with paintings of kitchen counters with mason jars and water pitchers. Each painting was breathtaking in its cerulean color scheme and realistic detail.

Chastity heard Charles's voice behind her, and she turned. He was in mid-conversation when he saw her, and he abruptly stopped speaking and took a step forward, his face lighting up with a boyish grin. The gentleman next to him looked startled, and glanced from his face to hers. She hardly had time to register any of this when another man clasped the viscount's shoulder.

"Charles," the man called out pompously—in English—as he reached out his other hand to shake. Charles had stepped back slightly, and his profile was visible to Chastity, revealing hardened features. Although she felt she should move away from what did not concern her, she could not.

Charles returned the handshake stiffly, speaking in chilly accents. "I'm surprised to see you here. I assume Manon has told you about the exhibit?"

"We came together. She's here." The Englishman gave a forced laugh, swiveling his robust frame to try and catch sight of her in the crowd. "She said you'd be happy to see us and maybe you could show us around your castle later."

Charles answered in a cold voice. "I regret that I'm unable to at present. If you wish to make an appointment with my business manager, I'm sure he can find the time to show you the château. And now I must—"

"These paintings are magnificent," the man interrupted, gesturing around the room. "I'll be buying a couple to put in my country house."

"This," Charles replied, seemingly with effort, "is a museum exhibit. The works are not for sale. I'll put you in touch with the artist's manager, and you can make arrangements with him. Now if you'll excuse me—"

"Charles, darling." Manon came up in a cloud of Poison by Dior, her red lipstick matching the beads sewn into the lining of her white dress. Her blond pixie cut was nothing short of elegant, and her diamond earrings glittered as she moved. Chastity focused on the paintings in front of her again. She heard the actress say, "I couldn't wait to surprise you. Isn't it wonderful that Bruce could join me?"

Chastity's mother sidled up to her, and whispered, "You're right. His face can change in an instant if he doesn't like someone."

"Oh, he likes her all right," she muttered, pulling her mother towards the exit. "Manon Duprey is his...Let's go, Mom. I don't even know why I came."

"We can do that, of course, sweetie—if you wish to. Oh, but look. There's Elizabeth. Let's go and say hello before we leave." Her mother had met both Elizabeth Mercer and Maude during their visits to the hospital to see Thomas. She steered Chastity over to where Elizabeth was standing.

"Chastity," exclaimed Elizabeth in a rich, warm voice. "How wonderful to see you out. And you look...beautiful." She shook her head back and forth, as if amazed by the vision before her. "Are you behind this?" Elizabeth winked at Chastity's mother—two conspirators.

Sherri smiled. "No, it was Dr. de Brase who invited us. He thought I might like to see some of the town since we've been spending most of our time at the hospital."

Elizabeth raised her eyebrows. "So you see Charles at the hospital then. He told me he would only be working there for a week."

"We used to," Chastity said, quietly, "but not so much anymore. It was thoughtful of him to invite us when he's got so much going on. Mom—Elizabeth, my mother and I were just leaving."

"Oh no, no. You're not leaving until you have some of the hors d'oeuvres with Maude, Michel and me. They're holding a table and there are a couple of extra seats." In a tone that brooked no argument, Elizabeth gestured for Chastity's mother to lead the way. "How do you find Thomas, Sherri?"

Chastity's mother spoke over her shoulder as she climbed the stairs. "He does seem to be improving rapidly. The doctor thinks he can come home soon with full-time care."

Elizabeth turned to Chastity as they rounded the stairwell. "That sounds like good news. Does that mean, then, that you'll be caring for him full-time?"

"Well..." Chastity chewed her lip. "I did want to talk to you about that. If our *mutuelle* covers it, I think I'd like to take advantage of having a specialist come and work with him while I'm teaching—

handle his physical therapy and all that. In some ways, I feel out of my depth with him. I'm afraid I'm not the best one to help him overcome the challenges. I just want to be there to love him."

"Hm." With a grace inherent to her, Elizabeth faced Chastity's mother at the top of the stairs. "You know your daughter and grandson better than anyone else. Do you think it's a good idea?"

"When Chastity first told me about her plan, I'll admit I wasn't keen." She considered her daughter kindly. "But if she can get home by late afternoon each day and have someone to share the burden of his moods and struggles, I can't think of anything better. I think Chastity has a good deal of foresight to know her limits."

Elizabeth nodded. "That's exactly what I think." Then gesturing forward, "We're in here."

The jazz music grew louder as they entered the spacious room, well lit with chandeliers. The wait staff was circulating with plates of champagne and hors d'oeuvres, and Chastity glanced at the table nearest her. "Oh no," she groaned.

"What?" Her mother looked around, perplexed, as Chastity scanned the room. "My dress is the exact color of the tablecloths," she hissed. It was true. Apart from the usual touches of white, all the tables were covered with royal blue linen, and all the decorations had royal blue accents.

Maude spotted them at the entrance, and as if sensing her friend's panic, rushed over. "Bonsoir, Chastity. You're here." She pecked her on the cheeks and grabbed her hand. Chastity's mother followed them to the table. "Michel this is Chastity's mom, Sherri Whitmore."

"*Enchanté*," He rose and greeted the older lady with two kisses.

On the opposite end of the room, Manon walked through the arched doorway, followed by an entourage of men that included Charles de Brase. His face was stony, as he listened to the gentleman he had been talking to earlier—a man who looked out of place next to the viscount with his orange spiked hair, black leather, and hoop earring. Manon was radiant in her white gown and blond hair, set off beautifully in a sea of blue. Chastity sunk into her chair, cheeks burning.

"So I've got five guys who'll mingle with the guests," Jef said, "and they'll keep an eye on whatever's going on in the room. I think that's where there's most likely to be action. They're well trained and will be a good complement to the officers." Charles nodded, offering no reply.

They stood at the table nearest the door, with Manon talking and gesturing to an enamored young man with red ears. Jef watched them before asking with nonchalance. "So. Who was that beautiful young lady in the gallery downstairs?"

Charles's reverie was broken. He glanced at Manon then back to Jef. "Oh, that's...it's, uh, Louis's English teacher. Her son was hit by a car, and I was the neurosurgeon on call."

"Was he all right?"

Charles nodded absently. "So far, yes. He's come out of his coma."

"Good." Jef gave a keen look. "I mean, I know you don't have eyes for anyone but Manon—what hot-blooded man could? But this woman —" He waited, questioning.

"Chastity Whitmore," supplied Charles.

"—Mademoiselle Whitmore," Jef resumed, "seems charming."

Charles ignored that comment and spoke with quiet deliberation. "As far as I'm concerned, things are over with Manon. I didn't invite her here tonight, and the only reason I haven't ended things is because I've promised to accompany her to the opening of her movie, and it would humiliate her if I pulled out when all the media has talked about us going together."

"Ever the gentleman," Jef said, drily.

"You should try it sometime."

"Ah, Charles." Jef shook his head. "What are we going to do with you?"

"Take Manon off my hands." Charles's face was grim. "You're a hot-blooded man."

“Sorry, old friend. I only have eyes for Adelaide. And—there she is.” His friend walked off without ceremony towards Charles's sister, and more out of curiosity than anything else, Charles followed him.

“Adelaide,” Jef whispered, worshipfully, taking both her hands in his and reaching up to kiss her on the cheeks. He was almost a full head shorter. “What do we need to do to get rid of this guy?” He jerked his head back towards Charles.

“Jean-François.” Adelaide’s low voice was filled with mirth. “What makes you think I want my brother to leave?”

“Why, so we can talk privately, of course. So I can ask you to accompany me to the spring ball that’ll be held at the château.”

“Ah.” Adelaide’s eyes twinkled as she extricated her hands from her adorer. Although her brother’s best friend had been perfectly respectful from the time she was married to when she was widowed, his life-long crush on her was an established thing. “Charlie, will you kindly tell your friend that he is much too young for me?” She added with a tinkling laugh, “as much as he flatters me.”

Just then, Charles saw Chastity whisper to her mother, grab her coat and stand. “Tell him yourself.” He left them abruptly and made a beeline for Chastity.

"*Mais—c’est qui ça?*" he heard his sister asking in hushed tones.

When the viscount made his way across the room, Chastity found that she could, indeed, blush even more deeply than she already was. She was kicking herself for entertaining hopes, kicking herself for coming, and was furious that her mother was moving with exasperating slowness.

“Chastity,” Charles called out, stopping short when he noticed everyone’s eyes on him. “Would you...like to see the paintings?”

She tried to slow her heart rate. “I have seen them. They’re wonderful. We were just on our way...”

“Let me introduce you to the artist.” He put his hand on her elbow and nodded to the rest of the table as he steered her towards the doorway. Chastity was thankful her friends didn't say anything embarrassing before they were out of earshot. "The artist is in the gallery down these stairs." Charles still had his hand on Chastity's arm, and he dropped it suddenly.

When they reached the bottom of the stairwell, he escorted her into the nearest room—a small alcove where the Cézannes were hanging. There was a tall, lanky gentleman talking to someone in the archway that led to the main gallery.

An elderly lady was taking her leave as Charles walked up with Chastity. He gave the introductions in English. "Mr. Mooers, this is Miss Whitmore. She's also from New York."

"Chastity," she said in a friendly voice, taking his hand.

"Randall. Where in New York are you from?"

"I grew up on 85th and Lexington."

"We're on 77th and Lex. Vivi." He signaled to an Asian woman who was crossing the room with two glasses of champagne. "This is my wife, Vivienne."

Chastity peered at her intently for a moment, and then at one of the two portraits hanging to the right. "The portrait," she said expressively, pointing at the obvious likeness.

"It's from when we first met." The petite woman gave a reminiscent smile. "I was at a café and he walked up and asked if he could paint me." Chastity went over to examine the portrait more closely, and Vivienne followed her while the gentlemen stayed behind in conversation.

Chastity saw another couple approach the artist. "Tell your husband I love his work." She examined the perfection of his brushstrokes. "I don't know why, but every painting is so cheerful. They make me happy."

"I'll tell him." Vivienne brushed Chastity's arm then floated over to her husband's side and turned her attention to the gentleman who was speaking. Charles chose that moment to leave the group and walk over to Chastity.

Chastity had moved to the large doorway that led to the main hallway where the exit was, her hands shoved low in her coat pockets. Charles stood at her side, and she felt heat coming from him—or maybe the heat was from her. He leaned towards her, and she caught a waft of aftershave with wood undertones. "I'm glad you were able to make it." His blue eyes searched hers.

"Me too. It's been awhile since I've gone anywhere besides the hospital and my apartment." Her voice died down, and suddenly there was a total sense of calm as the noises and distractions of the room faded. Though they hadn't moved, she felt a pull towards him. His eyes were on hers, and the corners of his mouth turned up as the silence stretched. Her own dimples started to form, and she took a breath to speak.

"Charles!" Serenity screeched to a halt with one word. The viscount's face grew unreadable again, and he inspected the wall beyond her instead of addressing the speaker. It was as if he were trying to garner his patience. Chastity's mother followed in Manon Duprey's wake, wearing her winter coat. She could have kissed her mom for showing up just then.

"It's my mother." She gave a tiny shrug. "We have to go now."

Charles held her gaze. "But I'll see you again soon?" He took a step towards her.

Chastity fought off the crushing sadness. *Why am I letting myself get drawn in? He will never choose me.* She gave a tight smile. "Maybe I'll see you at the hospital."

# CHAPTER 20

"She's here." Chastity jumped up from the couch and ran over to the intercom. "This should be fun," her mother said, patting Tommy's back. Her mom was wary of any movement that might jostle him or cause one of the tension headaches he was now prone to. Her grandson didn't answer but continued to push a small car over the tiny hills in his blanket.

Chastity opened the door and turned the lights on in the hallway before the elevator pinged open. A sturdy woman of uncertain age exited the elevator, hidden under coats, scarves, and hats. Her teeth were bright against her dark skin.

"Bonjour, Madel." Chastity shook her hand, smiling back at her. "Thank you for coming a little early for my first day back."

"It's my pleasure," the woman replied. "We can make sure Thomas has everything he needs before you leave."

"My mother is here, but I think if there's anything you two need to communicate to each other, Thomas should be able to translate it."

"We'll be just fine," Madel reassured her. "Bonjour, Madame." She nodded her head towards the older woman as she unwound her scarf and removed her coat. "Bonjour, Thomas." She directed her attention to her unresponsive protégé.

"Would you like some tea? We have fruit tea with honey." Chastity had gone into the kitchen and returned with the box in hand. When Madel nodded, it was her mother who took it from her and headed towards the electric water kettle. "You take care of seeing that Tommy has everything he needs, my dear."

Chastity sat on the large square footrest that extended from the couch where Thomas was sitting. Madel had pulled up a chair from the dining room table and was sitting next to him with a notepad, marking observations.

"Hello, Thomas. How are you feeling today?" Madel tapped her pen on the notepad. He shrugged. After waiting a minute without receiving further clarification, she prodded, "Where does it hurt today?"

"It doesn't hurt," was the sulky reply. "But I feel irritated."

"That's nothing new, is it then? We're going to do our usual routine today, but change some of the memory games and stretches. You'll get plenty of chance to rest in between. Do you feel up for it?" Thomas shrugged again, but nodded.

"Great." Madel clapped her hands on her lap with one of her sunny smiles. "I also brought you a new movie that I think you'll like." She turned to Chastity. "Has he been to the osteopath this week?"

"Yes, twice. She feels like he's making progress, and I do think Tommy is sleeping better."

"That's just what I'd hoped to hear. Osteopaths work wonders, and I'm glad you're getting coverage for his. Shall we let your mom get to work, Thomas?" Chastity's mother had come to stand in the doorway at this point, and though she didn't understand the conversation, she could see that Chastity was standing with her coat and purse in her arms. Thomas didn't answer, so she went over to take her daughter's place at his side.

Chastity tried to keep her voice steady as she addressed her son in English. "Okay, sweetie. Grandma's here and so is Madel. Is there anything you want for when I get back from school?"

"I want to visit the stables like that guy promised."

"What guy?" Her mind flashed back to Deauville. Could he be remembering that incident? His mind didn't often stretch to things beyond what was currently happening—at least not in any way he communicated. That would be a good sign.

"When we saw Mickey."

So it was the encounter in Deauville he was remembering. She couldn't forget such a name, or such a large animal. "It won't be today, honey." That was the only thing she could think of to say. She wasn't sure she'd be comfortable enough to ask Charles if they could visit his stables. Plus, it was too cold, and he was too unwell to attempt such a visit. Her son didn't say anything else in response, so she kissed him gently on the forehead then went over to hug her mom.

"I'm nervous," she whispered, as her mom squeezed her tight.

"You're doing the right thing." Her mom patted her hair. "I'll be here for another week, and by then it will be routine for everyone. Don't you worry about a thing."

Louis stomped along the muddy path next to the houses with no sidewalks. Without warning, he slipped and landed in the mud. Blood rushed to his cheeks, and he felt fury take hold of him as he reached over to grab his bag and get himself into an upright position. The fact that no one was there to see his humiliation, apart from an old lady in a housedress who was in the process of opening her shutters, did nothing to calm his rage.

First it was his dad. He chose today—the day when Louis had planned on ending things with Jean and Max and the whole drug scene to read him a lecture on the dangers of drugs and getting in over his head. As if he were a child that needed to be told what to do. He wasn't even done with breakfast when his dad started in on him.

"—and when I get back from London, we're going to have more of a regular schedule together to see how you're doing and start taking a look at some of your homework."

"I don't need a babysitter, Papa," he flashed back.

"That's not what I meant—" His dad had looked hurt, but Louis shoved that out of his mind. Served him right. He had no right to meddle now when for years he had been too busy to take notice of him. All that time when Louis was on his own and had no one to talk to besides Paltier.

And now his interview with Jean had not gone at all like he had expected. He thought he could end things cleanly and move on with his life, but he now knew it was not going to be that easy.

"I brought you something," Jean had said, tossing a bag of weed on his lap by way of greeting. "It's a freebie. To thank you for your service these last couple of months. There's more where that came from if you continue to pull in the same amount of orders." He seemed more cheerful than he had any right to be.

"Thanks," Louis mumbled, stuffing the marijuana in his bag. There was no reason to say no to something free. "I need to talk to you about that. I want out."

Louis looked at Jean now and was startled, then afraid. He had never seen such hardness in Jean's eyes before. When Jean spoke, his voice was deceptively casual. "Where's the money you owe me, Louis?"

Louis broke out in a sweat, though the late February air was chilly. "I'll get it to you. I just need some time."

"You shouldn't need time. It's simple. You give the goods, you get the money, you give it to me. Are you stealing from me?"

"No. No." Louis's voice cracked. "Someone stole from me twice after I made the drop. Both times it happened at the party. I think I was drugged—"

"Oh please. That's a likely excuse. You were drugged on the stuff *I* gave you—the stuff you got for free because I trusted you to bring in more clients." Jean's voice got louder. "If you think you can rip me off, you don't know who you're dealing with."

Louis stood suddenly from the park bench. He searched, but the quiet town brought no welcome sight of joggers, or anyone that could lend him a hand. "I promised I'd have it, and I will. It's just that being robbed twice...the amount is getting too big. I'm not sure how..." Louis cast about in his mind for something to say that would satisfy this guy. "Didn't you mention that I could do you a...a favor? Instead of paying you back?"

Jean had stood as well. "That favor was for the first couple a' thousand." He suddenly grabbed Louis's prep school tie and pulled it tight. He could feel the pressure on his throat. "Do not. Mess. With me," he growled.

Just as suddenly, Jean stepped back and laughed, patting a shaking Louis on the back. "I'll call in that favor," he said loudly. Two middle-aged men jogged by discussing when to plant spring bulbs, which seemed like such a ludicrous subject at that moment. Louis wanted to call out to them, but he had no idea what to say, and he wasn't sure he could find his voice.

The two of them were silent until the men were out of sight, but Jean seemed to have relaxed. In any case, he made no more threats. "Here's the deal. I'll let you do the favor instead of paying me the huge amount of money you owe. And I'm being generous."

Jean sat back down, indicating for Louis to follow. "This is what I want you to do. My uncle used to work as a gardener for your grandfather a long time ago."

Louis knit his brows together, but Jean didn't give him a chance to speak. "He had a set of gardening tools, wrapped in a leather pouch with a handle, and they had been passed down in the family. My uncle disappeared, and no one knows what happened to him. I want the tools, which are still in the château. They belong to my family anyway."

Jean paused, and Louis waited for more. When Jean said nothing further, Louis was perplexed. "But...what makes you think the tools are still there? The shed is a mess, but the gardeners tend to know where everything is. Those tools would have been thrown out or put to use by now."

"They're not in the shed. In fact, they're not outdoors at all.

They're in the basement."

Louis's mind drifted to the basement in the château, which—to a young boy—had been a disappointment. It was more open and light-filled than a boy with a good imagination could have liked. There was nothing very dungeon-like about it. *Except maybe the wine cellar...*Ever since he outgrew such fancies, he had barely set foot down there. Louis finally managed to speak. "How do you know?"

"My uncle told my aunt everything while he was still working there. There's a stretch of stone corridor near the wine cellar where it's not well lit. When you walk towards the cellar, you'll pass through an archway that has a ledge cut into the stone just above your head—it's where there used to be an iron gate that rolled up into it. The tools will be there towards the back of the ledge. You'll probably need a stick to reach it."

Many questions swirled through Louis's mind, but he settled on one. "Why didn't your aunt just ask for the tools? I'm sure my grandfather would have given them to her."

"Yes, but then you wouldn't have a way out of your own fix, would you?" Jean lit a cigarette. "When my uncle disappeared, the tools were the least of her worries and she forgot about them. Now she's getting old, and I'd like to get them back for her. She's nostalgic," he added by way of explanation.

"This is worth all the money I owe you?" Louis's voice was filled with disbelief.

"Don't question me too closely if you want me to *forget* the money you owe."

"I'll be shocked if they're still there." Louis folded his arms with belligerence.

"They had better be, or you and I have a problem," was Jean's calm response that left Louis more disquieted than he had felt at the open menace.

Louis trudged along, now on the street away from the muddy path.

His pants were wet and dirty, and so were his hands. He had nothing to wipe them on, and everything about this stupid day was going wrong. He didn't like it, but he knew he was going to have to take something from his house and give it to Jean. It wasn't stealing, precisely, but it made him uneasy. There were too many questions. Why were these tools worth so much money? Why did the gardener hide them? Because there would be no other reason to stash them there. Did Jean target him? Was that the reason he had approached him in the first place? Despite the unanswered questions and uneasiness, it was the only solution he could see to get himself out of this fix.

The school was in sight, and there was a group of kids a year older than him walking from the outlying buildings towards the main gate. Louis stopped on the street corner where the tall bare trees and parked cars lent the intersection protection. He dropped the book bag from his shoulder, and reached into the side pouch for his wallet. There was some cigarette paper folded in the bills. He glanced around before taking the bag of marijuana from his backpack and pinching a large amount into the cigarette paper. He licked the edge and lit the end, inhaling greedily, hungrily, as if he couldn't fill his lungs fast enough.

He held each hit of the acrid smoke as long as he could. *Everything's going to be okay. Everything's going to be okay*, he repeated to himself. After several hits, he was starting to believe it. Another group of students came into view from his left, heading for the school across the street. A petite brunette glanced over, and when she saw Louis, said something to the group in a soft singsong voice and walked over to where he was standing. Eloise Prynne's smile faltered as soon as she got close.

Louis stood, holding the joint slightly behind his right leg and waved at her with his left hand. He knew he looked guilty. "Aw, Louis." It was not hard to miss the disappointment in those words. Defiantly, he took another hit from the stub and threw it on the ground. "Are you going over?" he asked with false bravado.

It seemed she wasn't going to answer until she noticed his pants. "You're all muddy. Did you fall?"

"Yeah. It was stupid. I was walking on the muddy path, and I slipped."

She shook her head. "Let's go. History starts in five minutes."

Chastity was losing energy by the end of lunch hour. There had been so many emotions—fear of leaving Thomas, guilt over throwing her mother together with Madel when the two of them couldn't communicate, excitement at being back in school, exhaustion as she tried to act as if everything were normal in front of her students. Only over lunch was she able to pour her feelings into Maude's sympathetic ear. It had relieved some pressure, but she was eager to get through the three remaining periods and head home.

She stood against the wall as a flurry of students walked past her, blocking her from entering the classroom. Suddenly, she caught sight of Louis's head of dark, wavy hair, and before she had time to think, her heart leaped at the connection with his father. *I wonder if Charles has mentioned me to him. I wonder what Louis thinks of me.* Chastity blushed, thankful no one could read her mind.

Her heart tugged her inexorably onwards as she remembered how Charles had come to the hospital every day the week before. After she saw him with Manon, he should have put more distance between them; but rather than pulling back from her, he seemed to settle in. He became more...comfortable. The day before Thomas was discharged, her mom went for a walk as soon as Charles showed up, and the two of them sat, side by side. He read some medical research, and she...well, apparently she dozed. How strange it was that she could do that in his presence. When she thought of this, her heart seemed to sink and take flight at the same time. *I wonder what Charles thinks of me.*

"Welcome back, Miss Whitmore," sounded the cheerful voice of Eloise Prynne.

She smiled at the young lady walking next to Louis. As soon as they got closer, Chastity went still. Louis passed in front of her without even noticing her, and his red eyes and the heavy sour smell of marijuana were impossible to miss.

She groaned inwardly. *Oh Louis*.

# CHAPTER 21

"*Salut*, Tommy." Marc reached down, awkwardly, and wiggled Thomas's knee before straightening back up again. Thomas stared at the action figure he had in his hand without giving any indication he had seen his father. "Well, uh, I'll let you get back to your toys."

Chastity walked into the room, putting her coat on and digging through her purse at the same time. "Mom, I've got my phone. So if you need anything at all, you can reach me." Turning to Marc, "We're just gone for the afternoon, right? We'll be back in time for dinner?"

"Yeah, sure. It takes an hour and fifteen to get there, but then we're just staying a couple of hours for drinks. We'll be back by six o'clock easy."

"Okay, buddy." Chastity kissed Thomas and lifted his chin so she could look him in the eyes. "You and Grandma are going to hang out, and I'll be back, all right?"

"Okay, Mom." Thomas flashed her a rare smile, and her heart melted.

The March weather had started to warm up, and there was a smell of stables in the air, which was not unusual in her neighborhood. She smiled to herself. Never had she thought she'd associate the smell of horses with home. Perhaps she could get Tommy some riding lessons as soon as he got better since it was one of the few things that seemed to animate him. Then she had a sudden vision of him falling off a horse and shuddered.

"You cold?" Marc turned his head towards her.

"Yes, a little." She stopped short and gasped. "It just occurred to me that I should be bringing something for your parents."

"Oh, it's all right. They won't expect anything."

"No, no. I can't show up empty-handed. There's a florist right by the RER station and I'll get your mom a bouquet from there."

"That's probably a good idea, actually. I'm sure she'll love that." Chastity could see he was pleased and hoped he wasn't misinterpreting her gesture. She was doing this so he could be reconciled with his parents, not because she had any desire to win them over for her own sake. Her shoulders were beginning to tense in her efforts to be gracious and make peace with the past.

They arrived in the 16th *arrondissement* at Marc's parent's building, and he punched in the code. As soon as they stepped over the raised metal doorframe, they entered a cobblestone hallway with glass doors on either side, which continued on to an open courtyard. Marc buzzed his parent's apartment, and she heard his father's voice crackling through the intercom. "*Oui, âllo?*"

"*C'est nous, Papa*."

"*Entrez*." She followed Marc inside on to the plush dark-red carpet and up the winding wooden staircase with its short, narrow steps. The door to the apartment was already open when they got to the second floor.

"Ah, here you are." His mother was beaming as she kissed her son and reached over to kiss Chastity on both cheeks. She took the flowers. "Thank you. This is so sweet of you. I'll put these in water."

"Bonjour." His father reached out formally to shake his son's hand, and Chastity remembered he used to kiss him. This made her heart ache for Marc, and she was caught by surprise when his father leaned over to kiss her cheeks. "Welcome, Chastity. It's good to see you again." Marc's father had always been kind to her.

They walked into the large hall to the apartment, and Chastity peered into the kitchen where Marc's mother was busy arranging the flowers in a vase. She looked the same as she did in New York, except older. Chastity noted her high heels, which she had always worn, even at home on a Saturday. She thought she recognized the slim skirt and navy cardigan.

"There." Madame Bastien brought the flowers over to the table in the sitting room and showed Chastity and Marc to a small sofa. There were already round tables with chips, pistachios, and a few *petits-fours*.

"What would you like to drink?" Marc's father indicated the selection on the glass table.

"Brandy for me, Papa."

"I'd like some Cointreau, please."

When everyone had been served and had raised a glass to the general health of everyone else, Marc's father leaned back in the straight chair and crossed one leg over his knee. His mother sat forward in that focused, energetic way Chastity remembered.

"So, how's Thomas?" Chastity could see Marc's mother was determined to be pleasant and decided to reply in kind, giving a full answer.

"Thank you for the teddy bear you sent him. He really likes it. He's recovering quickly and has surprised the doctors. But I can see he has a long way to go. He's not himself. He gets frustrated easily when he used to be so easy-going. Truthfully, I can't tell the extent of how much he's lost cognitively because he doesn't communicate as much as he used to."

"We're hoping you'll be able to visit him soon," Marc piped up.

His father must have seen the alarm in Chastity's face because he said, "There's no rush. We'll be here. Let the boy get his bearings first."

"Surely a short visit—" his mother hinted.

"Uh, so...how long have you been back in France?" Chastity stepped into the breach, hoping to avoid what would be an awkward refusal.

"Oh, it's been about six years, right dear?" Madame Bastien smoothed her skirt and re-crossed her ankles. "Of course we had to wait until our Paris apartment was ready but once we decided to return, it didn't take long until everything was settled."

"Are the Ducamps still around?" Marc took a bite of his puff pastry and caught the flakes with his napkin.

"Oh, yes. You remember Marie Ducamp—she was about your age. She's married now and has two children. We see them with the Ducamps at the *boulangerie* sometimes. Séverine is lucky her grandchildren live so close by. She's able to see them often."

"What about the de Fleurys? I haven't heard from them in years." Chastity could see Marc was making an exceptional effort at conversation, but those words seemed to be the wrong ones because his mother puckered up and went silent.

"We've not had news from them in about six years now," Marc's father said quietly. "More Cointreau?" Chastity shook her head. Six years was about the time that Marc went to prison. She could see he had made the connection too.

Chastity tried a different tack. "So, I recognize some of the artwork from your New York apartment. Were you able to bring everything over?" From there the conversation steered towards safer grounds, and Chastity made every effort to keep it there. She wasn't ready to sacrifice her son's healing by arranging a visit with his estranged grandparents, but she did want Marc to be fully reconciled with his parents and would do whatever it took to help. He was not ungrateful.

"You were great," Marc said, as they walked towards the Metro on their way home. The sun was out, but it was starting to feel chillier, and she knew when they got off the RER in Maisons-Laffitte the daylight would have started to fade.

"I do want you to be on good terms with your parents, Marc. Nobody should be estranged from his own family. I'm glad I was able to help." She sidestepped a dog on a leash, and the conversation turned to the occupational therapy Thomas was undergoing. When they stepped off the RER, they walked towards her apartment in easy friendship.

Marc kissed her on the cheek at her door. "Good night, Chas. Thanks again. I appreciate it."

"Don't mention it." She smiled as he sauntered off, relieved that at least tonight, she wouldn't need to spell out that she didn't want more than a friendship. She knew she needed to tell him at some point—at least she thought she did because he had made it clear he wanted more. Maybe he had taken the hint and understood without her having to say it. He had been respectful today and treated her like a friend. Perhaps they could transition smoothly into this phase without any awkward explanations.

Chastity turned on her heel and inserted her key in the front door. She rushed towards the elevator, suddenly eager to give Thomas a hug.

Charles was dressed in a black suit with a gray vest and a burgundy silk scarf at his throat, whose elegant folds were held in place by a discreet pin. Manon Duprey was at his side in a skin-tight black dress with the back of the dress cut lower than her waist, but with black lace discreetly covering her bare skin. Her face resembled an angel with the large blue eyes and blond wisps that framed her face. He wouldn't have been human if he remained oblivious to her perfection.

He disliked the flashing bulbs as entertainment journalists took their pictures on the red carpet. He didn't like posing, and he didn't like the fake ambiance of people pretending to be happy to see each other. Their look of pleasure was purely for the camera and did not go any deeper than that. Although...Bruce Richard's lecherous delight was authentic. If Charles hadn't found his fawning so pathetic, he would have been amused.

Manon was in her element. She was never better than when people gathered around to adore her. She was gracious and charming. She could, at turns, look innocent and naïve, then sultry and seductive. Charles could see how he had been taken in by her. He had believed the innocent more readily than the seductive, and when accompanied by such an angelic face, well, he supposed he didn't stand a chance.

"Shall we go in, Charles?" Manon turned to face him, sweetly. She was on her best behavior, aiming to please, knowing he didn't like a lot of attention. She had even expertly fielded the question a journalist directed towards the viscount, joking that he was a private man, and if the reporter didn't stop asking questions, she would be left alone all evening without a date. The man took it in good turn, rallying that he would be happy to step in, and they were allowed to pass without Charles getting further accosted.

Charles sank into the plush chair, glad for the cover of darkness. On-screen, Manon was talented and perfectly suited to her role. At one point, he felt a lump forming in his throat when her character suffered humiliation that would eventually lead to her taking her life. Then he disassociated and stopped allowing himself to feel anything. He didn't want to show any emotion when the entire world would be watching him for a reaction.

Instead, he started thinking about Chastity. It hadn't been easy to get her to meet his eye after the fiasco at the museum. He could have shaken Manon for showing up just then. It had been the only time he had ever met Chastity outside the hospital, apart from the school meetings, and that night, he couldn't wait to see her.

He remembered how direct she had been at the school, back when they discussed Louis's problem, and how willing she was to fight to help him, despite Charles's own reluctance. With Thomas, it was different. Chastity came to him openly—soft, and entrusting him with her son's care. That evening at the museum showed yet another side of her. She was nervous, like a bird ready to take flight if he got too close. And just when he had gotten close...Charles shook his head in the dark, suppressing a sigh.

It took coming to the hospital every day, but she finally relaxed—even to the point of letting her head drop on his shoulder when she fell asleep. She'd been sitting on the chair next to him, with Thomas asleep in the bed at their feet. He noticed her out of the corner of his eye, jerking upright each time her head sank, and he'd leaned in until she finally let her head settle on him in exhaustion. He held his breath, not wanting to disturb her, afraid she would feel embarrassed if she knew. It was only five minutes of companionable bliss before she flew upright, a blush springing to her cheeks. He had shifted slightly so she wouldn't know...This was almost a week ago, and he hadn't seen her since Thomas was discharged because he was afraid to intrude on her private life. *Five days.*

Every facet of her held a different hue, and the sum was bewitching. He remembered her slamming the books on the table at their first meeting. Her lifting a tear-stained face from her son's bedside and jumping to her feet in confusion when she saw him. Her dropping the coffee cup when he had gotten Thomas to squeeze his hand. Her eyes lighting up when she told him her mom was coming to visit. Her rushing to leave the museum when she saw him walk in with Manon. (She had looked so beautiful that evening).

Her face, soft with regret as she said 'good night'. Her lips—

*My God*, thought Charles, thunderstruck. *I'm in love with her.* He started forward and drew a ragged breath. Manon linked her arm through his in the dark and pulled him closer, never taking her eyes off the screen. "I'm here, Charles." Her voice trilled with emotion. "My character is gone, but I am here."

# CHAPTER 22

Chastity and her mother stood near the security guard in front of the Plexiglas tube that covered the escalator leading to Departures. Chastity was fighting tears.

"All right, dear." Her mother offered a smile that belied her own emotions. "I can't leave your dad to fend for himself forever. The truth is, I miss him. Thomas is doing much better, and you're going to be just fine without me."

"I know, Mom. Of course I am." Chastity fell silent. *How am I going to do this on my own?*

"Have you spoken to Dr. de Brase lately?" her mom inquired, not-so-subtly.

"No, not this week." The image she saw of him on TV, holding Manon by the elbow, flashed before her eyes. "He's not the resident doctor for Thomas anymore, so there's no need for him to follow his progress now that Tommy is home."

"But he seemed to have an interest in you when he invited us to the art gallery," her mom prodded gently.

"Oh, Mom. You saw him on TV with that actress. How can you ask me about him? He was nice to take such good care of Tommy when he was his patient. But…I mean…I always knew he was just being nice. That—and being a good doctor."

"He still came back to the hospital every day the week before Tommy was discharged, and he wasn't his doctor then." It seemed her mother was not going to let this go.

"But we haven't seen him since. We're not from the same world."

"Hm." Her mother's face revealed nothing, but Chastity had a pretty good idea what she was thinking. She mistakenly thought the doctor—*Charles*—had feelings for her, but that could not be true. *She's just biased because she's my mom.*

"Give me one last hug," Sherri said. "You need to get back for the second half of school, and I don't want you to be late."

Chastity obeyed and gave her mom a tight squeeze, trying to keep a brave face. "I'll let you know what I decide to do, okay Mom? I have trouble imagining getting Tommy back to New York in the state he's in, and then getting him the care he needs once he's there. Let me know what your research turns up too, all right?"

They hugged one last time, and her mom held out her passport and ticket, went through security, and stepped onto the escalator. Chastity turned away with a heavy heart.

Charles strode to the school, whistling for a space, then furrowing his brows. He had set up a meeting with the principal to discuss the ball at the château next month but hoped to see Chastity while he was there. He realized, with regret, his original idea of asking Chastity to attend the ball with him would not work. At least, not yet. He could not, in good conscience, invite her until he had officially broken things off with Manon. He hadn't wanted to do that after the opening. It was only fair that her moment in the spotlight should be unspoiled. That meant he was not yet free to do precisely what he wanted.

Elizabeth ushered him to a seat while she shut the door. "Hi, Charles. What can I do for you?"

"It's about the ball next month," he said. "I thought it'd be a good idea to allow the upper level students to attend if you don't think that will cause problems with the rest of the school. In a way, it makes sense for them to be invited since my son is in their class. I've reserved a set number of tickets, and I just have to double-check the numbers with you."

"Are you offering the tickets to the students? Or will they need to pay for them? That'd be the only problem I can foresee as it might cause social divisions in the class if some kids can't afford it."

"I'm offering the tickets. It'll be my contribution to the school. I'd also like to pay for an instructor to teach them to waltz so they can dance when they're there."

Elizabeth raised her eyebrows in surprise. "That's very generous of you. I'm sure the students will be ecstatic. I'll have to think about where they can rehearse since we don't have a large enough space to fit them all."

"They can use the ballroom in the château for their lesson." Charles waved his hand dismissively. "Is Mademoiselle Whitmore in today? Perhaps I can speak to her about my idea."

The principal's eyebrow went up again, just slightly. "She is. Her class finishes in five minutes. If you would care to step upstairs with me, I can offer you an espresso, and we'll catch her on her way out of class." Charles nodded his assent.

The espresso machine hummed noisily, and two thin streams of foaming liquid poured into the glass cups. The bustle in the hallway increased in volume as students poured out of the classrooms. Charles stood in the doorway, trying to catch a glimpse of Chastity amidst the students.

There she was, hugging her books to her chest, listening as a student spoke to her. Nodding her head in reply, she laid her hand on the student's arm and said a few words before he flashed her a grin and took off. She walked towards Charles, her expression thoughtful.

"Chastity."

"Oh." She stopped short in surprise. "Hi...Charles." She blushed when she said his first name. "What are you doing here?"

"I had an appointment with Elizabeth to talk about the spring ball, and I wanted to fill you in on my plan." At this point, Elizabeth turned around with two steaming espressos. She handed one to Charles and extended the other to Chastity, who jostled her books into one arm and took the cup with a murmured thanks.

"Go," Elizabeth said. "The two of you can discuss it without me. I'm going to make another coffee and head over to accounting. Do you want me to see if I can find Margaret James to join you? You mentioned both English teachers."

"No need to bother her. Chastity, you can give Ms. James all the details later, right?" Charles had already turned to face her office, and Chastity nodded stepping ahead to lead the way.

"Here, let me take those." He reached for her books.

"No, it's okay. I'm afraid I'll drop them if I try to hand them over." Chastity made it to the table in the middle of her office before letting them go in a *whump*. She set her coffee cup down more carefully, shoved her books to the side, and indicated for Charles to sit.

He set his own cup down and took the seat across from her, leaning forward with his arms on the table. "How's Thomas? And your mom?"

"Both are well, thank you. My mother went home earlier this week, and Tommy seems to be doing well with the therapist we found for him." Charles thought she looked pale.

"How are you coping without your mom?" He noticed her eyes glistened before she blinked, but she answered calmly.

"It's hard without her, but I'm glad to come to work again. It's good to be here, and I can see Tommy is making progress with someone who's skilled at rehabilitation."

"I think it will keep getting easier," he said. There was a short, awkward silence before he plunged ahead. "Do you know there will be a ball at my house in three weeks?" Her eyes darted up, and he thought he saw a fleeting look of hope before her expression went blank.

"Yes, I'd heard."

"Well I..." He cursed his luck for not being free to ask her to go right then. "I'd like to invite the upper two classes from the school to go—my son's class and the one above it. The tickets will be free for them, and I thought it'd be a good idea to organize a lesson so they can learn how to dance the waltz." Charles grinned and leaned back, crossing his arms. "This is purely self-interest. I think it's the only way I can get Louis to learn."

Chastity chuckled. "It doesn't seem to be at the top of their list, does it? Teenagers learning to waltz?"

"Do you know how?"

"We had lessons in high school, believe it or not, but I was sick that day. So I'm out of luck."

"You'll have to come to the lesson then." Charles kept his voice light. He had hoped she'd reply immediately with a 'yes', but he was doomed to disappointment.

Instead of answering him, she changed the subject, piercing him with her gaze. "I'm sorry, but I have to ask about Louis. He was...I'm sure he was using again. This time I smelled marijuana on him as he walked by, and his eyes were red. It was during school hours. It's just —" She shook her head, "All the signs were there. I'm sure this time."

Charles felt the news like a punch in the gut. "When was this?"

"It was right after I started teaching again last week. I have to say he's been completely fine in class since then, although he's not participating much. Have you made much headway on your side?"

"I'm not getting far," Charles confessed. He rubbed his face and sat back, exhaling. "Every time I try to talk to him about it, he evades me. I don't know how to get him to open up and trust me. I can't help him if he doesn't admit he's in too deep."

"How has he been at home? With you?" Chastity met his gaze with a strange combination of warmth, friendship and support. The shoe was on the other foot now, and he was the one who needed her. The longer their gaze held, the more he wanted to take her hand that was on the table.

But the problem needed to be faced. "I was in London last weekend." Charles stared out the window, trying to remember. "The truth is, I'm not around much. I'm not around *enough*. I have no further plans to go to London, but the racetrack takes me away quite a bit. I've been involved in it ever since I began my sabbatical at the hospital, but maybe I should have taken a step back from everything."

Chastity sat back, leaving a scent of lavender soap in her wake. "I wonder if you could take him with you on your next trip? Do you have any plans to go away?"

"Yes. I'm going to Pontchâteau in two weeks. I'll be back just in time for the ball. I'd ask Louis to come, but even if it weren't for the fact that he'd be missing school, I brought him last fall and the trip was a failure. He seemed annoyed by my questions."

"Maybe he just wants to spend time with you, no questions asked. Maybe that's what'll get him to open up. And there's the weekend. He could go then." She paused, perhaps afraid she'd said too much.

"I've kind of made a mess of things," acknowledged Charles. "At first, I was too hands-off. Then I treated him to the Inquisition, even though I hated that as a kid." He sighed. "I'll invite him to come with me for the weekend."

Chastity smiled and nodded, then glanced at her watch. "Oh. I'm sorry—can I see you out? I have to prepare for my next class."

"Sure." Charles stood and reached for his briefcase. "I'm sorry to have kept you."

"No, no," Chastity demurred.

His brown leather coat was hanging over the back of the chair, and he put it on. Chastity led the way downstairs, and he realized he hadn't yet secured a promise from her to come to the waltzing lesson. If he was being honest with himself, he had organized the entire lesson just so he could dance with her.

"You'll let me know how everything goes with Louis?" she asked.

"Yes," he said. They were at the bottom of the stairs. This was his chance. He had to get her to agree to come. "I hope to see you at the dancing lesson before I leave, which, I forgot to tell you, is this weekend. Saturday at two o'clock. Elizabeth is going to let all the parents know." He faced her. "Will you come?"

Instead of answering right away, Chastity pushed the door open and walked onto the gravel path leading to the gate. She stopped short and turned. "If I can bring Thomas, I'll come." She held out her hand and smiled up at him.

Charles took her hand in his and held it. *Success.* "I'm glad. And yes, I'll make sure there's a comfortable place for Thomas to sit."

He was just enjoying the feel of her hand in his when she yanked it away.

"Chastity, there you are."

She took a step back as they both looked towards the gate. "Marc," she said.

Charles could hear surprise—and was that displeasure?—in her voice. She unlocked the gate, allowing him to enter. "Marc, I believe you remember Charl—Docteur de Brase?" The two men nodded at each other, unsmiling.

Chastity turned to Marc. "I'm surprised to see you since you know it's difficult to meet with anyone during work hours." Marc glared pointedly at Charles. "Difficult to meet with anyone but the parents and students," she amended.

"I came to see if I could take Tommy out for a short walk. I wanted to get the key."

Charles decided it was time to leave, and time to revert to being more formal. She had called him Dr. de Brase, after all.

"Good afternoon, Mademoiselle," he said. She gave a small wave as he hit the buzzer and pulled the unlocked gate open.

"Tommy's with Madel. It's better for you to call first," Charles heard her say.

"It's so nice out," was the answering protest. Then he was too far to hear the rest of the conversation. He wasn't sure he wanted to.

# CHAPTER 23

With the imminent rain, it was a good night for another attempt. For days, the moon had been bright in the cloudless sky, and although that was not what had stopped him from coming, he preferred the cover of darkness. He walked around to the back of the school, looked both ways, then climbed the chain-link fence and leaped to the other side. He hurried to the line of trees, but he was not worried. No one had seen him.

He made his way to the main building and jogged down the cement steps, which led to the basement. The lock was easy to pick, but it had been even easier to 'borrow' the key and make a copy of it. He slid it into the lock and turned the knob, grateful the school hadn't installed an alarm system. There was nothing to steal, he supposed, but he also credited his luck to the centuries-old building that housed Fenley. It had been there for so many years, and the school administration had every reason to believe it would be there for many more.

Cutting through the music room, he bumped into the edge of the table, which screeched against the tiles and made his heart thud. He stopped and listened, but there were no answering footsteps coming to investigate. This tomb of a building was a dream entrance to the tunnel, and he wondered how much it had been used in its day.

He crossed the computer lab and walked down the two steps leading to the boiler room, laundry room, and old servant's quarters that were unfit for public viewing. In the laundry room, there was an ancient stone sink at the far end, a relic from a different era. He bent down and removed the trappings beneath it that hid the tunnel. It was a simple matter of removing the frayed tarp, hooked to the underneath of the sink, and unscrewing the crumbling bolts that held the grate in place. When he crawled through the opening, he turned and propped the grate back in place. Even if someone discovered the fallen tarp, the grate afforded little view. It went a few feet before coming abruptly up to a stone wall.

He took his time. His habit was to arrive at the school around one in the morning, and finish his work by four. That way he was long gone before even the earliest caretaker arrived. He had not yet had a problem, not even a close call. With the bolts unscrewed and the gate down, he crawled through the hole over to the stone wall. He felt with his fingers along the edge of it until he heard a soft click, and he gently pushed the wall sideways so he could squeeze through. Once he was past the swiveling section of the wall, he made sure to turn it back in the unlikely event someone came into the laundry room. He had learned the hard way never to take any chances.

It was a relief to move past the section with the low ceiling and get to where he could stand and stretch. He hated being cramped in that small corridor and was glad the rest of the tunnel was not like that. He walked briskly now, no longer needing a map to find his way, despite the few tunnels that shot off from the main one. He had never bothered to see where they led, but maybe one day he would.

In a short ten minutes' walk he was there. The tunnel crossed from the school to the château directly, avoiding the detours a pedestrian was obliged to take because of the pattern of streets. He came at last to his handiwork—the wall he had been patiently chipping away at, removing the smooth rectangular stones one by one. He didn't dare risk making any noise, so he had to work away at the mortar by hand. Then, when he was finished with his night's work, he couldn't leave the stones lying in a pile, but had to put them back in place. Otherwise a draft would form in the tunnel and tip off that head butler who seemed to be aware of everything that went on in the château. Jean had done his homework, and he knew these things.

It was Etienne who sent him on this mission, reluctant as he had been at first. The former gardener was not likely ever to leave jail with murder on his record, even if he swore he had never set eyes on the prostitute. He latched on to Jean as the only other French inmate in a New York prison. Looking back, Jean realized the friendship had been staged with a goal in mind. He should not have been surprised.

They were sitting at a picnic table surrounded by barbed wire in place of trees, and prison guards standing in towers in place of birds, when Etienne first spoke of it. "The tunnel has been in place ever since the château and residence were built, but it's been condemned for the past couple of decades. People don't even know it exists anymore.

"You'll have the easiest time on the end where the school is. You can slip in and out of there easily. On the end where the château is, there's a wall." Etienne gestured, glancing up to see that the police officer in the tower nearest to them was smoking and not paying close attention.

"Anyway, I should've worked harder to break through the wall, since I had the only key to the gate, instead of relying on getting out through the door." He scowled at the memory. "You'll need to take it down, stone by stone, and that's going to take some time. The good news is that it's not visible from the cellar in the château. So your only risk is the noise. Be careful. Paltier—if he's still alive and working there—has eyes and ears everywhere in that place."

Etienne continued in a subdued voice. "So there's the gate, and I already told you how to get the key. That was the one smart thing I did before leaving." He glanced up again compulsively in a way that was sure to attract the guard's attention, Jean thought, before continuing.

"There's a room around the corner of the gate, but you don't need anything in there. I can only imagine it's still boarded up since I would have heard if there had been an uproar." Jean didn't dare ask for clarification.

"Up until this point, you're not visible to anyone in the château. You need to open that gate, and you need to break—" Etienne started to reach into his pocket, but the guard was staring at them, so he pulled out a cigarette from his pocket and lit it.

When the guard lost interest, he reached into his pocket again and pulled out a hand-drawn map and resumed. "This." He pointed to the rough sketch of a room with the gate on one side and a series of alcoves on another. "This is where you need to break the wall, and this is where you access the tunnel. Here. It's yours." He folded the map and handed it to Jean. "They had nearly finished plastering those alcoves when I was there. I hid the painting in the middle alcove when I heard everyone coming. I assumed I'd be able to get it before morning, but the investigation started right away, and I had to leave. Everything will have been sealed by now, and they obviously didn't think to look there for the painting or I would've heard."

Jean spoke for the first time after listening to this recital. "Why didn't you just grab the painting and run out the back door? You had such a head start."

"Pierre." Etienne shook his head. "The old gardener I worked for. I liked him well enough, but he caught on to what I was doing. He was there, and he wasn't going to let me go without calling for help."

"Where is he now?" Jean lit his last cigarette and pretended not to care about the answer.

"Don't worry about that. But it was enough of a delay. If I had left then, they would have found me right away. The smartest thing to do was to slip the painting through the hole in the alcove and act like I'd been standing guard at the door. In any case, it worked long enough for me to throw dust in their eyes, but not long enough for me to go back and get the painting."

"Okay, so this Cyril guy you were working for. Why does he still care so much about this painting? Nobody's gonna buy it since they could go to jail just for possessing it. Why does he want it so bad?"

Etienne blew out smoke as he shook his head. "It's not an ordinary buyer. It's a Russian who wanted to give it to his Dad, probably to get in good with him since he runs the mob. Anyway, the Russian guy had his agent contact the old viscount, but he wouldn't sell, so he decided to use Cyril. He always had a reputation for delivering, and when he failed, the Russian guy didn't let him forget it. Cyril is dangerous, but Vlad is worse."

Etienne had told him about the job once before but Jean hadn't yet committed to anything. Now that he had all the details, he wasn't sure he wanted in. "I'm just not sure I'm your guy," Jean had said. "I mean, I wouldn't turn down half a mil' that easily. But this doesn't seem easy. I'm almost out of here. I want to get on with my life."

Etienne stared across the yard as if he hadn't heard what Jean said. "Cyril found me, even if it took him twenty years to do so. He's got so many connections, I'd probably be dead already if I hadn't let him know I could help him steal the painting and get back his reputation." He looked straight at Jean. "I already told him you'd do it."

"What? But I never—"

"You need to try. Now that he knows I gave you the information, he's going to be after you no matter what you think you've decided. If you succeed, he's good for the money, and you can settle down to something respectable. Or you may find you have a taste for the more sophisticated stuff since you're not likely to get a job above minimum wage with your record. If you refuse, you may not have long to live and see what minimum wage is like. Cyril has no other way of figuring out how to get the painting except by using someone on the inside. He's determined."

"What if I just hand the map over to him when I get out and let him do it?" Jean's urgency was beginning to attract the attention of the guards, and Etienne leaned away from him.

"If you're that stupid, you don't deserve to live. Cyril hires other people to do the dirty work and he hires people to make sure it gets done. Even if you give him the map, you're the only one who can get the key to the gate. He doesn't like involving too many people, and he doesn't like loose ends. He's gonna make sure you complete the project, or you'll be the loose end." Etienne stood, and Jean followed suit, his eyes fixed on Etienne's face.

"And if I fail?"

"Don't." Etienne joined the line of convicts waiting to have handcuffs put back on. Jean stared after him for a minute before heading to take his place in line. Etienne was in for life, and Jean would do anything to make sure he had one.

He replayed this conversation in his head over and over in the weeks he spent scraping away at the mortar in the dark tunnel. He still hadn't fully committed when he first met Cyril, but he soon accepted his role in the theft as the only way out of a life of crime—and with his life intact.

He was now working away at the stones close to his waist. He would be able to climb over them noiselessly after this night's session, and the next step was to go unlock the gate and figure out how to retrieve the painting without waking up the household. He wasn't going to attempt it tonight; his mind wasn't in the game. However, the clock was running out. He had less than three weeks before Cyril had arranged to meet with the Russian buyer, and he needed to have that painting before then. Not so early that he was worried about someone finding it, but not so late that he missed the deadline. He would have to think this through more carefully.

# CHAPTER 24

It was all over the headlines, and Charles loathed to see his name attached to it. He had stopped off at a café while meeting his lawyer in Paris, and it was the cover photo that caught his eye. When he was finished reading, he threw the paper down in disgust. Thankfully he was in this anonymous city and not in Maisons-Laffitte where everyone knew who he was. As soon as he got home, he called her, anxious to put an end to things.

"Charles, Charles—" sobbed a distraught Manon. "It's not what you think. You have to give me a chance to explain. I can't believe I did such a stupid thing. We're so good together—let's give us another chance."

"Manon, please don't. It's over." Charles was walking briskly to inspect the *Cabinet des Mirroirs* in the château, whose multitude of tiny windowpanes he had ordered to be cleaned.

She gave a small sob over the telephone. "But we're so happy together." At this, he stopped short, and sighed.

"Manon, we're not happy together. If we were, you wouldn't be having an affair." He exhaled. "The truth is, it's not just you. I've known for some time that this wouldn't work out, and I should have told you sooner. I just...didn't want to hurt you." He cringed at the cliché.

She took an audible breath and let it out. When she spoke, her voice dripped acid. "I suppose there's no reason to beg." She waited to see if he would respond, and when he didn't, ended with a simple, "Goodbye, Charles." The line went dead.

He started walking again, his shoes clicking on the parquet in the echoing rooms. He wished he had time to process this before the students came over to his house later—with Chastity. But he was glad he had ended it with Manon and found his steps were lighter.

"Paltier," he called out, having spotted the balding head of his faithful servant as he headed downstairs out of sight. The butler walked back up a couple of steps and peered up. "The wine list you handed me is good. I assume you've already placed the order with your brother? I'm sorry it took me so long to approve it, but you know I trust your taste implicitly."

"Yes, monsieur. The orders have been placed, and the cases will arrive by next weekend."

"What would I do without you?" Since it was clear his employer didn't expect an answer, Paltier didn't give one.

When the doorbell rang, indicating that the dancing teacher had arrived, Charles asked Paltier to show him to the gallery and offer him refreshments while he went in search of his son. He found him coming out of his room, scrubbed clean. "I was just coming to get you."

"I'm ready." His son's face was brighter than his father had seen in some time.

"I'm glad you're up for this," his father said. "I wasn't sure you'd be too keen on learning to dance the waltz."

"I don't want to be the only one who can't." His son led the way down the stairs.

"Of course," Charles murmured. He followed in his son's wake, the corner of his mouth lifting.

When they reached the gallery, Charles greeted the dancing teacher, adding, "This is my son, Louis." The elderly man stood gracefully and walked over to Louis and bowed. Louis bent loosely at the waist and flopped back up again.

"*Non, non, jeune homme. Comme ça.*" The dancing teacher once again executed a perfect bow and snapped upright. Louis imitated him more seriously this time. "Bravo" was his reward.

The deep chimes of the doorbell sounded again, and Paltier was already on his way to answer it. Charles, unable to stay in place, followed him to the head of the stairs. A group of students poured in, laughing and chattering. Some fell silent when they took in the magnificent staircase. Louis walked over, and his father could see he was searching the crowd for someone in particular.

"Bonjour, Madame James." Charles welcomed the flustered English teacher, whose stout frame was at the head of the students advancing up the stairs towards the ballroom gallery. "I see you've gathered everyone in advance?"

"Yes, we thought it would be better than ringing your doorbell every five minutes." She was slightly out of breath as she walked to the top of the stairs. "I hope it's okay that I invited another teacher as a chaperone."

Charles glanced at the wiry, gray-haired man, herding the last of the students at the bottom of the stairs. There was no one behind him. "What an excellent idea," he said, distracted. "Is Mademoiselle Whitmore not coming?"

"Oh, she'll be here soon enough, but she's driving because it's too far for her son to walk."

"Of course." Charles's shoulders relaxed, and he took the stairs two at a time on his way up.

Louis, meanwhile, went straight over to Eloise Prynne and offered to show her some of the apartments on the first floor.

"You look...clean," she said, laughing, when they were out of earshot.

Louis flushed with indignation. "I'm always clean. I take a shower every day."

"Aw, that's not what I meant." She grinned, her expression kind. "You look clean, like, not on any drugs and not smelling like smoke. I like you like this."

"Oh." The two were walking down the long stretch of hallway, and Louis forgot he was supposed to be pointing things out to her. He watched her admire the antique furniture and beautiful architecture. On her left, through the small pane-glass windows, the fountain spouted water in graceful arcs, as the sounds of birds chirping reached them.

"I'm going to tell my dad about the drugs," he said, breaking into her quiet observation. "We're going to Pontchâteau next weekend for the races, and we'll have time together there. I know if I talk to him about it he'll make sure it stops."

"Good." She faced him earnestly. "That's good news."

"Will you come to the ball with me?" He blurted out the words before he could think of what he was saying and blushed furiously as soon as they were out.

She gave a dimpled smile, and her own cheeks were tinged pink. "I'd love to, but I've already told Pierce I'd go with him." When Louis's face fell, she added, "We're just friends."

Louis had seen the way Pierce looked at her and doubted it was friendship he wanted. He didn't know what to say, so he turned back dumbly without having shown her anything at all.

"Louis, I'd be delighted to dance with you, however." Her little nose wrinkled as she smiled. "If you'll ask me."

"Have you promised Pierce that you'd be his partner today?"

"M-mm." She shook her head, waiting.

"Maybe I could practice with you. But I don't really know how to dance."

"Me neither. We'll learn together."

. . .

"Your father's asking to come visit you while I'm at work and take you for a short walk. Do you want that, honey?" Chastity and Thomas were in their small car, about to turn into the château.

"No."

"Oh." Chastity was taken aback by the blunt refusal. This was news to her, but she didn't press the issue because she had driven through the iron gates and her beat-up Volkswagon was crunching over the pebbled driveway.

As soon as she stepped out of the car and lifted her face, she gasped. The château was immense, particularly when viewed from this close up. "Oh, dear. This old car is out of place here." She went around to open her son's door, and they made slow progress to the front entrance.

When she rang the bell, she saw Charles through the glass panes, jogging ahead of the butler down the stairs.

"Chastity." He took her by the arms and gave her two kisses, one on each cheek. Before she could recover from her surprise, he reached out for Thomas's hand and shook it gravely. "I'm glad to see you looking so well, Thomas."

"Let me take your coat, madame." The butler, who had been right behind Charles, stepped up to her, and she handed him her raincoat.

"Thomas, have you said hello?" she prodded.

"Bonjour, docteur. Bonjour, monsieur," he said, addressing the butler.

Charles leaned down and whispered, "This is Mr. Paltier and he can help you with anything you need. Standing, he coaxed, "Shall we go up? Thomas, do you need help?"

"No, thank you," was the dignified response, and the group walked unhurriedly up the steps so he would not be left behind.

Charles pointed over to the corner where a sofa had been placed with books and toys. "This is where you're going to sit, Thomas. You see the screen there? We can ask Mr. Paltier to pull the screen if all the movement starts to hurt your head, okay? If the noise is too much, we'll find a quieter place for you next door."

"I didn't even think of that." Chastity's eyes darted up to Charles. "Thank you." She watched Mr. Paltier observing the viscount as he walked the boy over to the sofa in the corner. It seemed the retainer's keen eyes missed nothing.

"Ladies and gentlemen." The dance instructor clapped loudly. "Find your partners and get into position." He was destined to be interrupted once more as the bell chimed. This time, the viscount did not rush down the stairs, and Paltier moved quickly from Thomas's side to the entrance. The teenagers chattered and laughed nervously at standing so close to their partners. When Paltier returned, he was followed by the young intern from the hospital. Chastity glanced at Charles, her expression a question, but he gave no explanation.

Noting the new arrival, the instructor called out, "What young lady does not yet have a partner?"

A student with a thick mane of black hair stepped away from her classmate and walked over to Dr. Okonkwo. "This lady doesn't."

"Fatima," was heard, amidst laughter. The teenage boy, who had just been dismissed, put his hands on his hips.

"You can share Becky." Fatima tossed her hair off her shoulder and smiled at Dr. Okonkwo. He looked amused, and a little trapped.

"Fatima, may I remind you that you are seventeen, and he is an adult." Margaret James's voice rang out from the middle of the dance floor.

"Seventeen is almost an adult," Fatima retorted as her classmates laughed. She smiled up at Dr. Okonkwo seductively.

"I am sorry to tell you, Fatimah, but I'm nearly certain he is already taken," Charles teased on the other side of her. Louis looked up in astonishment to hear his father joke with one of his classmates. Then he saw his father standing next to Chastity, and she thought she saw a slow comprehension steal over him.

The dance teacher resumed his lesson. "Gentlemen, you'll want to place your hand between the shoulder blades of your partner. Keep your elbow level with your shoulder." He demonstrated with his hands in the air. "Ladies, rest your hand on your partner's shoulder. This will help you sense where he's leading. Put your other hand lightly in your partner's outstretched hand. Like so. Very good," he added, as he observed the couples forming obediently.

Charles had his hand on Chastity's back, and her free hand was clasped in his outstretched one. They stood still while the instructor gave instructions for the steps, and she was conscious of his nearness. She could feel him looking at her, but she refused to meet his gaze.

"Chastity," he said. "I've been meaning to ask if you will come to the ball with me."

At this, she did look up, startled. She trembled in his hands. "But you are with... " Chastity stopped speaking. She had not missed the gossip about Manon's affair.

"I'm not with Manon. Trust me, it was over before this incident happened with Bruce Richards. I should have ended it sooner."

"Oh." She tried to buy herself some time. "I'm missing the instructions." The dance teacher droned on, and the partners around them began to move.

"Just follow my lead," Charles said. "You can't go wrong." His silence allowed her time to recover her composure while he led her gently in the most basic steps of the waltz. She peeked up at him again, and he chose that moment to lean down and murmur in her ear, his face warm against hers, "Don't worry. I'm wearing thick shoes."

She chuckled, and felt herself relax. He pressed again. "Will you come?"

"I don't know," she said. "Thomas..."

"I've thought of that," Charles said quietly. "If there was any chance he would enjoy it, I'd find a way for him to come and hire someone to help watch him. The truth is, the crowds and the noise won't be good for him. Do you think you can find someone you trust to watch him?"

"Mmm," she stalled. She was awkward and stiff in his arms, and he pulled her closer.

"There's his father," he offered—with a grimace, she noticed.

"Yes, but I haven't decided how much a part of Thomas's life he's allowed to have, and I'm uncomfortable leaving him alone with him," she hemmed. Charles was continuing to watch her attentively, spinning her in keeping with the dance teacher's instructions.

"Oh, why not." Chastity smiled, then laughed suddenly. "All right, I'll come. I'd love to be your date for the ball."

"That's a relief." Charles kept a straight face, but the muscles in his handsome mouth quivered. "Otherwise I'd have been obliged to ask Ms. James."

# CHAPTER 25

Jean prepared for his night, swiftly and professionally, fueled in part by anger. He was dressed head to toe in black and was wearing soft leather gloves, but that getup was customary. This time he would be carrying small explosives in addition to his mini pickax. He would also be armed.

He was going in to retrieve the painting this evening. All the months of preparation had led up to this. It was a week before the buyer was in town, and Cyril was already applying pressure to complete his end of the bargain. He had opened his offshore account to prepare for the funds coming to him, and he had found a way to disappear after the heist. In any case, he no longer had any reason to stick around.

He pulled the leather pouch from its spot on the shelf. It was in plain view in the apartment, but nobody would be looking for it. He untied the leather straps and opened the pouch on the table, revealing the rusted trowel and cultivator. The boy had proven himself useful. The other tools were hidden in the various pouches, but he didn't bother looking there. He took out the cultivator with the old wooden handle and unscrewed the place where the hinges were barely visible. When he had removed the end, he slid a narrow skeleton key from the hollow tube into his hand, which he then pocketed.

He was methodical in covering his tracks on the side of the school. And as he walked through the tunnel, his mind rehearsed each step he would be taking later that night. Remove the cut stones that were now resting in place without the mortar, climb over the reduced wall and unlock the iron gate. He would have to see about the rest when he got there. There was only so much he could plan for without having seen everything.

Cyril had shown up at his apartment unannounced earlier that night, barely greeting him before his interrogation. "How will you get through the wall where the painting is hidden? What are your plans to protect it from damage while you're coming back through the tunnel? Where will you store the painting once you get it?"

Jean knew Cyril was trying to keep him off-kilter by surprising him and testing him with how well everything was planned, but Jean wasn't threatened. He already had plans to take off following the theft and stash the painting in a safe place until the appropriate time. He was not stupid, and he wanted to survive this. Maybe afterwards he would be able to lead a cleaner life; although all things considered, there wasn't much incentive to work a menial job for almost no pay, and he knew his part would not get him far. Perhaps he would take on just one other gig.

"I'll bring it back here," he had said. "No one knows me, and there'll be no connection that could lead people back to me."

Cyril accepted this information too meekly for Jean to be able to trust him, which was why he had secured a gun. *How the mighty have fallen*, he thought with black irony. There was a time in his life when he never could have imagined ending up here.

He arrived at the stone wall, drops of sweat already forming under his arms, and began removing the stones as swiftly as he could without making any noise. He had gotten accustomed to working in complete darkness here where a flashlight would be visible from the basement of the château. When he finished removing the stones, he stepped over the wall and began to walk towards the intersection of the tunnel where the gate was. He stood next to the corner, not daring to breathe, and when he was sure all was quiet, he peered around it.

Everything was dark in the basement, but it was lighter in the section with windows leading to the garden just out of view. When he was sure no one was there, he hesitated before going directly to the gate, then decided to continue straight to the room Etienne had told him to ignore. It only made sense for him to see for himself what was inside.

He crossed the intersection of the tunnel and was once again hidden on the other side. He couldn't make out the outline of the door, but when he came to the end of the short tunnel, he felt for it with his fingers and found a tiny hole in place of a doorknob. He hooked his pinkie in the hole and tried to pull the door open, but it didn't budge.

Stopping to catch his breath, he wondered if it was worth it to look in a place unlikely to contain anything of value. But he had already started on this course, and he decided to finish it. He unhooked the crowbar from his belt loop and slid it between the door frame and the door. It was sealed shut with humidity, and the hinges squeaked when he wrenched the door open. Cold with dread, he stepped into the room and closed the door behind him. *Too late to turn back now.* He switched on the flashlight.

Dust-covered artifacts from centuries past lined the room—the kinds of things that might interest collectors if they were not in such neglected condition. It was clear there was nothing of value to the owner since this room had not been opened again since Etienne was here. Or maybe the owner never knew it was here. *Didn't Etienne say this was the only key?* As he followed the path of light from his flashlight he realized he had indeed wasted his time. There was nothing here but useless junk. That was when he saw a gleaming white bar. He walked over and knelt down to examine it.

It was not a bar. It was a rib. *Pierre.* Jean forced his pulse to stop racing, his breath to slow. Absently, he noticed that the dust didn't seem to stick to it, dulling its color. As he examined the rest of the remains, he found he could disassociate the bones from the former life that had inhabited them. Yes, it was a shock to find them, though Etienne had practically confessed, but these bones had no connection to his current mission. Satisfied that this was all there was to see, he stood and shone a path to the door. He switched off the flashlight and stepped out of the room, closing the door gently.

This time he walked directly to the gate without wasting time, slid the key in, and turned the lock. He had equipped himself with a small vial of motor oil—*If only I had thought to use it on the other door*—and he poured it over the hinges before he even attempted to push the gate open. It opened soundlessly.

Finally. He made his way through the short remainder of the tunnel, which opened directly into the basement, and stepped out into the open.

"Bonsoir." A quiet voice came out of the darkness, and Jean leaped in the air, gasping.

"Be quiet if you don't want to wake the whole household."

"What do you want?" Jean managed to ask.

"I should ask you the same thing. I've been expecting you. Been listening to you scrape away in the tunnel, night after night, and had a feeling you were getting close. You're here to steal from the viscount, aren't you?"

Jean had, by now, collected himself, and though his arms were relaxed, his every sense was alert. The man was not holding a gun, and he remembered that his own was in fairly easy reach. He glanced behind the man at the wall, and saw the sealed alcoves Etienne had been talking about. That was what he needed to break through. "I'm not sure why I should take you into my confidence."

"Well." The man paused as if he were thinking. "You see, one move on my part and I can trip the alarms. Yes, it was clever to come through the tunnel, and I'm not sure how you even know about it because it's not something that's generally known. I work here, and even I didn't know about it until I started hearing you in there. But you see, the viscount has alarms everywhere. Motion detectors. You'll trip them off before you even make it upstairs. I know where they are."

Jean's heart sank as the promise of half a million slipped away, not to mention the threat on his life that would now be a certainty. It was one thing to disappear from Cyril after producing what he wanted and getting paid. It was another thing to disappear without having handed over what was promised. Etienne had been clear about that.

"It was my plan to take something specific," Jean finally said. "So what do we do now?" He was too proud to beg, and he hoped the man could be bought.

André Robin could be bought. He wouldn't have dreamed of doing something so disloyal and out of character—not to mention, illegal—a year ago. But he was facing increasing pressure to pay his gambling debts and knew that physical harm would be the next step. "Something can be arranged," he finally answered. "What is it you want to take, and what's in it for me?"

Jean hated inviting someone else into his plan, but he didn't have a choice. He also didn't know how low of a cut this man would accept. After a brief pause, Jean answered, "An old painting buried in a wall down here. Twenty thousand euros."

*Ha.* André snorted quietly. "The Manet. The staff talks, you know, although everyone thought the painting was gone. But helping you get that Manet is not worth less than one hundred thousand to me."

Jean pretended to mull this over, but he already knew he would accept. He would be left with four hundred thousand, and he might even be able to shake the guy off his tail without having to pay him.

"Deal." He gave a nod, then rushed on. "We'll need to plant explosives in the wall to get the painting, then take it back out through the tunnel. You can seal the wall up after me and close the gate."

"Oh, no," his rival fired back. "I'll never see the painting, the money, or you again. We're going to do this correctly, and it's not going to be tonight."

"What do you mean it's not going to be tonight?"

"Even if we avoid the motion detectors, which I know how to do—figured it out before I started hanging out here at night—the sound of even the most quiet explosive will set off the sensory alarms. The viscount doesn't take any chances."

Jean sighed, now looking at his opponent with more respect. "So what do you propose?"

"We wait until the spring ball, which will be held in the château next Saturday night. The alarm system will be shut down, and although I heard the chief of staff talking about heavy security, they won't waste it down here. No one will look twice at me being here. They've already asked me to be on hand to direct people for the fireworks display."

"Fireworks," Jean repeated, alert.

"And that is when you'll set off the explosives. This way, you have time to prepare my payment, and I can either facilitate your escape or hinder it, depending on whether you have the money or not."

Jean rolled his eyes. "I can't get your share until I get mine. And I won't be coming here with a suitcase full of cash."

André, who until this point had been in full control of the situation, was now at a loss. "You can't put it in my bank account or they'll wonder how it got there." He started to stammer. "I...I'm going to have to find out where you live so I can get the money afterwards. That's the only reason I'm doing this. I don't want to get mixed up in anything complicated. I'm an honest guy, you know."

"Yeah, me too," muttered Jean. He wanted a cigarette, but didn't dare light one. Now he began to assess his self-appointed partner more shrewdly. The guy could prove to be a greater liability than he had previously thought if he couldn't keep his cool. He could ruin everything.

"Okay, here's what we'll do," André said, blinking rapidly. "I'll help you get in and out. But when you go, I'm coming with you. And I want to keep the key to the gate until then."

Jean thought for a minute, rubbing his chin, and then came to a decision. "Sure. That's fine. We can do it that way. But then you'll need to build the wall back up after I step over it tonight, and close the gate for me since you have the key. It's better if you're familiar with the tunnel anyway. Come on."

"You're lucky you have me for this, you know," his partner said, the rush of danger infusing his voice with nervous gaiety. "You would never have been able to pull it off yourself." André shook his head and gave a shaky laugh. He led the way past the gate into the dark tunnel, when suddenly he stopped short. "But why would I need to rebuild the wall after you when you can do it yourself? I just need to lock the gate—"

His reflection was too late. Jean had slipped the crowbar out of his belt loop and into his hand, and he brought it down hard. André slithered to the floor without a sound, and Jean dragged him to the room. *I knew there was a reason I came in here*, he thought, exultantly, although he was shaking. Closing the door behind him, he switched on the flashlight and searched for the piece of burlap he had seen earlier. He wadded this into a ball to form a makeshift silencer and finished the job. Then he stood, shaking and sweating, before doubling over and emptying the contents of his stomach.

Determined, Jean wiped his mouth and left the room. He took one last glimpse into the basement as he closed the gate then turned back to the wall he would have to rebuild after he climbed through. He had been hoping this would be the last time he would have to see that wall, but it was not to be.

*I may not have been able to do this without you*, he thought grimly. *But now you've told me everything I needed to know.*

# CHAPTER 26

Louis knocked on his father's bedroom door and entered when his dad called out. His father, in shirtsleeves, with the elegant suit jacket draped over the chair, was in the process of tying his wide cravat. He lifted his chin and glanced at his son in the mirror. "Very nice. You did a great job on your tie."

"Paltier," was the only answer afforded by his son.

"Ah." Charles smiled. "You'll learn soon enough." When he was content with his appearance, he turned around. "What is it, Louis?"

Louis frowned. "I heard the staff talking about how that gardener, André Robin, disappeared?"

"Yes, that's right. Thierry told me about it as soon as I got back Wednesday." Charles didn't add that he was perturbed that history should repeat itself, and that a gardener could disappear right around the time another ball was planned at the château. "Don't worry about it, okay? He probably just took off, and we already have someone to take his place for the fireworks."

Louis didn't budge and Charles, sensing that he had more to disclose, waited patiently. "I haven't told you everything about the drugs, Papa," Louis said, presently.

Charles's breath caught and after a split second, said, "Have a seat, *mon fils*." He took one of the two hardback armchairs in his bedroom that faced a small round coffee table.

Louis wasn't even seated before he began in faltering speech. "I told you I had been using pretty heavily, and that I had finally told the dealer I didn't want to do that anymore. I was going to stop." His father nodded. "I didn't tell you that I had gotten into dealing drugs. The man I was meeting with—Jean—it's the only name I know. Anyway, this guy convinced me to become a seller in the school so I could get my drugs almost free. He said it would make the other kids respect me." Louis buried his face in his hands. "I know how stupid that sounds now."

"Tell me everything, Louis." Charles spoke gently, but inside he was seething.

"I started selling. This kid Max at school, he found most of the clients—the kids—but I was the one dealing with Jean. It started to get stressful for me, so I started using at school to handle it. Then I had a problem." His father waited in silence, and Louis took a deep breath before rushing forward. "I was robbed twice at parties in the neighborhood. I'm almost sure I was drugged because I didn't have that much alcohol or pot, and I don't remember a lot of the evening."

"Were you harmed in any way?" Charles felt bile rising in his throat.

"No, not that. But—" Louis hesitated. "Both times they stole the money I was supposed to return to Jean. So when I went to meet him, I didn't have it."

"What did he do to you?" Charles's voice hardened.

His son pulled back, his face white. "He threatened me. He told me if I didn't want him to come and tell you, I needed to do him a favor." Louis cried out when he saw his father about to protest, "I should have told you."

"Always, always tell me, Louis," his father said, agonized. "I can protect you from people like that. So you didn't do the favor then?"

"No, I did, Papa. That's what I wanted to tell you. He wanted me to get an old leather pouch of gardening tools from the basement that he said belonged to his uncle. So I went and got it and gave it to him. Then I told him I didn't want to meet him anymore. I wanted to get on with my life. He let me go."

Charles stood suddenly. "Show me where you found the tools." He led the way towards the door and strode down the hallway with his son in train. When they reached the musty corridor in the basement, Louis pointed to where he had retrieved the tools. Though he knew he wouldn't find anything there, Charles reached up and felt for a clue. In silence, he made a quick tour of the rest of the basement, but it was too large to go over thoroughly, and he didn't see anything out of place.

As he was walking through one of the rooms, the iron gate caught his eye on his left, and he walked over to it and shook the gate. It was locked and did not budge. "I don't even know where the key to this thing is, but in any case the old tunnel has been sealed on both sides." He faced his son. "Did you look at the tools before you handed them over?"

"Yeah. I took each one out, but they were just regular tools. There was nothing there."

"Regular gardening tools?" Charles exhaled. Turning back towards the stairs, he pulled his phone out of his pocket. "I don't understand this, but we don't have time to worry about it today. There's too much to do." He jogged up the steps. "Have you eaten lunch?"

"Oui, Papa."

"Okay, can you take a look at where they're setting up the fireworks and see if the new gardener has any questions?" They had reached the top of the stairs, and Charles paused.

"Sure." Louis shifted, ill at ease. He seemed startled when his father pulled him into a hug.

"This is no longer your problem, it's ours," Charles said, holding him tight. Louis remained stiff for just a moment before hugging him back. Then Charles let go and started to walk away. After a few paces, he spun around. "Hey. Do you have a date for tonight?"

"No." Louis's expression was still troubled but his lips quivered towards a smile. "But I have a date for the waltz."

"Smart girl." Charles smiled broadly and started to walk away again.

"Papa," Louis called out and he turned back once more. "Are you bringing anyone?"

Now Charles was the one shifting uncomfortably, though the corner of his mouth lifted. "Eh...how well do you like your English teacher, Mademoiselle Whitmore?"

"Miss Whitmore? Uh...I thought it might be her. It's a little weird, but I'll try and get used to it." Louis gave a crooked grin.

"I'm picking her up in two hours if I can manage to get everything done. Now off with you. Go help me with the fireworks, at least." His son raced off, reminding him of the boy he was not all that long ago. Charles grabbed his phone, and hit one of the contacts.

"Hi, Jef. Aren't you supposed to be here already?"

"I'm a block away. Be there in a minute." With that cryptic reply the phone went dead. Charles hurried to the second floor where the Chief of Police had been closeted with Thierry and Paltier. A team of casually-dressed workers were rushing from one room to the next with large vases of fresh flowers, cases of champagne or wine glasses, and small plates for the *amuses-bouches*.

There would be oysters and lemon, smoked salmon on buttered toasts, leaves of endives with soft cheese and caviar, Russian blinis with creamed tarama, stuffed quail eggs, and toasted baguette slices with fig jam and foie gras. Two burly men were setting up the ice fountain in the middle of the *Maréchal Lannes* apartment. There was a security guard in every room of the château to keep an eye on the workers.

As Charles made his way back towards the gallery, he spotted Paltier and signaled to him. His butler left the police chief with Thierry and hurried over to the viscount's side, following him down the stairwell.

"Paltier," Charles said finally, after they had gone down a flight.

"Oui, monsieur."

"Have I told you I'm giving you a week off after this event is over? You've really outdone yourself."

His faithful retainer gave a prim smile. "That will be most welcome, monsieur."

As they passed the front gate the door opened, and Jef entered, elegantly attired. Adelaide, Isabelle, and Samuel spilled in behind him.

"Now I know why you were late." Charles shot him a wry look. He kissed his sister and niece and shook hands with Jef and Samuel.

"Why stick to business when you can mix it with pleasure?" Jef replied, with unshakable good humor.

"Adelaide, I was going to call you—" Charles paused, smiling. "I see you finally met my intern."

"Yes. Isabelle managed to overcome her shame of me and introduce us at last," his sister replied, in placid good humor.

"Ma*man*."

"I'm glad you were able to get back for the weekend, Isabelle. If you and Samuel don't have anything particular you wanted to do, I'm sure Louis would be glad to see you. He's outside helping the men who're setting up the fireworks."

"Sure. We'll go. Maman, will you take my dress with you?" Isabelle handed the slippery bag to her mother, and she and Samuel went back outside.

"Addy, do me a favor and keep Maman and Eléonore occupied tonight, all right? I don't want them to suspect that I'm...staying clear, but..."

"You're staying clear," his sister finished for him. "I can't imagine why," she teased.

"It's so my date doesn't get peppered with questions," he retorted. "Jef, can you come with me? I want to show you where I want your men."

"Date? It's not Manon?" he heard his sister ask as they disappeared down the corridor leading to the basement.

"How many men do you have?"

"Three others besides myself," Jef answered. "I was planning to cover the area in the ballroom—"

"—so you can dance with my sister. Why am I even paying you?"

Charles shook his head, but a smile hovered on his mouth as they jogged down the stairs.

Jef was unperturbed. "For the three excellent security guys I'm providing." Then, in a serious voice that years of friendship had taught Charles to ignore, he added, "Plus, you're a socialist at heart, and you want to redistribute your wealth."

"I don't know why they let a scrub like you into Saint Thérèse," his friend said amiably, heading over to the downstairs kitchen.

"It assuaged their guilty consciences for being so privileged." Jef broke off suddenly. "Why do you want us down here? There's no entrance."

"I don't think anything will happen here, but I just want one security guard to watch this back staircase coming off the kitchen, and I want another man to cover the door leading to the garden. You can put the third one wherever you see fit."

Jef was examining the room, and he turned to look up the back staircase, now professional and fully focused. "I forgot this was here." He started walking towards the door leading to the garden.

"No one is to come down here, except family and private staff," Charles said, following him.

"I'll take care of it."

# CHAPTER 27

Chastity struggled to pull her zipper the remaining distance to the top of her dress. At the same time, she was reliving her difficult conversation with Marc last week when she broke it to him that their relationship would be nothing more than friendship. She knew she had to. Between her growing feelings for Charles—her heart pounded when she thought about seeing him—and the fact that Thomas had said point-blank he didn't want to spend time with him, (she still needed to ferret out what that was about)—she knew this was not a relationship that could continue. Marc had not taken her refusal to let him be part of Thomas's life well and had stormed off. There had been no word from him since.

When she finally got her dress properly secured, she forced her mind back to the present. She was ready. Her hair was pulled completely off her neck, with little rhinestone bursts clipped into the auburn curls, and she had spritzed perfume delicately behind her ears. Her eyes were more heavily made-up than usual, but in the soft lighting, it made them stand out. Now she had her rented designer black dress on with discreet slits up the sides, and spaghetti straps holding the bodice. She would take no chances with matching tableware this time.

She completed her toilette by clasping a thin, almost invisible gold necklace to the back of her neck, which held a garnet heart. Smaller matching hearts swung from her ears as she bent close to the mirror to examine her appearance.

"You look nice, Mom." Thomas was sitting in his usual spot on the sofa when she walked into the living room.

"You do," confirmed Elizabeth. "Charles will be proud to have such an elegant date." As if on cue, the door buzzed.

"I can't thank you enough, Elizabeth." Chastity walked over to the buzzer. "You should be going to this thing. I should never have taken you up on your offer." She spoke without conviction.

Elizabeth smiled and stood to put her arm around Chastity's shoulder. "I've attended plenty of events like this. I'm glad to hang out with Thomas. He's promised to show me the rock collection he's building."

"Oh, yes, he just got another shipment in the mail." Chastity was distracted and breathless, waiting the interminable time for the elevator to arrive and the door to ring. She didn't open the door until the bell chimed.

Charles was already smiling when she opened the door, but he sucked in his breath at the sight of her. He leaned in to kiss her on both cheeks and murmured, "You are beautiful." She hoped her face was not as hot and red as it felt.

"Elizabeth." Charles greeted her as he walked in the room. "Thank you. This is really kind of you to stay with Thomas." He kissed her in greeting, a departure from their usual handshake.

"My pleasure. Besides I've been wanting to spend time with Thomas ever since he left the hospital."

The young subject in question turned his eyes upwards and was regarding the viscount fixedly. "Docteur?" Charles came and sat down next to Thomas. "What is it?"

"Can I come visit your stables?"

Charles raised an eyebrow. "So you like horses, do you? Then, of course. Any time you want. I'll tell the stable manager to expect you."

He glanced at Chastity then back at the boy. "You don't mind that I'm taking your mother to the ball tonight?"

Thomas shook his head and slid off the couch to get something in his room. "Tommy, we have to go, darling," his mom called after him. "Come back and give me a kiss, and then you can show your collection to Elizabeth."

She hugged him and grabbed her black sequined clutch as she shrugged into the short coat that matched her dress. "Thank you," she whispered again to her friend on their way out.

The afternoon was warm enough that her blazer would suffice. Charles pressed his key chain, and the BMW beeped on the street in front of them. "It's not far," he said, "but I didn't want you to have to walk in dress shoes." He opened the door for her, and they drove the short distance to the château—she, almost seized with nerves, and he, relaxed as they finally turned onto the pebble stone driveway.

"Stay here," he commanded when she reached for the door handle. He got out of the car and walked around to the other side, opening her door and extending his hand. She tried to keep her composure and not tremble from nervousness as he pulled her to her feet.

There were a few other couples arriving at the same time. "There are eighty people invited to the dinner," he told her. "The rest of the guests will arrive for the dancing afterwards." He leaned towards her. "May I take your arm?"

Grateful for his steady presence, particularly when walking over the pebbles in high-heeled shoes, she attempted to find her voice. "You've even decorated the windows with lights. It's beautiful."

He opened the heavy door for her. "I've seated us with your friend Maude and her husband because I may have to leave you from time to time to take care of details. Now I understand why my parents were so exhausted after these things. Ah—I'll have to introduce you to my mother too, I suppose. Don't let her scare you."

Chastity giggled and followed him into the downstairs apartment that was set with ten round tables, half of which were filled with guests, and more streaming in all the time. She spotted Maude and

Michel with relief and gave them a small wave. Charles held her chair for her, said hello to her friends, then left to greet the mayor and some of the other people coming in.

"I didn't know he knew who you were," she whispered to Maude.

"I would say the same thing to you," her friend retorted with a smile, "but I've been long convinced otherwise." She added in an undertone, "We were only invited for the dinner part because of you, my dear."

Charles had not been wrong when he said he would not be able to stay seated. In fact, he excused himself more often than she had expected, always with an apology and a warm smile that made Chastity's heart skip a beat. She found she couldn't relax.

When the dinner was over, he helped her to her feet. "I'm sorry, but my mother wants to meet you and I don't think we can avoid it." Charles pulled her hand through his arm, and the warmth of his proximity helped her stop trembling. "I promise not to leave you," he said with a wink.

Chastity was suddenly facing a stately, dignified woman, to whom she addressed a "Bonsoir, Madame."

"Bonsoir." His mother looked her over critically. Her face was reserved, but not unkind. "You're American, then. You seem to speak French well enough."

"I went to the Lycée Français in Manhattan."

"Ah. I have friends whose children went there. Do your parents work with the French consulate?"

Adelaide's voice came from behind. "Maman, the mayor has been dying to say hello. May I bring you to him?" The dowager acquiesced with a regal, "Bonne soirée, mademoiselle."

Chastity glanced at Charles, her eyes full of mirth. "Does she know my parents run a dry cleaning business?"

"I don't believe she does." Charles grinned and he caught her gaze. He made no move to go upstairs. The noise around them—the buzz of people talking, dishes clattering, scraping chairs—seemed to cease. He stood, immobile, his expression serious as his gaze went from her eyes to her lips. Her heart thudded. *He's going to kiss me.* Then he blinked and the spell was over. He cleared his throat and gave an attempt at a smile. "The dancing will start soon. Let's go up."

Nobody was on the floor yet, but Chastity observed everyone and noticed Louis talking to Eloise Prynne. That was Pierce Burns to the right, who did not look happy. Dr. Okonkwo was there standing next to a French girl, and she couldn't decide if they were together. Was that the viscount's niece? The intern gave a small wave, and Chastity returned it.

Soon, the musicians had drawn some of the more intrepid couples in, and there were pairs swirling to the music. Chastity noted with private amusement that her students would only join in when it would be more conspicuous to stay on the sidelines than to be on the dance floor. Charles was talking to a gentleman on his left whom she recognized from the museum. While they talked, his arm stole around Chastity's waist, and he pulled her into the conversation. "Jef, I don't believe you've met Chastity."

Eyes twinkling, his friend kissed her on both cheeks. "My pleasure."

"*Enchantée*," she returned, unable to resist a grin. She could see the long-standing camaraderie between the two men, and sensed his friend approved of her.

"I've known Jef since we were kids," Charles explained. The two gentlemen resumed their conversation, but he did not remove his arm from her waist.

# CHAPTER 28

Cyril was ill-at-ease, waiting at the entrance to the tunnel. He hated being in the deserted school when it was not yet fully dark, but he had no choice. The drop would be at eleven o'clock. He was also annoyed with himself for being so claustrophobic he couldn't do the job himself. That's how he had gotten into trouble in the first place those twenty years ago. He should have just done it. He knew, even as he chastised himself, that he never could have. A childhood spent locked in a cellar with rats left him utterly incapable of setting foot in a closed, dark space.

He might have underestimated Jean. The man had not been surprised to see him when he exited the tunnel the other night. "Don't bother killing me or you'll never get the painting," was all he had said when Cyril confronted him with a gun. "I've seen exactly where it is, and I know how to get it and when to get it. You won't like it, but it has to be the same night you meet with your buyer."

He didn't like it. He didn't like leaving things to the last minute, and he didn't like the lack of control he had over this situation. If he didn't deliver the painting this time around, things would end badly for him. It was no longer about his reputation; over the years he had become indebted to Vlad and no longer called all the shots. Now he worried that Jean had managed to find a different way out of the tunnel.

Jean, meanwhile, had reached his destination and had torn down the stone wall as quietly as he could. He climbed over it, and was now sitting on the floor with his back to the wall, just around the corner from where the gate was visible. The basement was absolutely quiet, though he could hear noises coming from upstairs, telling of the large crowds. The gardener—whose identity was revealed to Jean via a short blurb on page ten of the local newspaper simply by going missing—had not steered him wrong when he told him to attempt it this evening. He willfully relaxed his muscles and slowed his breathing as he waited.

Charles and Chastity were standing on the edge of the crowd of swirling people. "Let's dance." Charles didn't wait for an answer and took Chastity into his arms. He applied pressure on her back to pull her close and led her in the waltz. She didn't exactly float in his arms, but she was much freer and more relaxed than she had been at the lesson. "You're getting good at this."

She stared at his vest, and it allowed him a brief respite from his feelings. He didn't dare look at her too long or their first kiss would end up being a very public one. He was silent as he led her in step to the music, but finally teased in a formal tone, "You are trembling, mademoiselle."

She responded in kind. "I am nervous, monsieur."

"Don't be," he said, simply. "You're with me."

Jean pressed a button on his watch to show the time; it was nearly 9:30. He stood quietly, intending to move as soon as he heard the fireworks. It had not been difficult to find a schedule of the events for the evening since it was open to the public. It wasn't until 9:35 that he heard the first *boom*, and at that he went swiftly to the gate, opened it, and only paused at the end of the corridor to make sure no one was there before crossing the room. No one came, and no alarms went off as he walked to the exposed wall. Prepared, he took the small explosive device from the pocket of his vest, and began unscrewing the section that held the tripwire.

"Isabelle, where is Louis going?" Samuel saw him slip out of the crowd as soon as the fireworks started.

She looked at him in alarm. "Oh no, no, no. If he's going off to use drugs again, we have to stop him." They broke away from the crowd and just caught sight of Louis as he rounded the château, heading towards the side entrance. "Come on. I think I know where he's going."

The fresh night air, as they stood facing the fountain, helped clear Charles's head. He hadn't felt anything like this in so long he had trouble thinking clearly. He stood with Chastity in the exact spot he had occupied at the last fireworks display over twenty years earlier. He put his arm around her again and breathed in the perfume she was wearing. His senses came to life, and his body buzzed with contentment. He felt the curve of her waist, and as he pulled her closer, caught the soapy scent of her hair. *So that's where the lavender comes from.* The fireworks started, and he was hovering between two planes of existence. In one, he was falling hard for a woman for the first time in almost two decades. In another, his mind started to unravel the problem that was nagging him, which seemed to call to him as if from a dream. *Boom, boom, boom* echoed from a distance.

Suddenly, he gasped. The gardening tools.

"Chastity, wait here," he whispered, then skirted the crowd to enter through the front doorway, which had been left open. She obeyed for only a few seconds before following him.

. . .

Samuel was now in the lead, trailing Louis. He saw him head towards the basement, say something to the security guard, and slip through the door.

Isabelle stopped suddenly, her mouth open. "That's the back stairwell that leads to the old kitchen. Where's he going?" They rushed up to the guard, who put his hand out to stop them, looking at Samuel suspiciously.

"He's with me," Isabelle said. The guard didn't register any sign of recognition. "Come on. Jef knows me. He came here with my mom tonight. I'm the viscount's niece." She stomped her foot impatiently.

"*Excusez-moi, Mademoiselle.*" The guard mumbled something about just doing his job. He stepped to the side and they rushed through.

The mini explosion had worked perfectly, and Jean had been fortunate enough to time it with an explosion of fireworks, which was not something that could be planned. He had set the device high enough so no sparks would damage the painting, but now he needed to pull away at some of the plaster so he could reach in and grab it. Even when he stretched his arm down as far as he could, he wasn't able to feel the edge of the painting. He focused on working as quickly as he could, while making as little noise as possible. He just needed to pull this off and get out of here.

Charles raced down the main staircase of the cellar, not registering the click of high heels behind him. It occurred to him that he should have had a guard stationed here, too, so he could get some reinforcements, but he didn't want to waste time calling for any until he was sure his hunch was right. He remembered, once when he was young, Pierre showing him how the key to the shed could slide into the handle of the gardening tool and screw in place. It had been made that way as a safeguard so the gardener wouldn't drop the key in the flowerbeds while he was working. There must have been another key hidden in those tools, but what could they open? He knew the answer was in the basement.

Jean reached down until he managed to grasp the edge of the painting with his fingertips. He pulled it to the edge of the hole, and paused to breathe before slipping it through. He brought the delicate canvas to the light sconce and examined it for damage. Ah. The cellar was dry, and the painting was in near perfect condition. He released his breath. This was all going to work out.

Footsteps. He leaped to his feet and took out his gun. Holding the painting in one hand and the gun in the other, he started to run back towards the iron gate. If he could get through and lock it, it would buy him enough time to make his way through the tunnel and out the secondary exit he had discovered, which exited at the stables. Before he could get to the opening, the viscount came running up from the left. Viscount de Brase stopped short and showed his hands as soon as the gun appeared.

Before either could say a word, two more pairs of feet skidded to a stop.

"Jean," Louis shouted, coming in from the right—angry, but not all that surprised.

"Marc," yelled Chastity, coming up behind the viscount, almost speechless with astonishment. The color drained from her face as the revelation hit her. "Jean-Marc," she said with a shake of her head, remembering the christian name his parents gave him that none of his friends used. "How could you?"

He was not destined to answer because Samuel, who had been following Louis, crept along the wall out of sight. He had picked up a large vase from a nearby table and, edging towards the thief, smashed it over his head, sending him crumpled to the floor.

With the thief in a heap at his feet, Samuel turned to Charles. "I'm sorry about your vase."

Charles exhaled and gave a small laugh. "I didn't like it anyway." He peered past Samuel. "Oh. Hi, Jef. Nice of you to show up."

"Adelaide saw you all leave." His friend had the decency to look sheepish. "Looks like you handled it just fine without me." He took out a pair of handcuffs, and pulled the thief's wrists behind him roughly, just as he was starting to come to. He snapped the cuffs in place. "Christoph, get the guys down here," he said on his radio. "We're in the basement."

Charles walked over to Samuel and shook his hand. "I owe you. How did you know to come down here?"

"We were following Louis," Isabelle piped up. "Louis, what were you doing down here? Did you know this was going to happen?"

"I was late getting to the fireworks, and when I was walking around the crowd, I saw a flash of light coming from the basement window. So I left and went to investigate. It looked like the light was coming from the old kitchen so I went there first, and when I didn't find anything, I came here."

A crowd was beginning to form, although the guards had carried out their instructions and had allowed only staff and family downstairs. Charles watched his brother-in-law assist his mother into the room, her eyes fixed on the painting that lay on the floor.

Jef was still on his radio. "Rémy, go talk to the police officer in charge about getting someone over to the Fenley school in case there's an accomplice waiting on that side of the tunnel. Be discreet, though. We don't want him to get wind of it."

"Good call, Jef." Charles hadn't underestimated the benefits of working with someone who knew the château as well as he did.

Chastity watched as the viscount's mother cradled the painting in her hands—the one that had caused her late husband's demise. Her hooded eyes were filled with tears. "Maman, you need to sit down," her eldest daughter urged and led her to a chair.

Then she looked at the father of her child—the man she had even allowed to spend time alone with him—and she was filled with nausea. Jef had an arm on his elbow, and Marc refused to look at her. Charles was not paying any attention to her either, but was alternating his focus between the officers around him, and his mother, who was now leaning on him for support.

*I don't belong here*, thought Chastity. Her face was hot and her pulse was racing. She couldn't lift her eyes from the precious painting that now lay on a table between two guards. Her gaze darted to the viscount's mother who had begun to find her speech. "How did this...? How could he...?"

Chastity didn't wait a moment longer. *No one will even notice I'm gone.* She stifled a small sob and slipped away noiselessly.

# CHAPTER 29

Rays of sun streamed through the sheer white curtains of the apartment, and Chastity cracked the windows for the first time to let the fresh spring air filter through. *It's dusty*, she thought dully, watching the particles floating and falling, highlighted by the sunbeam that shone through the opening in the curtains. She moved mechanically, making a sandwich for Thomas and setting it in front of him, and taking nothing for herself apart from a ripe peach.

*He didn't call. He didn't miss me last night. He didn't even call this morning. It's over.*

Her heart was heavy. She thought back to her walk home, shivering in the biting wind, stumbling in her pinched shoes, and heartbroken at the turn of events. The viscount's mother was so shocked that the old painting had been there all along, and that someone had broken into their house again. Jean-Marc had been there because of *her*. Charles, or Monsieur de Brase—she would have to revert to his formal name—probably thought she was an accomplice. Thinking it over as she walked home, there was no doubt in her mind that if Louis knew him, it was because her ex had been supplying him with drugs.

He must have done it to get into the château. How had he known about the painting? Did he get back in touch with her for the same reason? She had so many questions and no way of discovering the answers since she planned never to talk to him again.

Louis's father was not likely to come back to the school as long as she was there. She would finish the remaining three months without needing to run into him even once. She was certain he would avoid her now. *At least I hope so*, she tried to tell herself.

"Why, you're home already? Didn't Charles accompany you?" Elizabeth had been surprised and concerned when Chastity walked, windblown and alone, through the door much earlier than expected. Thomas had only just fallen asleep.

"Oh no, there was an attempted art theft," she managed to say. "It just seemed better to come home on my own because he had a lot to manage with the police officers and his family. Can I tell you more about it on Monday? I'm just so tired right now."

"Of course."

Chastity could see her friend wanted to ask her more questions and was glad when she refrained. Elizabeth gathered her things and walked to the door. "Get some rest," she said, and gave her friend a hug.

When she was gone, Chastity unzipped her dress and took her makeup off. She collapsed on the bed, hot tears streaking down her cheeks, until she finally rolled into the pillow and sobbed quietly.

"Mom, are you sad today?" Thomas's small voice jolted her back to daylight and to reality.

"I am sad," she answered, clearing her throat. Her eyes were heavy, and it was impossible to try and hide it from him. He accepted her admission and attacked his sandwich again. She stood and brought her tea cup to the sink, but Thomas's next words stopped her dead in her tracks.

"Are you sad because my father's a criminal?"

"What?" She spun around. "Why would you say that?"

"I heard him talking meanly to a kid at school and threatening him. I heard him say something about drugs." He took a sip of his water.

"Honey, why didn't you tell me?" Her eyes filled with tears that she blinked away.

"I didn't remember. And then I didn't know." Thomas wrinkled his brow. "Or—I didn't know it was him at first, and then I didn't think to say anything."

"How did you figure out it was him?" his mother prodded.

"I heard his voice when I was sleeping in the hospital, and it made me remember his voice at the school when I couldn't see it was him." He picked up his sandwich matter-of-factly.

"Oh." She could find nothing to say.

"Is that why you're sad, Mommy? Do you want me to be nice to him?"

"Don't talk with your mouth full, sweetheart. No, baby. I don't want you to be nice to him. We're never going to see him again."

The door buzzer rang, and Chastity jumped to her feet, her heart beating wildly. Could it be...? She went over to the intercom. "*Allô?*"

"It's Charles," was the clipped response. His voice sounded hard, and her hands turned to ice. *Maybe he's coming to accuse me of having something to do with the theft.* She buzzed him in, forcing herself to breathe.

Charles noticed the red eyes and wan expression as soon as she opened the door, but he ignored it. He had already decided he would play it cool and not scare her away. "I came to take Thomas to the stables, if that's okay. I gave him my word I would."

Her eyes widened, and they both glanced towards Thomas at the table. "Oh you're eating lunch? I suppose I'm a bit early, but you see, I've been up since early morning." He glanced at Chastity and noticed that color rose to her cheeks at his unconscious reference to everything that had happened last night.

The truth was, he had barely slept at all. He had noticed her absence right away but couldn't protect her and oversee the arrest and investigation, so he had to let her go. They had found the body of André Robin, and another skeleton that was assumed to be Pierre Maçon. It didn't take long for Jean-Marc Bastien to confess to the murder in hopes for a more lenient sentence, and they were still trying to figure out the extent of everything Cyril Leonard was involved in. The list was long.

Thomas jumped out of his seat. "I'm done. I'm ready to go."

"Put on a warmer sweater, honey, and then you won't need to wear a coat," Chastity said.

"Perhaps you'll need something warmer too," Charles suggested.

"Oh." He could see she hadn't expected to be invited, and he had to fight not to take her in his arms. "I drove because I wasn't sure the excitement plus a walk would be good for Thomas."

"I think you're right," she managed. "I'll go see that he finds the proper clothes." Charles watched her walk down the corridor, putting her hands up to cool her cheeks. The windows were ajar, and he went over to close them. It was a safe neighborhood, but it didn't do to invite temptation.

After spilling out of the car minutes later, Thomas was almost jumping up and down. She had not seen him this excited since the accident, and she turned to Charles, her face flushed with gratitude. "I don't know how you were able to get away at a time like this—or how you knew what this means to him, but thank you."

He laughed and shrugged. "Oh, I was a horse-mad young boy at one time." He didn't look angry. In fact, he looked like he was… having fun. Chastity tried to wrap her head around everything, but nothing made sense. His behavior made no sense. He should hate her.

"Mickey," cried Thomas, going over to the now-familiar horse, whose head nodded over the stable door. "Did he win the races?"

"No. Black Star took first place," Charles answered. He went over to Mickey's head and patted it. "Mickey's racing days are numbered. He's had a very successful career and will retire soon. But we've got a good foal that shows promise. Solid back, strong muscles in the hindquarters. Would you like to see him?" He signaled to the older man just rounding the corner of the stables.

"Yes," was Thomas's enthusiastic reply.

"Grégoire, can you take Thomas to see Bold Liberty? Just for a few minutes?"

"Sure thing." Grégoire grinned at Thomas. "Come along, young man."

Man and boy walked towards a large paddock, and meanwhile Charles leaned over to whisper to Chastity. "I warned him we might be coming and that Thomas shouldn't do anything over-taxing."

She had only time to breathe a "thank you" before her son called out to her. "I'm going to get to ride a pony, Mom."

"Excellent, Tommy," she called back, trying to keep her voice even, although everything inside of her was fluttering. A few minutes later, Thomas reappeared, wearing a borrowed black riding helmet and polished ankle boots. A groom, leading a smart-looking pony, stopped and held the lead rope while Grégoire carefully hoisted Thomas onto the saddle. He walked in the direction of a fenced sand schooling ring with Thomas hanging on to his every word. Just before the gate closed behind them, Tommy looked back at his mother and grinned triumphantly.

They were alone.

Charles moved closer, and she could feel his warmth seeping through his clothes. She was nearly breathless as he faced her. "You left last night without saying goodbye," he said.

"I'm sorry. I knew you were busy. And I was just so shocked. I couldn't believe that Marc was behind all that." When she met his gaze, he took a step closer, and her last breath fled.

But she had to be sure he knew everything. "He was the one who got your son into drugs—I'm sure of it. I just...I didn't know how to face you after that. I can't imagine what you must think of me."

"Can't you?"

She heard the smile before she saw it and glanced up doubtfully.

The fact that he was smiling dared her to hope. Still. "I decided to go back to the States at the end of the school year."

Charles shook his head. "Chastity, stay." It almost sounded like he was pleading.

She swallowed the lump in her throat and replied without conviction. "I can't stay. I have no one to help me with Tommy. I have to go home."

"Really?" he said. "Because I have something of a reputation for knowing how to care for people with a brain injury." This made her laugh, tears on the ends of her lashes.

"Chastity, stay," Charles said, again. He closed the distance and wrapped one arm around her waist, pulling her close. With his other hand, he lifted her face to his, his expression questioning. He must have seen assent because he bent his head and kissed her decisively—and after a moment, more deeply. Chastity leaned into him and he wrapped his arms around her more securely. She couldn't process anything but his warm lips on hers.

When he finally released her, he gave a shaky laugh. "I have wanted to do that for such a long time."

Tears started pouring down her face again, and she wiped them with the back of her hand. "I need a Kleenex," she sniffed. She rubbed her nose on her sleeve. "I'm a mess."

"Good. Perfect people bore me." Chastity gave him a watery smile in return for his own. Charles pulled her closer, and his gaze grew intent, his fingers intertwined in her curls. He kissed her red nose and fixated on her lips before he dragged himself away. "Please stay," he said a third time, "because I plan to marry you." His crooked smile softened the surprising declaration, though his eyes were serious.

"What? No," she protested, but she was crying and laughing.

"You think it's too soon," considered Charles. "But I never thought I would feel this way about anyone again, and it's taken me fifteen years. So I wouldn't say it's too soon. I'd say it's about time."

"Oh, Charles—"

He didn't give her a chance to say anything else but took her face in his warm, firm hands and kissed her again. Eventually, warmth settled over her, and she relaxed into him. "*Mon amour*," he whispered, pulling her into a tight hug and kissing her forehead.

She rested her cheek on his blazer and sighed. Her trembling disappeared, leaving her with a sensation of peace for the first time since she could remember. The extreme emotions left her weak, and she wondered if she would be able to walk on her own. She dared to peek at him, only to discover that his blue eyes were already fixed in an intense regard on her. He bent down to kiss her again, when all of a sudden, he was shoved out of the embrace. There was a loud snort.

"Mickey, you traitor." Charles laughed. Then, looking down with a grimace, he cried out. "*Oh-ay*. You pushed me right into a pile of..." Chastity doubled over with laughter as the large horse bobbed his head up and down at the viscount, who was now trying to scrape his Italian loafer on a tuft of grass.

Just then, steps sounded outside, and Louis walked in. Charles's eyes widened in surprise. "Louis, I haven't seen you here in ages."

Louis grinned, looking like a much younger version of himself. He dropped a holdall on the ground and went back to stand by the pony's head. Behind him they could see Grégoire lifting Thomas from the pony's back. "Actually, I thought I would come and ride today. It's been awhile. Hi, Miss Whitmore. I saw Grégoire in the outdoor arena and walked back with them. Thomas told me he's your son?"

Suddenly, Chastity felt faint. *What will Louis think about all this?* "Hi, Louis. Yes, he is." She spoke cautiously. "It's a lovely day for a ride."

Thomas walked towards the tack room with Grégoire leading the pony in his wake. "Mom. It was amazing. This big kid said I rode him really well, and he knows this pony. Can we come here all the time?"

Chastity laughed and gave a discreet swipe at her still-moist eyes. "Yes, honey. I think we can do that."

"Yippee," was the gleeful response.

Louis came out of the tack room, carrying a saddle and bridle and speaking over his shoulder. "He seems to be really comfortable with horses. He's a natural." He disappeared in the stall containing a dappled gray horse, who let out an excited whinny. "So you haven't forgotten me then, Viva."

Charles paused in his efforts to clean his shoes and raised his eyebrows at Chastity. He flashed her a broad smile and mouthed, *You see that?* Leaning on the wall outside Mickey's stall, he called out to Thomas. "Bravo, Tommy. As soon as you're strong enough, we'll have you here riding every day."

Then, winking at Chastity, he glanced back down. "*Ho*, Grégoire, you're just in time. Hand me that rag over there, will you?"

# AUTHOR'S NOTE

Hi friends, thank you for reading *A Noble Affair*.

I used to tutor at the lovely private school Fenley is modeled after, although—of course—only its existence is based on fact. All the ways I brought it to life were fiction. Whenever I drove over the bridge to Maisons-Laffitte, the château would greet me, and I would imagine the centuries of stories it could tell. Not surprisingly, the château is a *patrimoine*—a national monument—and is empty, save for its caretakers. No handsome young viscount awaits to sweep a neighboring American teacher off her feet.

When I toured the château and studied its history for my blog, I discovered there was indeed a tunnel between the château and the school to allow the noble family to escape should there be an uprising. This detail is what triggered the idea for my story.

All characters are fiction, and any resemblance to reality is purely coincidental, except for Randall Mooers and his wife Vivienne. Randall is a real painter, and I met him through Vivienne when I was living in New York. His paintings are the most beautiful I've seen of any living painter. You can check out his work on the Randall Mooers Fine Arts website. Randall and Vivi – thanks for giving me permission to use the real *you* in my book.

I write a blog on the topics of faith, France, and food, and you can read the posts at aladyinfrance.com. If you'd like to keep up to date on my author news, you can access the newsletter signup on the sidebar of my other website, jenniegoutet.com, which is dedicated to my books in the genres of contemporary and Regency clean romance, as well as memoir.

## ACKNOWLEDGMENTS

I'm thankful to my husband and three children for understanding when I need to sit at the computer and work. (Even if it doesn't look like I'm working because Facebook is open). You remind me that life also exists outside the stories. That is a blessing.

I'm thankful to my blog readers who put up with this story in raw, unedited format, chapter by chapter for weeks until I finally pulled it at the last minute without letting you know how it ended. That was not very nice of me. I hope this past year-and-a-half was worth the wait for the finished product.

Thank you to my three initial beta readers: Emma Le Noan, Lizzie Harwood, and Emily Molinié who had to wade through some pretty raw material so that they probably abandoned all hope of anything salvageable coming out of it. I listened to you and changed almost everything you said, which greatly improved the initial rough draft.

I also want to thank my remaining beta readers: Julie C Gardner, Charlene Ross, Kim Tracy Prince, and Jaima Fixsen. You guys dealt with slightly more polished material and were able to address the fine-tune plot and character inconsistencies. You guys are the best. I changed almost everything you said, too, and my book is much better as a result.

A huge thanks to Deborah Gilboa (known nationwide as @AskDocG) who took time out of her segments on the Today Show and TEDx talks to correct my medical inconsistencies. Medical advice and parenting expertise aside, I'm glad you're my friend. I probably won't have to bother you for the next book since it's a Regency. Unless there's a bloody sword fight...

Thank you, Eloise Lorraine Duncan, for your lessons in teen text lingo. I'm sadly outdated, but now it's not quite as obvious. I hope you like your namesake in the book.

I want to extend my thanks to my father-in-law—who prefers to remain in obscurity—for saving me from making embarrassing blunders by inaccurately portraying French culture, or the customs of nobility, or by using the wrong French words. *Quel horreur!*

Last, but not least, here's a shout out to the two writing groups I'm part of—Paris Author Group (Didier, thank you for the dash) and Words Aptly Spoken. It's nice to have people who get it, and you are those people.

Made in the USA
Monee, IL
08 April 2021

65068623R00125